UNDERCOVER HOBO

By

Walter LeCroy

By the author of:

The Border Body Dumps
The Border Nightwalkers
The Ghost of Mount Chinati
Paula Maxwell

Recondite Press
Ralls, TX 79357

Although many of the places and events in this novel are real, the characters are fictional and not intended to refer to real persons, living or dead. The opinions expressed by the characters in this novel are for the purpose of characterization and plot. They do not reflect the actual views of the author or publisher. Neither the author nor the publisher condones the trespassing upon railroad property or the unauthorized mounting of freight trains. These practices are not only very dangerous, they are violations of federal, state and some local laws.

Recondite Press
P.O. Box 506
Ralls, TX 79357
Email: borderdrama@gmail.com

Cover design by the author and Ms. Loretta C. LeCroy

Printed in the United States of America

Text Excerpt:

Rocio's brow furrowed again. She rubbed her chin and said, "Ross, I've been thinking, Hon, maybe you could save a lot of time and risk-taking by just catching a plane to Los Angeles. That's where Reverend Tasker's Skid Row rescue mission is—the place he and others last saw Leah and Grifty."

"That would be a shot in the dark. There are a lot of freight yards, hobo jungles, soup kitchens, and rescue missions between El Paso and Los Angeles—Tucson, Yuma, El Centro, Colton—and I intend to scour as many as I can. As soon as I get on a freight train, I'm on their trail. Hey, Hon, the hobo grapevine is one of the most prolific sources of information imaginable and has been around before the Internet. All hobos seem to know one another, either by sight or by reputation. I may not need to go all the way to L.A., but if I wind up there, I'll need a little railroad grime on me to help me blend in with the people I'm going to be dealing with."

"You could go out to the meat packing plant and wallow in a pig pen—then catch a plane," she said with a smirk.

"Yeah, right, they let passengers covered with pig poop board planes every day— Hey, Hon, sarcasm isn't helpful here..."

PROLOGUE

The streetlights of El Paso's Alameda Avenue glowed brightly at midnight, on either side of the nearly deserted street, contrasting sharply with the solemn spirits of the two occupants of a black SUV that sped eastward. Passenger, private investigator Ross Spencer, and driver, his wife and partner, Rocio, rode silently, knowing one another's thoughts. Ross wondered how long it would take to clear up this case and be home with Rocio again. He reached into his shirt pocket, withdrew his pocket journal, switched on the dome light, and made an entry:

Shortly after midnight, Monday, October 10. Leaving El Paso from the Alfalfa Freight Train Yards to catch out west. Final destination, California.

Rocio watched him replace the small journal in his shirt pocket. "You didn't forget your cell-phone, gun, or flashlight, I hope."

He patted several spots on his body. "No, Hon. I double-checked this afternoon and I think I have everything. Everything is in either my backpack or bedroll—or I am carrying it in my clothing—or somewhere on my body."

"Passport?"

"Check."

"Binoculars?"

"Check."

"Rations?"

"Enough for emergencies."

1

"Pen scanner?"

He pulled it from is shirt pocket and held it up admiringly. "Yes—and this little gadget is also my camera and voice recorder."

"Flash Drive?"

"On my key ring."

"Plastic hand and leg restraints—and duct tape?"

"Well-concealed in the secret compartment of my backpack."

"I hope you don't have to use those."

"Nor I, but I have to prepare for contingencies."

"I saw cigarettes in your backpack. You don't plan on *smoking* as a disguise, I hope."

"No, Sweetheart. I brought a pack along because cigarettes are a lot like beer. They can be an icebreaker and induce a prospective source of information to loosen up and start talking."

"If he or she is a smoker."

"Right—nicotine is the strongest drug you can buy that's legal. If a targeted source of information is a nicotine addict that needs a fix, I'll be ready to legally accommodate him."

The two fell silent again. Ross could now see the distant, tower-mounted lights of the Alfalfa Freight Train Yards. Their hazy lights brought back memories of frequent violence. This yard was one of four major railroad-switching yards in El Paso where he had worked as a border guard, dislodging illegal aliens from boxcars and hobo jungles. Management's assignment of Ross and other "schoolboys" to dangerous, lonely and isolated duty forestalled complaints from non-student agents that "schoolboys" were getting favored assignments. Student agents accepted that sarcasm as minor tribute for a modicum of rapprochement. It was a token concession to bitter supervisors for their own unspoken regrets for failing to get an education when younger; for their lost opportunities to find a better job; a job that did not require mostly night work and one that did not have a minimum retirement age of fifty. He remembered that those jaded, lower-ranking supervisors could recite the agency's rutted, policy clichés faultlessly; but after some forty-years of alcohol and tobacco abuse, a brain becomes its own obstacle to new learning.

Those dismal-looking freight yards brought back many memories, and one still haunted Ross: one night a young, inexperienced drifter had crossed his traveling companions in a hobo jungle. They had beaten the offender to near death with a broken, sledgehammer handle they call a "goon stick," slashed his throat and lain him face down on top of the railroad tracks under a boxcar of a train ready to pull out. The assailants knew that a body run over by a train leaves little usable evidence as to cause of death. He and his patrol partner had moved the body off the tracks and called the police. They were certain that they and the police had rounded up the culprits, but since not all of the hobos seen earlier with the victim in a hobo jungle could be located, the police let the prime suspects walk, and the victim died the next day.

Rocio turned the SUV north onto a dark street called Pasco Court and continued slowly east for a block between two junk yards, each side fenced with vertical, scrap-metal panels. She approached a dead end where only a guardrail and a chain link fence stood between the vehicle and the railroad tracks. She wheeled left into a turn-around area. The SUV's headlights lit up a large, man-size hole in the chain link fence.

She put the vehicle in park and looked at her husband. Even in the dim light from the railroad yards, he could see that her dark eyes were moist. Those tear-dimmed eyes brought back sadder memories of when he had first met her, soon after she had become an Iraq War widow, when she had come into his office and implored him to help her find her kidnapped sister in Juarez. She leaned forward on the steering wheel, facing her mate, and said, "I'm going to miss you Sweetheart."

"I'll miss you, too. After we complete this gig, we'll go on vacation to Vegas or somewhere."

"Promise?"

"I Promise...and promise me you'll be careful, too."

3

"You know I will." They embraced, kissed and whispered their last goodbyes. She pushed him back, held him at arms' length and implored, "Call or text me every day, Sweetheart."

"I will—at least once a day."

Ross got out, strapped on his backpack and carried his bedroll in his right hand. He felt Rocio's eyes upon him as he headed toward the hole in the fence, an illegal entryway into the freight yards made with wire cutters, most likely by illegal aliens and other hobos. He poked the bedroll through the hole in the fence, and then went through, stooping and sidewise. After passing through the fence, he was on railroad property, and now an official trespasser.

A chilly, autumn breeze stirred up debris and dust that stung his eyes. Time had blotted from his mind some of the realities of hoboing. The real, recognizable smell of human feces of the hobo jungle rudely greeted his nostrils. He squinted to protect his eyes from the dust while hoping that his stonewashed dungarees would be enough to protect him from the autumn chill. For the present, his blue flannel shirt kept him comfortable. He pulled down tighter his jungle-style hat. He walked briskly for a short distance, then halted and looked back. He could still see the parking lights of the SUV on the other side of the fence, and he realized that Rocio still sat there, watching. He turned back to face the railroad yards, took a few more steps, and finally heard the engine of the SUV start. He stopped again and looked back across the top of the abandoned canal levee in time to see the tail lights of the SUV disappear between the two-junkyard fences, headed south. A sinking feeling of loneliness abruptly settled in the pit of his stomach. Self-doubts pervaded his mind. He began to wonder what insanity had induced him to accept this gig. Had he really agreed to take on the notorious rail-hopping FTRA gang and try to wrest from them, and return to her mother, a disoriented, misguided, teenage female? Cops and railroad agents are barely aware that the FTRA exists, some of them still deny its existence, and as long as that gang's activities remain covert, officers do not have a lot of inspiration for doing anything about them. Most of the victims of FTRA violence are youthful runaways with a romantic image of freight train hopping. The normal news channels barely mention them, and no investigative journalist has ever tried to penetrate their sanctum—not like author Hunter Thompson did with the Hell's Angels motorcycle gang. It cost Thompson some beatings, but even the media knows that the FTRA would not play games or let anyone out alive who knew their innermost secrets. FTRA members, and their victims alike, are usually unwashed, disheveled, freight-train travelers of great distances. They have severed ties with family and organized society; and they do not *want* anyone to find them. Acquaintances of rail-hopping drifters expect them to live whimsically and seldom tell anyone of their travel plans. Often, they will hop a freight train without knowing, or caring, where it is going. No one misses them if they disappear, because acquaintances *expect* them to frequently disappear, and reappear unexpectedly at rescue missions, soup kitchens or hobo jungles where they may exchange tales with fellow hobos from recent travel. However, a report of a "missing hobo" would be an oxymoron. Their residences are literally where they lay their bedrolls and backpacks.

Ross' eyes fixed upon the spot where the taillights of the SUV had disappeared as if the glowing red lights had been a tether to a spacewalk that had broken away from the master ship. Self-doubts surged. When he had worked in these yards as a border guard, not only had he federal authority to be there, he always had a partner and companion to "walk out" trains preparing to roll out of the yards. Now, he was all alone. Loneliness can be a fearsome emotion. His mind raced back to his pre-school years when his older brother started to school and left him behind. He knew exactly where both hands on the clock would be when the rural school bus would bring his sibling home. When very young, he never enjoyed being alone, and he remembered an occasion when his mom had sent him to the field to take his father's lunch. On the way home he became aware of the vast open plains around him, was overtaken by loneliness and walked down the turn-road, crying. No one knew but he, and his 6-year-old pride was not injured; afterward, he felt better. He would get used to solitude years later when he, instead of his father, sat on that tractor from daylight to dusk, plowing and listening to the drone of the engine that he kept hearing while trying to sleep. There were rare times, like the present, when memories as a six-year-old came back to haunt him

Here in these freight yards there was no emotional outlet to alleviate loneliness. He shook his head violently as if to shake off negative feelings. He imagined that he could hear a woman's voice, but it was not Rocio. "It's heads up time, Ross. You are now in a jungle that is unforgiving for even minor mistakes, and your undivided attention is necessary." Suddenly he realized that the voice was that of his brave, first wife, Olga, who had died in his arms after a gun battle while rescuing imprisoned women from a cartel brothel. She had awakened him with those words when he had dozed off on Mexican bus ride. They had been on their way to a twin-plant midnight shift change. There they would transfer to a specific commuter van and issue justice to the driver, known as a *rutero,* and his accomplices. The driver and accomplices had raped and murdered several girls on the *rutero's* outskirt, commuter route.

When sub-contracting with Olga, it had been a relief to have someone else making the decisions. He remembered that Rocio had misgivings about the ways and means of accomplishing the objectives of this present job. That memory triggered self-doubts. Was the method he had chosen—to go undercover as a hobo—the best way to find a modern-day Svengali and a disoriented teenage girl? He knew his decision was not based entirely on the lucrative fee, but also on a secret, unfulfilled dream, long suppressed by middle class pressures to fulfill the American Dream. The secret suppressed dream, to be a hobo, still lay in his bosom in extended hibernation. After disciplined, programmed, military life, he had longed for total freedom from the herd—but an older brother with a job waiting for him intervened. As a city cop, he had succumbed to the curse of insecurity that drives people into debt and into middle class conformity.

For self-assurance of his sanity, he began to retrace the events leading up to the decision to accept the contract that had put him here in this lonely railroad yard at midnight. The chain of events had begun October 3, the day the Christian, missionary, widow, Rachel Waters, had walked into his office...

UNDERCOVER HOBO

CHAPTER ONE

From the office storage room, private investigator Ross Spencer brought a paper cup filled with coffee. Circling behind his chair, he offered some to his prospective client, Mrs. Rachel Waters.

"No, thank you, Mr. Spencer--coffee is among those vices that our religion spurns."

He then offered coffee to his wife and partner, Rocio. She sat at her own desk, next to the small office's entrance. She too declined, "Thanks, Hon, but maybe a little later in the afternoon. I'm sort of coffeed-up right now." She pulled out a file folder and some pre-printed forms, preparing to take notes. Ross shrugged and said, "Then I guess I'll indulge in my vice alone."

With both hands, he gingerly placed the paper cup of hot, black coffee on his desk and sat down in his modest, manager-style chair, facing Mrs. Waters. He had recently decided to keep a pocket journal of all important encounters and events. He made an entry.

El Paso, Texas. Monday, October 3. Interviewed Mrs. Rachel Waters, potential client.

He set the pocket journal aside on his desk, got up and pulled the shade on the west window, and sat down again at his desk. He cleared his throat and said, "You say your daughter's name is Leah, Ms. Waters?"

The graying dowager nodded. "Yes, Mr. Spencer, and I am convinced that Leah is mentally ill or possibly addicted to drugs." She rummaged in her handbag for a tissue, found one, and dabbed at her right eye.

Rocio inconspicuously began to scribble notes.

Almost sobbing, the prospective client continued her lamentation. "Most certainly, Satan has taken control of my daughter, body and soul."

Ross nodded sympathetically and asked, "How old is Leah?"

"She is Seventeen." Ms. Waters switched the tissue to her left eye.

"And how long has she been missing?"

"About six months. She had just turned seventeen when she met up with that terrible young man with whom she ran off. I asked the police if they could charge him with some kind of sex crime, or abduction, but they said seventeen is technically the age of consent in Texas—and in California where I think she may now be. It seems that laws are deliberately ambiguous these days."

Setting his coffee cup down, Ross sat up straight and explained, "Technically, eighteen is the official age of consent in both states, but in both states, age seventeen is indeed a gray area of the law. The issue of emancipation comes into play. Both states also have *close-in-age* statutes that might make a stronger non-consenting case, if she is more than three years younger than the person with whom you think she ran off. In Texas, if that were the case, it would be a felony. In California, it is only a misdemeanor. In either case, the authorities might use it as a lever to develop the essential elements of other crimes that are more serious. From what I gather so far, there is a good chance her companion and inducer is twenty-one years old, or more. The police will have to sort that out after we locate Leah—and him."

Rocio shuffled papers and continued scribbling notes. Ross decided against recording the interview, since most clients

9

dislike recordings. He asked Ms. Waters, "Has Leah ever given any hint of...being troubled?"

Ms. Waters replied, "Oh, no," and declared emphatically, "We adopted her in Miami as a year-old baby, sixteen years ago, and since then she has been our life. At age nine, she accepted the Lord Jesus as her personal savior. My late husband, Herbert, and I thought she was on her way to becoming a fellow missionary with us. We need youthful missionaries, you know."

Ross nodded, sipped coffee and peered across his desk at the aging woman who was now looking down and re-folding the tissue. "Then I gather Leah was an only child?"

"Yes. We never had any children of our own. As missionaries, we traveled all over the world and we always took Leah with us. Like Herbert and I, she could speak several languages, and for most of her life, she seemed happy with our lifestyle. We had taught her to be a Christian, and we thought she was. For his baby girl to join a group of atheistic heathens was more than my poor husband, Herbert, could handle."

He nodded again and set his cup on the desk.

Rachel Waters continued her acrimonious grief. "The stress must have caused Herbert's fatal stroke last summer. Needless to say, it was very hard on me, too, but my faith and counseling from my Christian brethren helped pull me through—so far, anyway." With a weak smile, she put the tissue back in her purse.

He studied his prospective client's appearance. She came across as an honest Christian and he saw no reason to doubt her, or suspect her as a troublemaker. She was short and full-bodied with dominant strands of gray supplanting a trace of blonde hair. Her face sagged a little at the jowls, and he guessed her to be sixty-five. Her eyebrows angled downward at the outer corners, framing her deep, blue eyes in a natural, baleful look. She had an austere hairdo, wore a frumpy, one-piece, gray dress with matching belt around her trackless waist. New, unadorned, black shoes with medium heels added little to her short stature. Ross declared, "I hope you realize,

Ms. Waters that trying to locate a missing person can be expensive."

"I suppose you are wondering about my ability to pay for your services?"

"Well...mostly *willingness*."

"A few years ago my husband inherited a lot of land in West Texas with oil on it. He was the sole heir to his father's estate. I have money. Finding Leah is presently my only obsession and worth it all, if necessary."

"I take it that you and your husband decided to retire here, in El Paso?"

"Yes. There is much need for the Lord's work here. When the Lord blessed us with the windfall, we had just opened a rescue mission in a poor *colonia* across the border in Juarez, and we had planned to add a drug rehabilitation dormitory and treatment center to it. We had even hired two professional counselors, but the drug cartels forced us to close the mission."

Ross nodded and added, "Drug rehab centers are considered bad for the drug business. I have read about several closing due to crime and graft. The cartels killed all the patients and the staff in some of them."

"Yes, there used to be several in Juarez, now there are none that I know of. Satan was victorious, but Christians are resilient and we will be back."

"Drug traffickers see drug rehabs as breeding possible future informants. Killing off witnesses, real or imagined, is part of their routine."

Ms. Waters nodded again in agreement. "After we closed the mission, we just did volunteer work, until the Lord called Herbert home. Now I just do volunteer work in the local missions and in the charities. With Herbert gone, staying active in the Lord's work helps me to cope with the loss of the two people I loved most. I pray daily that He will help me get Leah back."

"What do you know about the man that Leah..." He hesitated, trying to select the least offensive word, "...the man with whom Leah is believed to be *traveling?*"

"Very little, except that, from all I have heard about him, I can reasonably conclude that he is an atheist, a reprobate and into drugs as a user and trafficker, like so many of those transients. The Reverend Alfred Tasker, a missionary I have known for years, works at one of our missions on Skid Row in Los Angeles. He recently sent me an email and told me that he had seen Leah with a male companion at his mission. Since the companion is a known drug user, Reverend Tasker had already banned him from staying overnight at the mission, but he said that the two of them occasionally show up for the free meals his mission offers every day. The Reverend does not deny food to anyone. He thought that Leah and her male companion were living in hobo jungles around L.A."

"How did Reverend Tasker arrive at that conclusion?"

"Reverend Tasker has worked with transients for many years and he is familiar with their habits. Over time, he has developed a network of informants. He has provided permanent employment to some of them, which he calls his Home Guards, and gotten them off the streets. Many people down on their luck come to his mission for free meals and a couple of nights of free lodging—two consecutive nights of free lodging are their limit —two nights every thirty days. The sermons they have to listen to before mealtime are just a boring necessity to some of them. However, some do listen and the missionaries do save a lost soul now and then. My late husband and I both have been infrequent volunteer preachers in his mission."

"The missions are sometimes good starting points to look for missing people. Do you have a name for the man Leah is supposed to be traveling with, Ms. Waters?"

"I know only his nickname. The street people call him 'Grifty.'"

Rocio was copying everything, but Ross scribbled the name on a notepad to help make it indelible in his memory.

He asked Mrs. Waters, "When was the last time you heard from Reverend Tasker?"

"I have stayed in touch with him daily, by phone, but he hasn't seen Grifty—or Leah—since he sent the email. They must be getting food somewhere else. The reverend learned from one of his converts and helpers in the mission that Grifty hitchhikes or hops freight trains to many different towns in different states where his acquaintances say that he has multiple SNAP card accounts under different names. Reverend Tasker says that many addicts feed their drug habits by fraudulently exploiting the welfare system to get extra money. However, Reverend Tasker says that Grifty always seems to gravitate back to the Los Angeles area. He mentioned on the phone that the homeless people on L.A.'s Skid Row quickly noticed Grifty's new companion—Leah—because she was so pretty."

Was, he thought, picking up his coffee cup and drinking. His vast, personal knowledge of railroad travelers reminded him of what living on the road for a considerable length of time can do to an attractive female—or male—for that matter. Abuse of drugs, malnutrition, alcohol, poor, or nonexistent, hygiene and disease, especially STDs, usually go with such a life. He offered Ms. Waters a mint from a jar on his table. She refused and he popped one into his mouth.

Ms. Waters nervously shifted positions in her chair and continued her lament, "Reverend Tasker had said that Grifty was suspected of being a crystal methamphetamine and ecstasy addict—and possibly a violent man. The reverend said that he is a suspected member of a train hopping gang called the FTRA. He said that Grifty sometimes wears a red kerchief around his neck with their symbols on it."

He set down his coffee cup. "FTRA, huh?—The Freight Train Riders of America."

"I believe that is what Reverend Tasker called Grifty's gang."

He pondered Ms. Waters' statement. If this Grifty is a member of *that* gang, then I'd say her daughter is in more peril than she can imagine. Those thugs throw other hobos off trains just for the hell of it. Most of them are ex-cons, some still on the lam, with violent criminal histories.

Ms. Waters continued, "The reverend also said that a previous young female, traveling companion of Grifty committed suicide, under suspicious circumstances, and for that reason, the reverend had hoped to gain Leah's confidence so he could discourage her from consorting with him. Unfortunately, she had shied away from the mission after that. He said it seemed to upset her that the reverend had recognized her, even though she did not remember him."

Another pattern consistent with many runaways, he thought. Oblivion and anonymity is part of their objective. Most of them want to sever all ties with their former lives. Some young runaways have what seem idyllic lives, but someone, or something, usually drugs, causes a short circuit in their brains. "I see you know quite a bit about the drug culture, Ms. Waters. Do you know anything about Grifty's physical description?"

"Reverend Tasker described him as a slender man, about six feet tall, perhaps in his late twenties with stringy, unkempt, dishwater blonde hair. He often wears railroad-type coveralls and a baseball style cap."

"How can you be sure that Reverend Tasker is not mistaking some other girl for Leah?"

"Reverend Tasker has known Leah since she was very young, about eight years old. He, my husband, and I had done missionary work together in Korea. Leah was very pretty and had features that anyone would remember—even eight or nine years later. She was a pretty blonde with long hair and unusual, baby blue eyes." Ms. Waters handed Ross a snapshot of Leah. "You can keep the photo for your personal reference, Mr. Spencer. In the envelope, there is other information concerning Leah that you might find helpful."

The investigator pulled the pictures from a small manila envelope and perused one of them for a moment. Indeed, Leah was very pretty. The typewritten sheet of paper gave physical details. She appeared to be average height and build, had a quarter-size birthmark on the base of her inner, right bicep, and an old, one-inch diagonal cut scar on her left knee. Ross got up, handed the envelope to Rocio, and told her to make a dozen color copies of the snapshot and duplicates of the other information in the envelope.

"Where did Leah met Grifty?"

She sighed deeply and began, "He reportedly came into El Paso to renew one of his SNAP cards. According to Reverend Tasker, he may have fraudulent, SNAP card accounts in many different names."

Ross observed, "Some of them may not be living. Identify theft by drifters often follows the deaths of persons with whom they might have been traveling. Identities of cadavers who are transients are easy to steal because often no one will ever miss him or her. From stories I have read or hear, identity thieves among the rail riders often murder their victims, take their IDs and have new cards made with the photo of the thief replacing the real owner of the card."

"Yes, Mr. Spencer, a detective told me of that nefarious practice by some transients. He said that multiple SNAP accounts are how some of them get enough money to feed their drug habits, and they will kill other transients to get extra SNAP cards."

"El Paso seems like a long distance for Grifty to travel—just to renew a food stamp card."

"He had another reason. He also came to contact an old friend he used to hang out with in Los Angeles."

"How did you find out about that?"

"The police detectives that are investigating the case told me."

"Did they tell you the name of Grifty's friend?"

"Indeed they did. His name is Lorenzo Castillo."

While Ross and Rocio scribbled notes, Mrs. Waters went on talking. "I asked them if I could have Leah arrested as a runaway, and they said that it is possible but that it is only a so-called status offense and she'll just be turned over to me if

I am handy, and maybe released after a couple of days if I am not there to take custody. I think that if I could talk to her and let her know that she is forgiven and try to find out why she ran away, I might persuade her to stay at home, finish school...and..." Her voice trailed off into silent thought and private sorrow.

"What else did the detectives tell you about Lorenzo Castillo?"

"He was on probation for drug possession in California. They said he got his probation transferred here because his mother was ill. He worked at the Kwiko Taco Eatery not far from the school where Leah used to attend."

"Does he still work there?"

"No. He left just yesterday because he had finished his probation. His probation officer called me late yesterday to tell me. I had stayed in contact with his probation officer since we both believe that Castillo may eventually give us a lead as to where Grifty is—and that may lead us to Leah. Although the probation officer said he can no longer keep track of Castillo, he believes he may be headed back to California to re-join Grifty."

"It sounds like the probation officer gave sound, mature advice."

"I think so. He recommended that I hire a private eye, since they no longer have Lorenzo under supervision. At first, I was tempted to leave the case in the hands of the police, but I realize they are not going to drop everything else and dedicate themselves to finding Leah. Upon Reverend Tasker's recommendation, I decided that a private investigator is probably my best option. He did some research and suggested I come to you."

"I appreciate Reverend Tasker's opinion of me, and I think he gave you good advice to come to a private eye, due to the large number of missing teenagers, not just in California, but all across the nation. Is there anything else you think I might need to know about Lorenzo and Grifty?"

Ms. Waters looked down at the floor and rubbed the side of her face pensively for a moment. Her eyes lit up for a moment and she said, "This might be if some help: The police told me that they believe that Grifty and Lorenzo have gotten several high school girls, including Leah, hooked on drugs, especially methamphetamine. An anonymous informant told Detective Quinada that Lorenzo was still dealing, even while on probation. He was supposed to be selling small amounts of marijuana in the restroom hallway of the Kwiko Taco, out of sight of everyone in the eatery. The police said that small-time, street-level traffickers are hard to catch and that they are not top priority."

"Small-time pushers usually know all their customers and do not sell to strangers for fear they might turn out to be an undercover agent."

Ms. Waters seemed to ignore the investigator's remark. She shook her head slowly in despair and lamented, "Poor Leah. At age seventeen, she is so vulnerable—she cannot judge character. I went down to the Kwiko Taco Eatery late yesterday to see what I could find out, and one of the girls who worked there told me Leah got a tattoo before she left with Grifty. It was probably Grifty's idea. I guess it was his way of putting his brand on her, at least that's what the police detective suggested."

"Did the girl give you any description of the tattoos?"

"No, and I didn't press her. I don't know if the police followed up on that lead."

"The tattoo might help me to positively identify her, but we have quite a bit of other information here." What he left unsaid, communicated itself silently. Her countenance darkened and her eyes moistened again. She gazed silently for a moment in the distance, through the window behind Ross, toward a tall building across a parking lot. Ross did not have to tell l her that sometimes the police and PIs wind up looking for, or finding, cadavers instead of living people.

Ms. Waters lamented, "Sometimes I blame myself for teaching Leah that all people are basically good at heart. I have changed my ideas about that in recent times. Indeed, I now believe that some people—more than we realize in this day and time—are possessed by Satan himself—and they come disguised as human beings, and in that disguise they can easily cast their demoniacal spells and pain and suffering upon the vulnerable and innocent." Ross imagined that Mrs. Waters had spent some time in the pulpit, judging from her glibness and lines of speech.

The two P.I.'s exchanged discreet, esoteric glances and Rocio rolled her eyes in her familiar, sardonic 'tell me about it,' gesture. Nobody had to tell Rocio what evil lurks in the minds of some people. After all, a Juarez drug cartel had kidnapped her sister, and they had worked together, along with his deceased first wife, rescuing her. Then they had brought their boss' brand of "justice" to the murderers of the young factory workers. The murderers had tossed their bodies into isolated trash dumps near the border. Some Christians do not understand the complicated and often dangerous mental workings of psychopaths, like the types with whom he and Rocio often come into contact. Their types proliferate in border cities throughout the southwest. If a psychopath says he is converted, he is probably planning a diabolical deed that requires establishing the confidence of the targeted victim. There are plenty Elmer Gantry types out there that exploit the vulnerability of the faithful.

Ross tossed his empty paper cup into the wastebasket, and announced, "We would be glad to handle the job for you, Ms. Waters. Would you like to discuss a contract?"

Ms. Waters breathed a sigh of relief. "I'm so happy to hear that, Mr. Spencer. Just tell me how much money you need."

"Our fee will be two hundred thousand for a basic retainer for two months. I would work on this case exclusively, and as I mentioned to my wife, it would entail undercover work, travel to other states, and maybe to other countries, riding freight trains, staying in hobo jungles, homeless shelters, rescue missions, welfare offices and eating in soup kitchens. Undercover work entails expenses, so I will need another fifty thousand for incidental, or per diem, expenses. If we haven't closed the case within two months we'll have to re-negotiate the contract, both parties willing, depending upon our mutual prognosis—but let's hope it won't take that long."

Ms. Waters leaned forward in her chair and in a pleading tone said, "I was referred to you by a Christian organization. I trust you, Mr. Spencer."

"I appreciate that, Ms. Waters. As a former border agent, I am familiar with all the haunts, travel patterns and modus operandi of transients that I just mentioned because arresting illegal transients was my job for several years. Frequently my job led to assignments inside railroad transfer yards and areas near them where transients hang out. We have four major railway transfer yards here in El Paso, but from what you tell me, I think very little will be done here."

"Ross has hopped many a train," observed Rocio with a smile. "However, it was not for travel—but to get the travelers *off* the trains."

"That is among the things that Reverend Tasker told me. Could I now have a cup of water?"

Rocio brought Rachel Waters a cup of water from the cooler in the storage room, and Ross observed, "Most illegal aliens could be defined as hoboes, at least part of the time, but usually with different goals. I figure that the fee is commensurate with the hardships and the dangers of the environment and the types of people with whom I will be dealing and interacting. In addition to normal expenses, money is necessary to buy information and establish rapport with informants."

"It sounds fair to me," said Ms. Waters, putting her water cup on Ross' desk and removing a checkbook from her purse. She wrote out a check for two hundred and fifty thousand dollars and handed it to Ross.

Rocio took a contract form from the file drawer of her desk and brought it to Ross. He handed Rocio the check and heaved an inaudible sigh of relief, for often potentially lucrative contract negotiations die with low fee demands from bargain hunters that usually will get nothing that they pay for.

Ross said to his new client, "As soon as we get the contract executed, we need to go over to the domestic relations court and get a court order granting me temporary, co-custody of Leah, when I find her." He looked over toward his wife. "Rocio, would you please look up the California law for time limits on detaining 17-year-olds."

In about three minutes, Rocio had the answer on her computer. "It looks like seventy-two hours, Love...but there are a lot of ifs, ands and buts."

Ross explained to Ms. Waters, "That's what I thought. Like most other states, California authorities can detain her for up to seventy-two hours, until the legal parents arrive to take custody. I will have only the authority that you give me in a court order for temporary custody. We can work out the details on how to get her home after we find her."

"*If* you find her," said the sad lady, and added, "I'll pray that we can talk some sense into her head."

"I'm always the optimist, Ms. Waters. If you can't' get to California in seventy-two hours, I may rent a car and physically restrain her until we at least get to Arizona. We will have to improvise. I agree that the best approach is as you just suggested, trying to talk some sense into runaways. However, once they are hooked on drugs, and once they have experienced a period of freedom and imaginary self-reliance, convincing them to give it all up and come back to a normal life is problematic. Coming home to humiliation and ostracism is not an attractive alternative to a free life style, and if you can detain them, they'll tell you anything to get a chance to escape and go back to living on the street where they can score some more drugs."

"I will gladly agree to protective custody, or anything that would help me bring Leah home," said Ms. Waters. Her baleful eyes looked even sadder than when she had first come into the office. From her desk file drawer, Rocio dug out another form. Ross took it and handed it to Ms. Waters. "You need to fill out this petition to grant me temporary custody and then accompany me over to the court house to file it with the court of domestic relations. The court should approve it in a couple of days. We need to make it valid until Leah turns eighteen. After that, she will become an adult and legally emancipated. How much time do we have until she turns eighteen?

"She'll be eighteen next spring, April 4."

"We have a window of about six months within which to work."

"What then?"

"Then your only hope to return her to normalcy would be to get a court to declare her incompetent, at least temporarily, and extend your legal custody. Let's hope we can find her before all of those things come into play." Ross pulled out a printed form with a copy of his photo imbedded and handed it to Mrs. Waters. "After you fill out this form, I want you to write a brief note of introduction of me to Reverend Tasker in the square at the bottom of this form. To insure privacy and security, you should send it to him certified mail, restricted delivery. Sometimes employees sign for, and open, the office mail and for that reason we need to be sure to restrict information to those that have a need for it." Then Ross addressed his wife, "Rocio, I think that you and I should visit the Kwiko Taco Eatery tonight, what do you think?"

She turned slightly in her swivel chair, looked at him askance, smiled, and said, "I was wondering when you were going to take me out to dine again."

He turned back to Mrs. Waters and said, "We joke around a lot here, but we take our mission very seriously. Actually, we'll probably just enjoy a cup of coffee or soft drink at the fast food place, and dine somewhere else later."

"I understand."

"As soon as we can get the court order for custody and make a few purchases, I think the best approach would be for me to hit the open road toward L.A. to see Reverend Tasker, but I'll have to discuss that with my partner, Rocio. If we use that approach, along the way, I'll see if I can pick up any intelligence, or with a lot of luck, find Leah somewhere in between El Paso and L.A. If the trail leads me all the way to L.A., there

I might find some homeless men and women, and possibly witnesses that can provide information in addition to what Reverend Tasker might develop. Now let's discuss what you might provide that will help me identify her, or prove to the police that she is Leah. I'll need her social security number. It might help us locate her, and then help me to positively identify her after I find her."

"I don't mind giving you her social security number, but I don't understand how it will help locate her."

"We have confidential sources that can tell us if she is working somewhere, provided she *is* working—and provided she is using her *real* social security number. The number can also be useful if she applies for some sort of....benefit."

In spite of Ross' euphemistic effort to assuage the "welfare" word, anathema to most middleclass Americans, it visibly perturbed Ms. Waters. Ross quickly continued, "I don't ask my sources where or how they get their information, but I can assure you I use only reliable ones, and they must necessarily remain confidential."

Rachel Waters acknowledged with a nod. The sad, desperate mother pulled from her purse a small writing pad and, from memory, wrote down Leah's social security number. Then she began filling out the letter of introduction form.

"We'll need to exchange phone numbers with which we can contact one another 24/7," said Ross.

She dug in her purse and pulled out a calling card, and Ross gave her his. She said, "I will call Reverend Tasker today to let him know you are coming and that I am providing him with your letter of introduction."

"By the way, has Leah ever been fingerprinted, Ms. Waters?"

"Well, sort of. My husband and I used to be participants in the Polly Klaas Foundation, and we have a fingerprint kit. Herbert took Leah's fingerprints just before he died, but he smudged them pretty badly, and I tried to get Leah to go down to the police station with me and let them re-print her, but she refused."

"Why?"

"I think she picked up some bad habits and bad advice from some of her peers at that public school she was attending. She was getting very rebellious at about that time. I had wanted to send Leah to a private, faith-based school, but Herbert had argued that she needed to mix with, and get to understand, potential converts to our faith. He thought a public school would be a good experience for a future missionary. "

"I see."

"I can give you the smudged fingerprint card, if you think they can be useful."

"It most probably will be useful. Smudged prints are nearly always readable, with a little difficulty. Also, bring me a certified copy of Leah's birth certificate, if you have one."

"I have one at home."

"Bring it and we can get the county clerk to make copies, certify the copies, and give you back the original. Do you have and dental records of Leah?"

Rachel Waters sat silent, looking intently and questioningly at Ross. He knew what she was thinking: coroners are usually the only ones that use dental records for identification—of cadavers. He quickly explained, "They would be for positive identification, Ms. Waters, in case she tries to deny who she is when I find her. As co-legal custodian, I may be able to force her to get a dental exam, if she gets stubborn."

She assented. "I'll go by our dentist's office on my way home, get copies of her X-rays and bring them tomorrow."

Rocio was able to schedule a special custody hearing for the next day, and Mrs. Waters showed up on time at the office. She brought Leah's fingerprint card, birth certificate and dental records. Ross made four copies of all the documents in the duplicate of the office folder, and added these items to the biographical data inside a plastic, waterproof envelope that he would carry in his backpack. "If I need more copies to give to other agencies, I can make them before I run out," he said.

23

The court hearing went smoothly, and after Ms. Waters had left for home, Ross said to his wife, "Well, we have legal custody, if we need it, so it looks like we'll soon be ready to roll."

"*You'll* soon be rolling—on the steel wheels of a freight train," injected Rocio, almost sarcastically.

Ross smiled at his wife's humor. It was comforting that she was not pouting, for that would mean she wanted to go with him. "It sounds exciting, doesn't it? Last night I dreamed I was in a huge, dark, freight yard, enclosed by high walls with warehouses at the tops. I wanted to catch a freight train out of town with a bunch of friendly hobos, but I suddenly remembered that I had left the car parked downtown and I needed to get it and bring it home to you before I caught the freight. By that time, the train was moving and picking up speed, making a dismount dangerous. Since it was so dark, I had to jump around on the train from car to car to find one with a ladder that was safe for dismounting. When I got off, I could see a half-open door at the top of a wall that seemed to offer an exit from the train yards. To get to that door, I had to climb a huge, shaky scaffold. When I got near the top of the scaffold, the door slammed closed. I figured a railroad agent in the control tower had pushed a button to teach me a lesson. That was when I woke up—in utter frustration. It was weird. How would you interpret *that* dream, Hon?"

She gave him a severe look of reproof. "So you remembered—after you had parked *our* car down in the slums—that I might *need* it—or it might get damaged, or keyed? How considerate! And by the way, I didn't hear you say you had my consent to hop a freight train *last night* in a dark freight yard with high walls."

"It was just a *dream*, Hon."

She forced a worried smile, kissed him on the cheek and said, "I think that dream means that you are in for some difficult times, Hon."

CHAPTER TWO

At the Kwiko Taco Eatery, Ross discreetly asked the young, female server, "You're Cathy Cañedo, aren't you?"

She nodded nonchalantly and held her notepad and pen ready to take their order. She did not seem surprised that Ross knew her name. Ross gathered that, like most attractive servers, she was probably flattered with the thought that more former customers remembered her name than she did theirs.

"Where's that cook you used to have here? I think his name was 'Lorenzo," or something like that."

The youthful, raven-haired server looked up from her order tablet. "Lorenzo? I haven't seen him in a while. He told me he had finished probation and was going back to California. I think he has family out there."

"Did his old pal, Grifty go with him?"

"Grifty? I don't know. I barely knew Grifty. I haven't seen him in a while either, but I knew the girl that ran off with him, Leah Waters. She had been a regular in here. She said she met him on an Internet social media service." She chuckled and said, "I overheard her talking to another student in a booth over there by the window one day, and she was bagging about having met a real live hobo on the Internet. Can you imagine that? I mean bragging about *that*."

"I've heard of such things."

"Do you know Grifty?"

Ross held out his right hand, palm down, and rocked it back and forth. "So-so. Was Leah a friend of yours?"

The server began to show discomfiture at all the questions. She answered, "We were not really *close*, but I liked her." She lifted her order pad a little higher, signaling her impatience. Ross and Rocio gave her their orders: Coffee and an order of Nachos.

When the server left the table, Ross whispered to Rocio, "I think we've got about all the free information we're going to get. Try to lure her to the restroom hallway with that advance twenty-dollar tip, then tell her we'll give her fifty more if she'll meet you somewhere and help you work up a composite drawing of Grifty."

When Cathy Cañedo returned with their order, Rocio discreetly handed her a rolled up twenty, and with bated voice, introduced herself. The server took the twenty and Rocio advised, "That's your advance tip, and if you will meet me in the restroom hallway for a minute, there's much more where that come from. I need to ask you a question. It will take only a moment."

Cathy Cañedo looked askance at the cashier. He was reading a thrifty-bargain shopping paper. She whispered, "Give me a minute, and when I go in there..." she said, nodding toward the restrooms, "You follow me."

As soon as the server got a break from work, she gave an eye signal to Rocio and disappeared behind the hallway door. Rocio got up and met her in the narrow hallway.

When she got back from the meeting Rocio told Ross, "We're in luck. She's a criminal justice major at the community college and she really digs this kind of stuff. She does not fully comprehend everything that's going down, but she is sympathetic and agreed to meet us after work at the Big Beefy Burger over on North Loop. She's off duty here at five."

"Money talks better than people," said Ross with a smug grin.

Two hours later, Ross and Rocio met Cathy Cañedo at the hamburger place on North Loop, about mile from the Kwiko Taco. The three selected an isolated booth and ordered Cokes around. Rocio opened her computer notebook and downloaded a composite-drawing, software program. Cathy had a better than average memory and was able to pick out quickly the most prominent facial features of Grifty. Rocio soon had a composite facial image of Leah's mesmerist. Rocio asked her about Grifty's physical size and stature and she said that he was probably in excess of six feet, slender, with dishwater-blonde hair, displayed a snag, upper incisor, and sported rings on both ears. He had many tattoos, most of the details of which Cathy could not remember. She recalled, "Every time I saw him he was wearing a dirty red baseball cap with a marijuana leaf patch on the front—and I remember he also had a marijuana leaf tattoo here." She patted her upper right arm. "It was a green marijuana leaf—like Leah's."

"Leah had a tattoo?" asked Rocio.

The server patted her right upper arm: "Yeah, she got it just before she disappeared. It was a marijuana leaf—just like Grifty's."

Rocio scribbled notes of everything Cathy Cañedo said and added them below the composite image. Wrapping up the interview, Rocio asked Cathy whether she had heard anything about Grifty that might be significant: whether he had ever worked or held a job of any kind.

Cathy said, "Well, I remember Leah saying something about Grifty once worked as a carney."

That piqued Ross' interest. "He was a carney, huh? That seems consistent with everything we've learned so far."

Rocio decided to accept Cathy, the CJ major, into their sanctum as a trustworthy comrade-in-arms, and launched into cop talk. "Since he learned to rip off welfare, I'd say he would abhor any kind of work."

Ross agreed, "I've never seen a druggy really look for work. Some hold up pity signs saying, '*Will work for food,*' but if anyone offers them work, they laugh and decline. What they want are handouts, and if they get in a good location, they can rake in a couple hundred bucks in a day—but of course it's not as lucrative as welfare fraud."

After the meeting with Cathy, Rocio gave Cathy the promised fifty, plus a ten-dollar bonus.

When they pulled away from Cathy's' home, Rocio said, "Hey, those Kwiko tacos were not bad, Ross. Maybe we should do this again, sometime."

Ross looked at her quizzically.

"Seriously, I liked them."

"Fine, now I know where to take you for your next birthday."

"You're mean, Ross."

"He kissed her on the cheek and said, "You know that I'll take my office manager to the nicest restaurant in El Paso."

"Office manager...sounds important."

"It is. Rocio, and while we're on the subject, I want you to promise me that if anything comes up, like a lucrative contract that requires immediate field work, you'll call me before agreeing to any contracts. If we accept such a case, we'll want to put one of our intermittent investigators on it."

"I can do field work, too, you know," she said with a pout.

"Absolutely you can, Rocio." In a worried voice, he added, "But while I'm away, we need to stay in touch and be available for phone calls or text messages 24/7. You are my man Friday in the office."

"*Woman* Friday." she corrected.

Ross ignored the pouting verbiage. It was her way of displaying displeasure at his imminent departure. He understood. Her first husband had gone off to war in the Middle East, and had come back in a coffin.

The two sleuths spent the next few days going over notes and double-checking the Internet, including the interactive social media networks, to no avail. They made several copies of the composite drawing of Grifty and gave one to the local police agencies with a request to notify the two sleuths if they encountered him, or locked him up on some drug charge. They did not yet have enough on the sleaze ball to swear out a warrant for him, but they hoped that some alert cop might remember their request and let them know if they encountered Grifty or his known associate, Lorenzo Castillo. It was a routine, but necessary, exercise without much hope for success, but they did have a few friends on the P.D. and thought it might pay dividends.

After multiple unsuccessful efforts of Internet browsing for Leah's name, Rocio heaved a sigh of frustration and said, "Of course not even a naïve teenager is going to use her real name on the Internet. If and when we learn her street name, we might find something."

"We are bound to get a break eventually, Hon."

Rocio got up to get a cup of coffee and added, "This afternoon I'm going to have lunch with my relative from down at the welfare office and get her to check to see if Leah has applied for a SNAP or EBT card, or otherwise made contact with them. Their records cover all the U.S."

"Good girl. Of course, Grifty is skilled at anonymity, and probably street wise enough to get Leah a new counterfeit birth certificate, a new name and a new social security card. This is hardly his first rodeo in young, female enticement into running off with him."

"Probably not. As a carney he probably did a little of that. Young girls, especially in small, rural towns, learn too late that carnies are mostly a bunch of intermittently-employed, anonymous drifters, many with shady backgrounds. They use the glitter of the carnival to entice them to accompany them on to the next town—and beyond. Even in Mexico, in my hometown, that was a problem."

"Welfare and identity fraud probably would not impress young girls as much as the carnival glitter—until they learn how crafty and bold one has to be to engage in the practice—not to mention the easy money and a clever way to avoid working for a living. Everything these drifters do impress the young and naive."

"It can become a way of life until they get caught. Nevertheless, few get caught. A hobo once told me that welfare abuse by FTRA members is rampant because it is a lot safer from the possibility of physical violence than the usual theft and robbery."

"Not to mention that the jail sentences are much shorter, in the unlikelihood that they get caught."

"Your source has a window upon the underbelly of society, Rocio. She knows better than we do that engagement in welfare fraud is lucrative enough to feed expensive drug habits."

"It could take us eons to get information though regular channels with Freedom of Information Act applications. It is offset by the restrictions of the Privacy Act, and ultimately they can say that their information is protected and unavailable."

Ross nodded agreement. "The Government protects our entitlement class better than the gold in Fort Knox. We are fortunate to have your inside connection, and we must protect it at all costs."

Without looking up from her computer screen, Rocio muttered, "I've heard that there really isn't any gold in Fort Knox."

"Well, I have heard the same thing, and if it's true, I think we just broached upon the reason: domestic and foreign abuse of so-called safety net programs, which they say is two thirds of our national spending each year."

"The tail is wagging the dog."

"Yep, but that tail does not protect us from foreign invasions. I hear that they are now sending out social security checks with little notes saying that the well will run dry in 2033 and benefits will be reduced."

"Then I guess they must guard the empty vaults at Fort Knox to prevent national panic. If the mints ever run out of paper, ink and money presses, we're all up the creek without a paddle."

They laughed together and Rocio suggested, "That reminds me. Just to be meticulous, maybe we ought to check the Social Security death notices."

"That's an idea, but Social Security death notices are of limited value. They are not updated but once in a blue moon and we need very current information. They still depend upon the relatives of beneficiaries to report deaths—and send back the checks."

"It's nice to live in a country where we can still use the honor system, right, Hon?"

Ross looked at her studiously and after a moment, her poker face cracked into a laugh. "You had me worried there, Rocio. For a moment, I thought you might be serious." He got back to business. "We might as well check the obituaries of all the major southwest newspapers."

Rocio nodded, "Yeah, but they are of limited value since the homeless seldom have any relatives that care, even if any can be located—and if the bodies have never been fingerprint-ed, they might be buried with whatever alias the authorities choose among their identify cards."

"That's an unpleasant thought, Ross. Let's hope Leah is still alive. If she is deceased, they may have buried her with an assumed name, under whatever ID she was using at the time. Our cemeteries have plenty of Jane Does, like those we dis-covered on that gig in Juarez."

"At least our Jane Does have a six-foot-deep place to rest. In the border cities, missing young factory-working females lie either in isolated, roadside ditches, or in shallow graves."

"A gruesome thought to the uninformed, but we learned its truth, didn't we?"

Ross grunted agreement. "To someday learn that Leah has been long dead and that her body had just not yet been dis-covered—or identified—by the authorities would be a very sad end to this investigation."

"Especially to her mother."

After lunch, Rocio returned to the office to report that her relative had found no recent welfare applications, at least not in Leah's real name.

Ross suggested, "Well, since it hasn't been a fruitful day on the computers, I guess we can spend the rest of the afternoon doing my shopping at the thrift stores."

"You make it sound almost exciting, but it reminds me that you will soon be out there living among the dregs of society—and dressed like them. It is *not* a very comforting image."

"I know, but if I'm going undercover as a hobo, I need to blend into the environment. If it makes you feel better, I'll take my small travel kit with a couple of safety razors, but use 'em only if I have to mingle with the respectable side of society. Mostly, I'll be sleeping with the homeless under the stars, which reminds me I need to pick up a sleeping bag."

"You are not going to buy *that* in a thrift store, are you?"

"No, Hon, for *that* I'll go to a sporting goods store and get a new one. I don't want to share anyone's scabies."

"I hoped not. I'm going to double-launder every piece of clothing you buy in a thrift store, anyway, to be as safe as possible."

"I may become unshaven and grubby, but trust me Hon, I won't forget personal hygiene."

Inside the first thrift store, Ross started filling up a shopping basket with dark clothing.

Rocio asked, "Why all *dark* clothes? It seems sort of sinister..."

"Most professional hobos travel mostly at night nowadays, and dark clothing blends in with the darkness."

"I don't like black. It reminds me of funerals."

Ross ignored the remark and said, "I'll have our seamstress sew in a breakaway holster with snaps under the left shoulder of all the shirts, custom-sized for my 9 mm semi."

They got back into the SUV and Rocio asked, "Isn't your permit to carry a concealed weapon good only in Texas, Ross?"

"If I get searched outside of Texas, I'm screwed if they find my weapon. You might be coming somewhere out west to bail me out of jail. I'll keep my weapon in my backpack, except maybe when I wind up in a boxcar with some unsavory characters—then, I'll want it handy—in my special pocket."

"You mean unsavory—as in *FTRA*?"

"Exactly, and I'll try to avoid that scenario. However when you're improvising, it can lead you into some strange situations. Boxcars are like a Shakespearean tempest—they make strange bedfellows. When working the freight yards as a border guard, I've called coroners to come and pick up bodies of hobos that chose the wrong boxcar, or the wrong traveling mates. You've heard the old cliché, but nobody really *can* sleep with one eye open."

"Knowing you, Ross, I'd say that you will sleep with both eyes open, but at six feet and a hundred and seventy pounds, you should be able to use your fists to avoid using a gun against criminals you might run into."

"A lot of experience in street fighting is fine in an emergency, if some lone criminal tries to overpower and rob me, but if I'm facing more than one, the best way out may be to run—I'm very fleet afoot, you know."

"*You*? Run from a *fight*?"

"Hey, Sweetheart, discretion is the better part of valor. Our client is paying us to use our best judgment, and all vanity is suspended. Criminal-type hobos like the FTRA usually run in packs, like wolves, especially when hanging around hobo jungles. This is not that border-body-dump mission in Juarez all over again. If I have to use deadly force in this country, the mission, for all practical purposes, is over. I might eventually beat such charges, but it would require a good lawyer, waste a lot of time, and draw unnecessary attention to us and our mission. Unlike Mexico, we don't have anarchy conditions as we had back then when the cops hid from the cartels. Cops in this country are professional, more efficient, and they are not short-handed. If I blow my cover in a display of vain machismo with some psychopath and get the cops on my case, we haven't been fair to Ms. Waters. Say where do you want to dine tonight?"

Rocio looked at him worriedly, noting his abrupt change of subject. "Why don't we try Chinese food?"

"Chinese it is."

While Ross steered the SUV toward their favorite Chinese restaurant, Rocio said, "Be sure to eat well and stay in shape on the road, Ross. It will give you the physical advantage—if superior intellect fails."

He leered at her suspiciously, and then gave her the benefit of the doubt that she was being sarcastic. "Uh-huh, that's important, but I was thinking. I need to think up some kind of false identity, some kind of story to tell when talking to others while on the mission."

"Yeah, I guess it would not be cool to tell everyone you're a private eye."

"Yep, most on the people living on the fringes of society have pasts that they want to leave behind, but I think my personality is more suited to a different role—you know, sort of a nerdy, struggling writer—one named Jake."

"I suppose that role would compensate for not appearing mentally deranged like a lot of drifters. I'm a little skeptical about a writer named *Jake*. It doesn't sound like a writer's name."

"Very few do and that is the reason many writers assume pseudonyms. Once you succeed, even Koontz sounds like a writer." Ross cocked his head pensively, considered Rocio's observation, and decided, "Jake will have to do because I'm already acquainted with my alter ego, Jake."

"But how many writers are out there consorting with bums while gathering material?"

"As a border guard in the freight yards, I did occasionally come across a writer or two traveling on the rails. In fact, I can even remember a couple of college graduate students, at different times, sitting on the front porches of hopper cars, and working on theses. I envied 'em. As I've mentioned to you before, and if I had followed my instincts, after the Army I would have actually lived the life of hobo—and if I had, when I grew old, I'd have written about it, instead of taking up fishing, or something less mentally demanding. After retirement from this job, I still may indulge in writing."

"I remember your telling me about your latent ambitions—or lack thereof—to be a hobo, but I thought you had forgotten about it. There are other subjects about which to write. We both already have a lot of interesting experiences to draw from. Maybe we can do *that* as a team too someday, maybe co-author a book—about subjects other than hoboing."

"Correct! Hey, every writer needs an editor and critic or co-author and I know you wouldn't pull any punches, but you wouldn't be as harsh as...well like my older sister."

"What *about* your sister?"

"Oh, once I had a class project in the sixth grade to write a poem. At that age, it was, of course, doggerel, but I still remember my sister's cackle. When coming home on the school bus, she found it where I had folded and stuck it in the pages of my English textbook. She read it to her friends, and they all got a good laugh."

Rocio laughed aloud. "That's funny. If you were expecting praise from an older sister, it's because you forgot your place in the family pecking order."

"No wonder so many kids run away from home. They're probably all younger siblings."

Rocio brought the subject back to the business at hand. "Leah had no older siblings to put her down, yet she ran away with the most loathsome scumbag imaginable."

"Yeah...she had a wonderful family, as far as I can tell. We will leave that puzzle to the sociologists. Our problem is just to find her and bring her home..." He paused a moment and said, "I recall that hobos liked to talk with border guards..."

"You're not thinking of impersonating a federal officer, are you?"

"Hell, no—first of all, that would be a felony, then as a border guard, I always had a partner while working in the freight yards. I was just mentally making a short trip down memory lane, thinking that my experience of communicating with hobos should help. Most of them liked border guards because we helped keep the illegal aliens from taking over the freight yards and giving them all a bad image with the railroad agents. They cooperated with railroad agents and reported cases of illegal aliens breaking into boxcars and stealing cargo. Hobos think that the illegals have made it rougher on *all* rail riders, like those that used to break into and rob boxcars at the Anapra, New Mexico siding. The siding stood only a hundred yards from their sanctuary, the Mexican border. Once they got their loot across the border, they were home free. Illegal aliens and the FTRA have both given hobos a black eye. Those gangs and stepped-up security, especially since 9-11-01, makes freight hopping much more challenging than a few years ago. I hear that railroad agents are suspicious of everyone nowadays."

Rocio's brow furrowed again. She rubbed her chin and said, "Ross, I've been thinking, Hon, maybe you could save a lot of time and risk-taking by just catching a plane to Los Angeles. That's where Reverend Tasker's Skid Row rescue mission is—the place he and others last saw Leah and Grifty."

"That would be a shot in the dark. There are a lot of freight yards, hobo jungles, soup kitchens, and rescue missions between El Paso and Los Angeles—Tucson, Yuma, El Centro, Colton—and I intend to scour as many as I can. As soon as I get on a freight train, I'm on their trail. Hey, Hon, the hobo grapevine is one of the most prolific sources of information imaginable and has been around before the Internet. All hobos seem to know one another, either by sight or by reputation. I may not need to go all the way to L.A., but if I wind up there, I'll need a little railroad grime on me to help me blend in with the people I'm going to be dealing with."

"You could go out to the meat packing plant and wallow in a pig pen—then catch a plane," she said with a smirk.

"Yeah, right, they let passengers covered with pig poop board planes every day— Hey, Hon, sarcasm isn't helpful here. The fact is, I've been away from freight trains for a while and I need to refresh my memory on a lot of things. Occasionally, when I find someone I trust, I may show Leah's picture, to learn if he or she has seen her. I want to put out the best effort possible for our client. There's an implied guarantee of putting forth our best effort in every contract. I mentioned those hardships and hazards when I quoted our fee to her."

"That word, *grime* still doesn't sound very appealing."

"Don't worry, Hon. When I come back to you, I promise I'll be neat as a pin."

Rocio's face darkened. "Then I guess I may not see you for six months?"

"If this gig gets to be longer than I expect, you could fly out and meet me for a couple of days on occasion—if you don't mind staying in a cheap motel."

"We can afford nice motels nowadays."

"Yeah, but the world I'm working in is on the fringes of society and out in the boon docks. There won't be many nice motels, if any, near the working area."

"Don't forget to call me, or text, or e-mail me every day."

"I promise I will, Hon—we'll need to stay close in touch because things happen around offices, too. We have to keep the office open, you know."

CHAPTER THREE

Ross' flashback of the events of the past few days faded, but his eyes remained fixed upon the spot where he had last seen the taillights of Rocio's SUV. Loneliness began to set in more profoundly. His life mate's departure had brought back memories of emotions he had once felt as a small kid. After his older brother started to school, his daylight hours were long and lonely, and he watched the clock a lot, knowing exactly where the large and small hands would be when the school bus would bring his older brother back home. One day, his mother had sent him to the field to take his father a jug of ice water. When he delivered the water and left his father plowing the field, he started the trek back to the house. On the way back, the wide-open spaces of the plains suddenly engulfed him in abject loneliness and he had cried. No one heard him, of course, and his six-year-old pride was not injured, and after a good cry, he felt better. Didn't a Hank Williams mention a grown man crying from loneliness?

Now, however, there was no emotional outlet. He thought that he was beginning to understand the meaning behind that nightmare he told his wife about when he was in that canyon-like freight yard, trying to catch out when he remembered he needed to return the family car to Rocio.

Ross' memories of monophobia were interrupted by the clashing of railroad cars on the far side of the tracks—toward the westbound rails. Though he'd been away from the yards a few years, he knew that a switch engine was making up a westbound train. He walked faster toward the bushes and weeds where he had rousted out many an illegal alien, waiting to hop freight trains. He approached the area cautiously and

38

found a small clearing in the weeds on the north slope of the canal bank where he could sit and conceal himself. Just as he unstrapped his backpack to relax, the cough of a man startled him. He craned his neck, trying to see more clearly, and the bright, red glowing ember of a cigarette pinpointed the source of the cough. The man that had coughed sat camouflaged in dark clothing against the dark background of tumbleweeds. Ross took a small LED flashlight from his shirt pocket, lit him up and got a good look at him. In the light, he could see that the man was small, wore a dark, denim jacket with shiny, copper buttons. On the man's head, cocked at a rakish angle, was a slouchy, denim hat with a narrow, flimsy brim, turned up all around. The hobo cleared his throat and spoke in a sober, high-pitched Southern accent. "Howdy, Bo. Catchin' out?"

Ross laid down his bedroll and backpack in the weed clearing and said, "Yeah. You gave me a start with that cough."

"Not half as much as you gave me when you clicked on that flashlight, dude. I thought you were a bull."

"Sorry," said Ross.

"No harm done. Where you catchin' out to?"

"Goin' west—you waitin' for a westbound, too?"

"That I am," replied the diminutive hobo. "They're making up a westbound train now. I can hear them bangin' the cars together over east of here. At night, the crash of railroad cars always sounds louder—and you can hear it further."

Ross sat down in the weed patch near the hobo and asked, "You catch-out here often?"

"About once a month—I have a food stamp account here—as well as another in Tucson—and one in L.A. I'm hopin' to dodge the bulls, stay out of jail and head back to Tucson. Then I'll head for L.A. There's more free money from my California EBT card."

"It looks like you found a pretty safe place to catch out here in these weeds, bro."

"As safe as can be expected. By the way, most people call me Sandhouse."

39

"Just call me Jake."

"Jake? It doesn't sound like the name of a veteran of this game."

"Actually, I'm a writer and I plan to gather stories from hobos—like you—and someday try to put it all together in a book."

"That's interesting," Sandhouse's, voice rose in interest. He squirmed, removed his hat, scratched his head and said, "Every once in a while I run into a writer lookin' for stories. Most are young college students."

"I'll bet you have a few stories for them."

"Yeah, I try to help 'em out, but I don't bullshit 'em like some of these younger hobos and make up stories."

"I'm sure they appreciate your honesty."

"I wish I could write good enough to do a book. I could fill several books with what I know and what I've seen, but most writers are young and prefer to hang around people their own age, but they ain't gonna learn much about this profession from those young-uns."

"Then I'm lucky I met you, Sandhouse."

"If you hang around railroad yards very long, you'll probably get a new handle, Jake. Other hobos give out the handles. You don't get to choose your own."

Ross laughed. "How'd you get yours?"

"I used to sleep in sand houses in the freight yards in cold weather. They are always a warm place to sleep because the trains have to keep their sand dry for braking the big engines. In the winter the rails get cold, wet and icy."

"I've read how the sand is channeled under the steel wheels to give them traction, when icy."

"Yep, and that's why railroad tracks are always so shiny." He hesitated for a moment and continued, "Anyway, one night me and some other hobos got rousted out while sleepin' in a sand house in El Paso, and a bull asked me my name. I was drunk and feelin' kinda bold, so I just blurted out, 'Sandhouse Sam.' That bull slapped me to the ground and said, 'I meant your *real* name!' I didn't have an I.D. with me

40

so I gave him a fictitious name that I don't even remember anymore—not my real name, of course. Anyway, after the bull ran us out of the yards, us bo's all got to drinkin' wine under a tree near the freight yards. The other bo's laughed about me gettin' slapped for tryin' to jerk the bull around. The handle, *Sandhouse,* stuck, but not the *Sam.* Most bo's in the southwest will know who you are talkin' about if you mention a hobo named Sandhouse."

Ross heard human voices approaching from his right and whispered the news to Sandhouse.

Sandhouse whispered back, "It might be the bulls—they work in pairs." He put out his cigarette and said, "Just lie low in these weeds and they'll probably pass without noticing us."

In the darkness, Ross could see three shadowy figures, and soon two tall men with husky voices walked past, headed west, trailed by a female. She complained in broken English, "You *batos* walk *fast!* You want I *run?*" She was carrying what appeared to be a sleeping bag and her voice made her seem to be in her mid-to-late-twenties.

"Shut up, Maria—and keep up!" snapped one of the men in a husky, domineering tone.

Hustling to try to keep up, Maria, with her bedroll swinging sideways, said, "You *batos* promise me a feex."

"When we get on the train, Maria."

After they were out of earshot, headed west alongside the railroad tracks, Sandhouse said, "I think I recognize the voices of those two guys. If they are who I think they are, they're FTRA. I guess they picked up and an illegal Mexican woman at the soup kitchen to entertain 'em on the road. They're probably headed west, too, and we don't want to get on a rail car anywhere near them."

"You say you saw those guys at a soup kitchen?"

"Yeah, here in El Paso a couple of days ago. They're mean, ornery—hang out together—I didn't get to know their monikers, but I remember those voices. I think they practice talkin' in those deep, tough voices to scare people."

The conversation between Ross and his companion wound down, both now listening to the slam of boxcars, getting louder and closer. Ross looked up at the sky. He could not see a single star through the haze. The light and dust pollution formed halos around the yard's tower lights.

The switch engines continued to roar intermittently in the thin night air, chugging forward and backward. Ross began to relax and self-rebuke. Damn, Ross, you really should have done this when younger, carefree and unattached! Meeting people like Sandhouse was an adventure in itself. There must be thousands of hobos out there willing to share their stories. Any of them who had been riding the rails as long as Sandhouse, could probably write a best seller, if he could just master the mother tongue, or find a good ghost writer or co-author. Maybe, after retirement, he would indeed write a book about this life.

Ross reminded himself that he had to be careful and not let his dormant passion for hoboing distract him from his assignment. He said, "Say, Sandhouse, have you ever heard of a hobo named 'Grifty?' I think he was involved with the FTRA."

His traveling companion coughed up some phlegm and spat it on the grass on the opposite side. "I think I bumped into him at a soup kitchen in California a couple of years ago—a skinny guy with a snag tooth. I don't hang out with FTRA. They're bad news. Do you know Grifty?"

"No, but I've heard of 'im. You don't think one of those two FTRA guys that just walked past could be him, do you?"

"Hell no, I don't remember their handles, but both of those guys are a lot bigger than Grifty—and I'd know that high-pitched voice of Grifty's anywhere."

"I heard Grifty's quite a dude—sort of a legend in some places, and in the FTRA. He might make a good story."

"I doubt he'd be worth spending a lot of your time on. He sure ain't no legend, or I'd know 'im better. My impression of 'im was that he's probably more sneaky than tough, like most FTRA dudes."

"Fair enough, Sandhouse—then tell me a story I *can* write about."

Sandhouse chuckled, coughed, spat again and lit up a new cigarette. He began, "Well I started to ride the rails after I first tried roamin' as a hitchhiker. Hitchin' on the highways is a lot more dangerous than hoppin freights."

"How do you figure?"

"Hell, hitchin' puts you in a dangerous position. You have to stand close to the highway on the shoulder of the road. There are more than a few sadistic motorists on the highways."

"Sadistic?"

"Hell yeah, they'll throw rocks, beer bottles and all sorts of dangerous things at you when they drive by. If you wanta find out just how low and savage some people in this country are, just try hitchin' on the highways for a while."

"They sound evil, alright."

"Ha! Not just evil, they are crafty, too. They've got wheels and they know that a hitchhiker is a transient with no local community ties and they know hobos don't get any sympathy from local cops. Hell, the local police chief might be a rock thrower's brother-in-law."

"I hadn't thought of that."

Sandhouse grunted, "Uh-huh," and continued, "I remember once, I was headed west, thumbin' on the outskirts of Wilcox, Arizona. A cowboy with a big Stetson and his wife were driving past me in a pickup truck. They had a little boy about five years old standin' on the seat next to the passenger window. I was facin' the vehicle with my thumb out, and the pickup began to slow and I thought they were goin' to pick me up to maybe ride in the bed of the truck. I saw the dad tell his kid somethin' and then hand him an object. I quickly learned that the object was a rock. The kid threw that rock at me through the open window and if I hadn't ducked when I did, that rock would have hit me in the head. A kid that age can't throw a rock hard enough to hurt me ordinarily, but add in the speed of the pickup, and he could kill you, if he hit you in

43

the head. The man and his wife looked back through the rear window laughin' and the father tousled his sons' hair as if to congratulate him. I made up my mind if I ever saw that cowboy at a truck stop, or some other place, I was gonna beat hell out of 'im. When hitchin', I always carried a set of brass knuckles in a zipper pocket of my duffel bag and another pair in the waistband of my pants. They are weapons that even up things and make a fight with a big dude fairer; in fact, it gives you an advantage if you are quick, get in the first blow, and know how to use 'em. I'm strong for my size, and fast. When they underestimate me due to my size, it gives me the advantage of surprise. Ya gotta learn to detect the necessity quick, and sucker punch them before they do it to you—but as I got older I've learned to recognize trouble brewing and get the hell away from someone I might have to fight."

If the police catch you with brass knuckles, it is a felony, thought Ross, but he kept his thoughts to himself and said, "That's an Interesting story Sandhouse, but I find it a little surprising that you think ridin' the rails is safer than hitching automobile rides."

"Hell, yeah it is—I mean you can take up with the wrong man or wrong crowd, but you learn to use and trust your survival instincts and you learn who you can trust. No matter how careful you are, you gotta remember, your choices of rides are limited by the number of offers, and if you've been standin' out there in the hot sun, or the freezin' cold, for hours on end, you quit lookin' for red flags and you're willin' to take a chance and accept the next ride offered. You forget that any motorist can be a nut case, a serial killer, or a bondage, sadist freak. The ones you feel uneasy with, you try to get away from immediately. You obey your gut instincts and refuse a ride when you see a red flag go up. Now take yourself, for example. I suspected you were a writer or somethin' like that. You're too clean—hell, I cain't even smell cigarette smoke on you— and I can tell by the way you talk that you're educated. Even in the dark, I knew that you ain't a regular bo of the road. You're the kind of person another honest man can trust, not to say you can trust all educated people. They have their crazies, too. If I get hooked up with someone I don't trust, I just say, like, 'I gotta get out and take a dump,' or make some other excuse, and you tell 'em to go on without you. I'd rather sleep in culverts along the road for a week than take a chance on getting' injured or killed by a drunk driver...or travel with a pervert that sexually preys on males of all ages. I've had fellow bo's tell me that they've been raped with a gun to their head."

"I appreciate the advice, Sandhouse."

"On the other hand, there are dangers in rail ridin', but your precautions are different. Some of the meanest, orneriest men you can imagine are out here ridin' the rails, but it is easy to stay away from them. Again, you gotta use your gut feeling. Watch for the red flags. The FTRA nuts are a good example. Hell, I've come across dead bodies a few times. Usually, I just ignore 'em and walk on—you know why? If a drifter like us reports a crime like that, they make us the prime suspect. If I can afford a pay phone, I might make an anonymous call to the cops, but mostly I just keep movin at the sight of trouble. I'm not a fan of spendin' a month in jail on some trumped-up trespassing charge while they try to make me admit I'm guilty of somethin'—or maybe they think they can break me down and make me squeal on somebody else, even though I have nothing useful I can tell 'em. Some bulls and some cops just want to make a case and they don't really care if they have the right person. They just want a conviction. They don't believe anything we say anyway, and they'll accept lies if it fits their plans. There are a lot of innocent people in prison, but the cops figure, what the hell, people like us have *got* to be guilty of somethin', so they figure they are doing society a favor by getting' us in jail, anyway."

"Your caution is understandable, Sandhouse."

"Another thing you gotta watch for in this game are dudes that will try to eg you into a fight. They seem to thrive on violence, especially if they're high on alcohol, crank, or both; and some won't even stop at murder for kicks, if you know what I

45

mean. These FTRA characters will kill you for sport, for your ID, for your food stamps or the boots on your feet, if they take a likin' to 'em."

Sandhouse threw the butt of his cigarette into the weeds, stood up, looked around, sat down, pulled out a new cigarette, peeled a match off a paper package, leaned back into the weeds, and lit up again. His adrenalin seemed to be flowing from memories. He sat upright again, took a deep draw and puffed up a large cloud of white smoke. He coughed and spat again and continued, "A few bulls are brutal and will hurt you, too. A long time ago, there was one that worked these same yards. When I first met 'im, he was a curly-haired, blonde prick of a kid they called JJ. I guess he's either retired—or maybe the FTRA killed him."

"I've read stories about some bad apples out here ridin' the rails, Sandhouse. Right now, I'm thinking of an FTRA enforcer called Robert Silveria. He's doing life without parole, last I heard. Then there was Angel Resendez. They already executed him."

"Yeah, I've heard of both of 'em, but I never ran into to 'em. If I had, my survival instincts would have made me get to hell away from either of 'em." Resendez wasn't FTRA because he was an illegal alien. They don't let them join the FTRA, and his victims were ordinary people, often the elderly, that mostly lived near the railroad tracks—not fellow rail riders—not like most of the victims of the FTRA. Resendez used the rails as his primary transportation, but he was also a burglar that deliberately broke into homes while the occupants were sleeping, killed them and always had sex with the dead females. Now, take Silveria, he preyed mostly on his own kind—the homeless—or even members of his own gang—to take their EBT and identity cards."

Ross had heard, or seen, such freight-yard horror tales before, but it was good to keep Sandhouse talking. "I'll try to benefit from your experience while I'm ridin' the rails, Sandhouse. I suppose being arrested for trespassing, is just one of the minor hazards of riding the rails."

"You got that right, Jake. Most of the time, the railroads don't prosecute for trespassing. Hell, the jails are full of real criminals that rob, steal, beat up and kill people. Just don't give the bulls a hard time like I did when I got my nickname and you'll usually be okay, unless you run into a gung ho sadist like that JJ I mentioned earlier."

Ross already knew from his own background that transients and the homeless who become victims of violence are low priority for police departments. Riding the rails is a perfect place for a psychopathic serial killer like Robert Silveria. By the time the authorities discover their victims' bodies, they are usually hundreds of miles away.

After a few draws on his cigarette, Sandhouse broke the silence. "Like I say, I could write you a book if only I knew how to put one together. Here's somethin' you might want to remember: Highway hitchhikers are also often victims of robbers."

"That's rather surprising, considering the limited means of most of them."

"Hell, Jake, I've been a victim myself. About twenty years ago, I was hitchin' on I-10 about fifty miles west of Phoenix when this dude in an old beat-up clunker stopped and offered me a ride. He said he was on his way to Tucson, and I was on my way to El Paso to collect some food stamps. We traveled a few miles and he pulled into a greasy spoon café just off I-10 near Tolleson, Arizona. He drove to the rear of the building to park and that should have sent up a red flag to someone more experienced than I was at the time. He said his old car was usin' a lot of oil and he wanted to put in a quart. He handed me two bucks and told me to go inside and get two cups of coffee while he put in the oil. That seemed reasonable because the managers of those places won't let you work on cars in their parking lot. Anyway, since he was generous enough to buy me coffee, it threw me off guard. I took the two bucks and went inside. When I came out with the coffee and returned to the rear of the building, my ride was nowhere in sight. I checked the whole parking lot and it soon became obvious that he had left and ripped off my luggage."

"It still befuddles me that a thief would victimize hitchhikers, whom I can't imagine carrying many valuables."

"Some carry more than you think. I had a nice new jacket, which I needed, because the nights were already gettin' cold. I had a little extra cash for emergencies inside an envelope, a flashlight, a camera, a transistor radio and an electric razor—all of it in my duffel bag."

"He must have been running a flea market somewhere."

"Maybe so, but anyway, that ain't the end of the story. Just outside of Tucson at a truck stop, I met another hitchhiker who'd been ripped off by the same guy. It's not just some sort of fetish. They have motives. Sometimes hitchhikers carry food stamps, ID cards and a little money in their baggage." Sandhouse let out a sardonic chuckle. "Lookin' back at it, it's sort of funny how I let that guy rip me off, but I've talked to a lot of hobos, and you'd be surprised how many thieves rip off inexperienced hitch-hikers. Beginners soon learn to never leave a car without their belongings."

Ross and his new hobo companion sat silently for a spell, and soon Sandhouse said, "Jake, you see that engine with the bright light on the front of the engine, about half a mile east of here? That's gonna be our train."

Sandhouse started strapping on his backpack and Ross followed cue. He said, "I'm glad I ran into you, Sandhouse. Your experience is very helpful."

In a few minutes, the engineer sounded the highball, two short blasts of an air horn, indicating he was pulling out. Sandhouse said, "Freight trains gain speed really fast, so we'd better get across to the main, westbound track. We need to catch it while it's still goin' slow. I never try to grab onto one traveling more than about five miles per hour. I've known too many inexperienced hobos that got yanked under the wheels."

Ross let Sandhouse take the lead. As a border guard, he too had seen the victims of inexperienced train hopping. He did not doubt that Sandhouse had as much experience as he claimed, but he withheld his own views on the subject. A display of too much knowledge about train hopping could arouse Sandhouse's suspicions and cause him to clam up. Although he apparently doesn't know much about Grifty, other than a little hearsay, he might yet be a source of useful information.

The two traveling companions hustled across several railroad tracks to the north side of the yards, and as their train went slowly past, a grain hopper car approached. "Hopper cars are great," said Sandhouse. Let's grab the back porch of that one."

Sandhouse tossed his duffel bag and bedroll onto the rear platform of the car and Ross followed suit. While the train gained speed, Ross instinctively accelerated his pace, leaving Sandhouse behind, and grabbed the handrail of the hopper. He deftly planted his right foot into the lower right corner of the stirrup of the last rung of the ladder, simultaneously pulling himself up to the platform. He quickly moved his luggage over to the opposite side of the back porch to make room for Sandhouse. The seasoned hobo ran alongside the train, awkwardly for a moment, but managed to grab the handrails of the ladder before jumping onto the ladder with both feet, simultaneously. His right foot slipped all the way to the right corner of the stirrup, and he almost lost his balance. Fortunately, he had enough arm strength to pull himself up, out of danger. Ross felt an impulse to tell him how to do it safely, but that would blow his cover and Sandhouse would suspect that he had been hoodwinking him about being a novice rail rider.

When Sandhouse settled onto the south side of the back porch, he said, "Damn Jake, you made grabbing this car look easy. You sure you ain't ever hoboed before?"

"I read some Internet stuff on hoboing before I started out. It's no substitute for experience, though."

"You're a fast learner, Jake—without any practice, too. I'm gonna try to do it the way you did the next time I get on a moving freight car. You looked like you were giving that bottom ladder rung a karate kick, and then the first thing I know you're up on the platform."

While the train continued gaining speed, Sandhouse placed his bedroll against the slanted wall of the hopper car, leaned against it and stretched his short legs all the way to the edge of the back porch and said, "Keep your eye peeled on your side for the bulls and I'll watch this side. If you see a dark, green SUV driving slowly alongside the tracks, let me know and we'll jump off on this side and cut through the yards to a safe hidin' place. The same move applies to the opposite direction, if I see a railroad cop comin' on this side of the train, then we'll head for the bushes over on your side."

"How long do you think it'll take us to get to Tucson, Sandhouse?"

"Oh, I'd guess about an hour after sunrise. This train may stop at a siding out west of the town to let another train pass in the opposite direction. If that happens, we gotta be very careful because there may be bulls out there to protect the train from hijackers across the border. That railroad siding is just a few hundred yards from the Mexican border. If we get past the siding in good shape, and the train stops in Lordsburg, it will be just to change crews and we may have to hit the weed patch there—if there are bulls around. However, that would be nearly two hours after midnight and the bulls seldom work into the wee hours of the morning. From Lordsburg, we'll ball it on to Tucson. The old Southern Pacific trains used to change crews in Lordsburg, but since it merged with Union Pacific, I haven't noticed any crew changes in Lordsburg. The last one I took ripped right on through to Tucson."

"Tucson seems like a good place to study hobos and maybe collect some stories," ventured Ross.

"You bet it is. There are some good rescue missions and some good soup kitchens in Tucson—one is Casa Merced, not far from the main freight yard. I'll show you when we get there. In the morning, they dish out free donuts with coffee, and in the afternoons, they give us free sandwiches with coffee. I nearly always eat and drink coffee there when passing through. It's a good place to hang out when you're gettin' EBT cards renewed and you'll find plenty of people willin' to help you with your writin' project."

Sandhouse pulled a bottle of cheap wine from the center of his bedroll and offered Ross a swill, which he politely refused. The hobo said emphatically, "Wine is good tonic to help you sleep on a freight train. Once the loud noise of a railroad car becomes monotonous and humdrum, a little wine will put you out like a light. However, as I said, I would not sleep around just anyone. I know who I can trust."

Ross had to keep up his vigilance, for when people like Sandhouse tell you they trust you, it often means they are getting ready to impose on you and make you responsible in some way for their safety and care. Ross knew about the effects of cheap wine on hobos. They go to sleep so soundly, even on a bare metal floor, that it was difficult to awaken them to check their citizenship or IDs. He'd seen them sleep through the banging of cars when trains were coupling or uncoupling. Ross assured his companion, "If I feel like I need it to sleep, maybe I'll try a little wine later."

Ross did not plan to spend much time in Tucson, but he knew that soup kitchens and rescue missions are exactly the types of places that could produce information that might eventually lead to Leah Waters and her low-life mentor, Grifty. Who knows, he thought, he just might just bump into her in some skid row soup kitchen. If he did, he was not sure what course of action he would take. He'd have to improvise and try to gain her confidence until he got a chance to bring in the local authorities, to enforce his temporary custody order. If he did *not* run into her, he would continue visiting such places all the way to L.A.

By the time the train reached full speed, the wind grew chilly. A strong autumn wind from the north whipped around both corners of the front porch of the hopper, and in the yard's dim tower lights, Ross observed Sandhouse buttoning the top of his denim jacket. The veteran hobo then shifted into a fetal position, pulled his fedora down over his eyes and rested his head on his bedroll.

The train glided through a familiar, dimly lit tunnel, under the skyscrapers of downtown El Paso where he used to roust illegal aliens from behind recessed breaker boxes in the walls of the tunnel and from their other hiding places.

Clear of the tunnel, the train followed the northward bend of the river along the foothills of the western slope of Mount Franklin. It curved right, snaked to the left, then turned sharply west, across a high viaduct. Far below, Ross could see the headlights of early morning commuters speeding along I-10. He breathed a sigh of relief because the train's speed indicated it would not be stopping at the Anapra, New Mexico siding to let an inbound train pass. That was good. The train's cargo would not be subject to a raid by border bandits this trip, nor would Ross and his companion be hassled by railroad agents, nor threatened by Mexican bandits.

Ross began to relax, resting his head upon his bedroll, pulling his legs up to keep them from dangling over the edge of the platform. He looked skyward, but the anticipated beauty of a midnight train ride eluded him. They were still too close to El Paso and too much light reflected off the polluted sky to display any but the brightest stars. It was not a starry night like Jimmy Rodgers sang about in *Waiting for a Train*.

He took a deep breath, enjoying the clean countryside, thinking how lucky he was to be free from the futile cat and mouse games of the border guards. As a private eye, he was his own boss, now enjoying the freedom of the open road with the hobos he used to envy—and being paid well for it. It doesn't get any better than that. Self-reliance and achievement had softened his former cynicism and he even felt a tinge of sympathy for the less fortunate former colleagues he'd left behind. Those that remain are like gerbils on exercise wheels. They are just biding time toward retirement with no satisfaction of any accomplishment. The Council on Foreign Relations, the U.S. Chamber of Commerce, the Trilateral

Commission and all the other shot-calling institutions that call themselves "think tanks," maintain that all borders are artificial. That condition can obtain only if we erase our national culture by allowing a massive invasion of illiterate peons that cannot survive without socialism, and the shot-callers are working on that. He pushed aside gloomy thoughts of the past, took a deep, relaxing breath of fresh air and thought, Ah, how nice it is going to be, for a spell, to consort with those oblivious souls whose carefree lifestyle he so envied. Their lifestyles will remain the same, no matter what kind of Government takes over the country. If the welfare trough runs dry, they can always go back to panhandling.

The stars were becoming brighter as the train entered the open desert; the air became easier to breathe. He thought of his life mate, an Iraq war widow, young, beautiful, athletic, and mature enough to understand the meaning of violence and the necessity of bravely confronting it head-on. He did not worry about leaving her alone for a few weeks, as he would have, if he had married an average girl.

The next town, Deming, New Mexico, was some seventy miles away and there would be no sights to enjoy along the way, except the stars. He knew that sitting on the back porch of a hopper freight car all the way to Tucson could be tiring, but only if he failed to put it in the right perspective. He knew that, with the FTRA involved, this assignment might soon lead to violence again, but he was determined to enjoy this serenity as long as it lasted. *Carpe diem.*

CHAPTER FOUR

At daybreak, Ross stretched and looked over at a snoring Sandhouse. His hobo companion's mouth was open, exposing several gaps where teeth used to be. The night had passed much faster than seemed real, and in spite of himself, he realized that he had dozed off, too.

He had been lucky this time, but was determined never to fall asleep on a freight train again. As soon as possible, he determined to buy a vacuum bottle of hot coffee at a convenience store to ensure that he remained wide-awake and alert.

Daybreaks like this would make the most stubborn morning glories bloom. Golden shafts of sunlight broke through ragged, scattered, clouds, gilding their blue edges brilliantly across the horizon from east to west. The air mixed with the redolence of dew-moistened sage and creosote.

The train began to slow, passing by a few houses and businesses. Ross pulled out his pocket journal and flashlight and made an entry:

Approaching Tucson, Tuesday, October 11

As the train slowed, bright sunrays shined directly into Sandhouse's face, awakening him. He sat up stiffly and stretched his arms and legs. He rubbed his eyes and squinted into the bright, morning, desert sun.

"Not a bad night," he said with a yawn. "I slept pretty well. How about you, Jake?"

"I feel pretty good."

"It looks like we're coming into Tucson. We need to get off on your side, partner, before the train comes to a complete halt and before our hopper car winds up in the center of the freight yards."

"Where the agents are—where we don't want to be, right?"

"Right." Sandhouse began rolling up his bed, and with a long shoestring, tied it into a cylindrical shape. Ross followed his cue. Sandhouse said, "I'm going to cross over to your side of the porch so I can see something."

"What are you looking for?"

"A small park on city property near the railroad tracks. If we can get there, the bulls won't bother us."

Ross harnessed into his backpack and slung his bedroll over his left shoulder.

"There's the park. Get ready to jump, Jake!"

Sandhouse jumped off awkwardly and stumbled. He fell and rolled on rail ballast, but was safely away from the train's wheels. Ross went down the ladder backwards, swung his left foot behind his right, letting it touch the ground and pull him into a smooth, natural, fast walk. He went back to where Sandhouse was now standing with one pant leg raised to examine a skinned knee.

"Are you alright, Sandhouse?"

Sandhouse brushed the dirt off his clothing and said, "Yeah, just a skinned knee, but no broken bones. I usually get off these trains easier. You sure did it smoothly, Jake,"

"I seem to pick up on these sorts of things."

They ran north, across four lanes of a city street with fast automobile traffic. They set their luggage on a small, metal park table and waited for their train to clear, then waited again for an eastbound to clear. Transients had heavily scratched the metal, park table with graffiti, and Ross noticed the initials, FTRA, etched into one corner of the table top. "It looks like the FTRA has been active around here."

"Yep, Jake, this is part of their territory. Most of them won't bother you, but I don't advise hanging around them any longer than necessary. One of them alone is okay, but put two or more of them together, and they're more dangerous. Don't ever turn your back on one."

"How do you recognize them?"

"By the red kerchiefs on their necks with a silver slide. The slide, which they call a conch, will have the letters FTRA pressed into it."

"I wonder if there are any imposters...you know...just masquerading as FTRA."

Sandhouse chuckled and said, "Hell no. That would be the death sentence with the FTRA, if one of the enforcers sees it. They all have well known nicknames, and if they never heard the name of the imposter, he's in big trouble. The FTRA on the West Coast wear a black kerchief, but you probably won't see any of them, unless you get north of Los Angeles."

After the eastbound train cleared, Sandhouse grabbed his gear and walked out to the edge of the street, looking to make sure no more trains were coming. "C'mon, Jake. Let's cross over to the south side of these yards and head for that soup kitchen I was tellin' you about."

"Sounds good, Sandhouse." Indeed, it sounded like a good place to begin his search for Leah, or in the alternative, if he were lucky, to get information about her.

"It *is* good. Right now hot coffee and donuts are waitin' for us. I also have a mail slot there, and I need to check my mail."

"Free mail service to transients, too? Y'know, Sandhouse, all these amenities these days makes hoboing easier than I envisioned."

"When the staff of Casa Merced gets to know you, you can get a mail slot there, too, Jake. I also have one in L.A."

They crossed Kino Highway, a major thoroughfare, wound their way through city streets and soon found themselves at the Casa Merced soup kitchen. It was an inviting place with an outdoor dining area, equipped with metal tables covered by umbrellas. There was a line of people, mostly illegal aliens, standing on the south side of the establishment, waiting for a paper cup filled with coffee and a ration of two doughnuts.

Volunteers dispensed the nourishment through a small window that probably had once been the drive-up window of a fast-food establishment. The coffee smelled good, and Ross gladly accepted the beverage and food. "There is sugar and whitener on the tables," said the volunteer from the window. She was a middle-aged African-American woman who smiled frequently and made all beneficiaries feel welcome.

Ross thanked the woman, and said, "It's really nice of you to provide us travelers with this free coffee and doughnuts."

"Don't thank me. Various charities provide the food and drink. I am just another volunteer and I enjoy this work."

Russ followed Sandhouse to a table. Sandhouse gorged and seemingly inhaled the coffee with a loud, sucking noise. "You better take it easy with that hot coffee," said Ross. "Give it time to cool a little."

"I'm in a hurry. Gotta check my mail and renew my EBT."

When Sandhouse finished his coffee and doughnuts, he went inside the building, and in a few minutes emerged frowning as he read a printed, business letter. "Not bad news, I hope, Sandhouse."

"Naw, but this is my final notice to renew my EBT card. After I update the card, I can apply for a free cell phone."

"A *free* cell phone?"

"Yep, that's what the lady in the office said, too. She said I am entitled to a free cell phone and a lot of free minutes, but I gotta have an up-to-date EBT card to apply."

"It's beginning to look more and more like I should have followed through on my whim to become a hobo after I got out of the Army," Ross quipped.

Sandhouse folded the letter, put it in his shirt pocket, and declared, "Well, I'm outta here. The longer I screw around here, the longer the line is going to get at the welfare office. You wanta come along, Jake?"

"No. I think I'll hang around here for a while and maybe catch-out to L.A." He couldn't tell Sandhouse that wanted hang around the soup kitchen, hoping to make contact with someone that might know Leah or Grifty. Without a parting word, Sandhouse, preoccupied with his "business," disappeared around the corner of the building, headed for the welfare office.

After he finished his coffee and donuts, Ross went into the office of the soup kitchen and explained to the manager his real mission. She was a tall, bulky, leisurely-dressed, blonde woman in her fifties. Her physique indicated she could handle physical problems, if the occasion called for it. He pulled the billfold-size photo of Leah from his wallet and showed it her. "Her mother is an evangelist and is very worried about her. I promised to try to find her. She's supposed to have hooked up with some freight train riding gang."

The manager took the photo and studied it carefully. "She looks vaguely familiar. However, so many men and women come and go through here that we cannot keep up with them all, and they soon start to look alike. I can tell you only that I have not seen this girl recently. She is strikingly pretty. If I see her, I'm sure I'll remember her." She walked over to a copy machine and copied Leah's photo. "If you don't mind, I'll put this copy of her photo on the office bulletin board with your contact information. Only the staff will see it."

Ross gave the manager a calling card and a fifty-dollar donation. He put Leah's original photo back in his billfold and said, "I appreciate your time and trouble, ma'am. You can call my agency and get in touch with me anytime at the number on the calling card."

When he came back outside, Ross chose an empty table near the far, east side of the outdoor patio. He put on his sunglasses, pulled the brim of his hat lower and studied the transients who came and went. He relaxed on the white plastic chair and cupped a fresh cup of coffee between his hands. Soon, a slender, unaccompanied woman in her forties carrying a sack lunch and cup of coffee sat a table next to his. She carried a large, fabric tote bag with a strap that looped over one shoulder and a backpack that looped over the other. Her dishwater blonde hair was typical of the female transients. It was unkempt, brushed back and tied with a rubber band. She wore faded, tight-fitting jeans and a green sweater over a tank top that had once been red, but now was faded to pink. She sat down at a nearby vacant table. Ross smiled at her and she smiled back.

"Catching out today?" asked Ross.

"Not today," she said. "I have to stick around Tucson for a few days until I get my food stamps, how about you?"

"I may leave for L.A. tonight or tomorrow."

"You don't sound like you're in a hurry."

"It depends. By the way, my name's Jake."

She smiled and said, "Jake doesn't sound like a regular hobo's handle. They call me Horseshoe Annie." She got up, grabbed her luggage, and without invitation, moved over to his table.

"You have an interesting handle," said Ross.

"Yeah, it's because I carry a horseshoe in my backpack to wedge open boxcar doors so I don't get locked in. If one of those sliding doors slam shut on your car, you're stuck inside until someone hears you hollering. In the summertime, you can cook inside a closed boxcar. Just call me Annie for short."

"Did you ever get locked in a boxcar?"

"Yeah, once, a few years ago. Me and a guy that I was ridin' with got locked in one near Fresno. The car we were in was unhitched, and when the engine humped it forward, the door slammed shut. We were on the edge of a large yard, and we were stuck in that car for three days without food—just a jug of water between us. The only sunlight came through a crack next to the door. Finally, we heard the crunch of footsteps on the slag beside the tracks. The sound came from another transient, looking for a car to crash in for the night. He heard us yelling and got the door open. Since then I always use my lucky horseshoe to make sure I keep the door jammed in the open position. I always insert it in the bottom runner of the boxcar door."

"I find that interesting. I confess I'm not a regular at this game. I'm a writer and someday hope to record in a book such tales as I can pick up on the road."

"A writer, huh—you sort of look like a writer. You look too smart to be out here on the bum like most of us. Once upon a time I thought I'd become a writer, but after a year of college, I got on drugs—first, it was coke, then horse— and I soon just lost all ambition. I've tried all the drugs—crystal meth, cocaine..." She grabbed hold of Ross' forearm and added, "I hope I get to read your book, Jake. Someone smart and educated like you could inspire me to stay off the junk and do something useful."

The speed with which Annie confided in him made Ross uneasy. She released his arm and leaned back in her chair. She sipped coffee with a faraway gaze, and then said, "I could help you write about hoppin' freights. I just got out of rehab in Yuma a week ago, but I'm clean now and I'm determined to make it this time."

Yeah, right. The last thing Ross needed was to hook up with a druggie, even as a casual acquaintance. He decided to try to be sympathetic, and at the opportune moment let her down easily. He said, "I understand, but guess what, Annie—there are a lot of people out there who envy your freedom and experiences. I, for one, think that ridin' the rails is a great adventure. I've always admired those that reject the life of the herd and accept the challenge, the experiences and the thrills of hopping freights and living off the fat of the land, as the saying goes."

She held the Styrofoam cup with two hands, tried to force a smile, and Ross noticed that her hands were a little shaky. Horseshoe Annie bit off a chunk of donut, swallowed, coughed, spat phlegm, coffee and donut onto the gravel. She said, "It all depends on your point of view. I've been on the bum ridin' the rails for nearly ten years, been eatin' in soup kitchens like this, and stayin' in homeless shelters—when I can find one that has room for me."

"I'm sure you could tell me a few good stories, Annie."

"Ha! More than you can imagine. Mine would probably be enough to fill your book without your even talkin' to anyone else...but nobody ever tells everything they know to a stranger...and sometimes not even to a good friend. I could tell you some stories that would make your hair stand on end——some so bad I'd have to kill you, after I told you." She cackled, looking into Ross' eyes with her own bloodshot ones, expecting him to laugh, but he sat stoically, thinking she talked too much, far out of proportion to what he estimated to be her intelligence.

"Annie, maybe you should consider writing a book yourself. I've never read a hobo story by a female writer, but I've heard of a couple."

Annie smile, pulled a cellophane-wrapped bologna sandwich from her tote bag, unwrapped it, and answered, "Life on the bum ain't always everything it's cracked up to be. We are just another sort of herd—one that's hard to break away from."

Ross watched her chew on the sandwich, staring at the table, ruminating, chewing. After washing down a bite with coffee, she looked at Ross with a studious leer. "You say you're catchin' out tonight—or tomorrow?"

"I plan to."

"Jake, why don't you wait for me to get my SNAP card renewed, and then tomorrow we can go on to L.A. together. We still call it gettin' food stamps, but now, you know, they issue us debit cards, SNAP cards."

"Also call them EBT cards, right?"

"Yeah...say, Jake, you seem to know all about these welfare scams."

"I pick up a little here and there. A writer has to do that, you know."

She leaned back against the chair's backrest and said, "I guess so. Whoever thought up the idea of debit cards sure helped us street people a lot. Those that ain't re-habilitated need a lot of money to buy drugs, but I'll find still a use for all the spare change I can get, any way I can get it. There are convenience store clerks in every city who'll give cash—deducting an amount for the service, of course. It's actually too easy to convert EBT cards to cash—but it does *not* help anybody get off the junk, if you know what I mean."

The revelation did not surprise Ross, but riding on a freight train with a seedy female who probably still indulged in drugs, though in denial, in addition to engaging in welfare fraud, was not exactly what he had planned.

Annie blew a cloud of cigarette smoke into the air and suggested, "It's safer—you know—traveling with a companion—having someone to watch your back..."

Ross nodded, but he'd be afraid to turn his back on this broad, and even if he did out of some idea that she might provide useful information, he'd never dare tell Rocio about such an arrangement. He could see the rapidly approaching end of his relationship with this obnoxious, narcissistic, female derelict, but first, he would try to salvage wasted time by seeing if she *did have* any usefulness. He pulled Leah's picture from his billfold. "By the way, Annie, have you ever seen this girl?"

She pulled the pic closer to her eyes, and they lit up. "Why that's Leapin' Lorena! Where did you know *her*?"

Ross' heart jumped with hope. "She's a friend of a friend. I promised to give...Lorena...a message, if I run across her."

"That might not be easy, Jake. The last time I saw her she was in Portland, Oregon hangin' with some dude in the FTRA—he had, you know, a red bandanna and all that stuff. I heard he has an EBT account in Portland and a lot of other places."

"How long ago did you see *her*?"

Annie drank the rest of her coffee and threw her paper cup into a large, plastic can. "Oh, it's been a couple of months—like last summer. I used to hang out in Eugene and Portland, but I got tired of cold weather and all the rain the year around. Now I try to stay mostly in the warmer climates."

"How was...*Lorena*...I mean, health-wise?"

Annie shrugged and said, "Oh about as well as you can expect for a tweaker."

"A tweaker?"

"Yeah, they said she was hooked on crystal meth when I last saw her. No tellin' how many other drugs she's on by now—knowing that dude she was travelin' with."

Ross was sure he already knew, but he asked, anyway. "What was the dude's name?"

"I only know 'im by his street handle, *Grifty*."

Ross maintained a poker face, though his emotions were mixed joy and worry. From Annie, whom he had thought was a derelict with one foot in the gutter, and the other in the grave, he'd harvested important information. The source did not matter, for Annie had corroborated it with enough details to leave no doubt in his mind. *Leapin' Lorena* was now—or at least *had been*—Leah Waters. He said, "If I see her, my friend wanted me to try to persuade her to come home—back to Texas."

"Would that be her mother?"

Ross nodded.

Annie lit up a new cigarette and said, "Too bad. Lorena must have had an unhappy relationship with her parents to take up this kind of life. Does she have a father?"

"No. Her mother is a widow. That's another reason her mother wants to get in touch with her—to let her know about her father's passing."

Annie took a deep draw on her cigarette, shook off the ashes, and said, "Most of the people in this street life really couldn't care less about their family. If the family had loved 'em, they'd have stayed home. The longer they stay away from home, the harder it gets to go back to living the straight and narrow. If they are in a conflict with their parents, the last thing they want to do is swallow their pride, come crawling back, and admit that they made a mistake."

Ross nodded agreement. "Nevertheless, if I run into...Lorena...I'll fulfill my promise to try to get her to come home."

Annie's hand began to shake, and she pulled out her lighter and applied the flame to her already-burning cigarette. She fumbled for her sweater pocket and tossed the lighter inside. She looked away from Ross and said, "Good luck with that, Jake, but I think Lorena is too far gone. She'll die in the gutter of some slum, or in some hobo jungle from an overdose, before long—if some railway serial killer doesn't get to her first. Maybe you will get lucky and run into her. She and her dude will probably be back in L.A. before long, if they are not already. L.A. is really Grifty's preferred turf. " She reached over, turned Ross' wrist and checked the time on his wristwatch. She got up and said, "Ya sure you don't want to come to the welfare office with me, Jake? I could tell you a story or two on the way."

"I appreciate the invitation, Annie, but I think I'll stick around here for a while. By the way, how did Lorena pick up that 'Leapin' handle?"

Annie laughed dryly. "They say that when she first started hoppin' freight cars, she really sucked at it and fell a few times trying to leap into moving cars. They said she finally got the hang of it, though." The aging, female vagabond harnessed into her backpack, grabbed her bedroll, slung her tote bag over a shoulder, and, carrying all her worldly possessions, said, "Well, Jake, I'm outta here. The longer I wait, the longer the EBT line will get. I'll be back in about two hours and meet you so we can plan our trip to L.A. Is right here, okay?"

Ross shrugged. "Why not?"

She ambled off west, on 25th Street. He watched her swaying, well-proportioned and almost alluring hips. She must have been pretty at one time. Now, her unkempt hair and lined face, unmasked by any kind of makeup, offset any attraction her figure might have had for men outside of Skid Row. She was skinny, her complexion sallow, and her face was fraught with the strain from living on the hard edge. He watched her disappear around the corner and began to think of a way to ditch her without causing a scene.

Ross decided to look for a cheap motel, take a bath, change clothes, call Rocio and then get a good night's rest. Tomorrow, after a good breakfast, he would take a roundabout path to the freight yards and catch-out early.

A homeless man in baggy khaki pants and khaki shirt hanging, out over his beltline, distracted Ross' from his planning. The man brought his ration of coffee and doughnuts over to a table next his. He settled onto the fixed, plastic seat of the table, belched and then broke wind loudly. Ross, ignoring the man's gross contempt for social skills asked, "Say, bro, where could I find a cheap motel near about?"

The short, fat, old hobo displayed a bald head when he removed a diesel-smoked baseball cap, held it by the visor, and swatted a table fly. He put the hat back on and vigorously scratched his crotch with both hands. His almost toothless mouth seemed to be chewing on some imaginary food. He said, "There are some cheap motels over on Sixth Avenue—about four or five blocks from here."

"How do I get to Sixth Avenue?"

The hobo washed a bite of donut down with coffee, smacked his lips and said, "Just go west on Twenty-seventh street right here in front of the soup kitchen." He pointed west.

Ross put on his backpack and made and entry in his log:

October 11, noon. Prepared to leave Casa Merced to rent a motel room. Will check the welfare department tomorrow morning to see if I can learn anything. If nothing pans out, in Tucson, plan to catch-out west tomorrow.

Ross grabbed his gear, left the soup kitchen and followed Twenty-seventh Street west to Sixth Avenue. He came around the corner and quickly spotted a suitable motel, with a sign in front that read, *The Elysian Inn.* Apparently, it had once been an elegant tourist haven, like so many cheap motels on major thoroughfares before the interstates bypassed them. Immigrant managers, mostly Asian, due to their cultural austerity and perseverance, have retuned many of them to economic viability. Owners had painted these buildings desert beige and lined the perimeter with palm trees at wide intervals.

Ross' rented a room near the rear of the compound for two nights, with an option of canceling the second night in case of exigencies. Only a low, cinderblock wall separated his room from a trailer park. He kicked off his shoes, relaxed on the bed, clicked on the TV with the remote, and found a cable news channel. The budget motel brought back memories of a stay in Albuquerque's old Route 66, bypassed by I-40, while on a Border Patrol assignment. A tweaker couple in the room next to his, stayed up talking all night, until they left for breakfast at 6 a.m. When checking out, he complained to the management. With a heavy Asian accent, the female manager assured him that there was only one occupant in the room next to his, a single lady that had "seemed very nice." On another per diem occasion, to save money, he'd stayed in a cheap El Paso motel. An illegal, Mexican tweaker in the room next to his had practiced on his double bass, pizzicato, all night. "Why didn't you complain?" the Middle East manager said. He knew damned well the immigrant from the Middle East would probably have done nothing. Our audacious barbarian invaders intimidate everyone, especially immigrants other than those from the western hemisphere. With the copious flow of crystal meth, the whole nation is becoming like Las Vegas; it never sleeps. In a low-budget motel in Amarillo, an Asian female manager's answer to his complaint of noise by other occupants was a question: "Have you stayed here before?" The answer was "No," but if it had been "Yes," her defense likely would have been that the motel was no noisier now than it ever has been. With that reply, she disappeared into her office.

Asians are by culture, "caste conscious." Order and degree still prevails in the Far East, and everyone is either born into, or, in the case of Americans, lumped into a nebulous social class. If you stay in a cheap motel, you are a "Dalit," once translated as "slum dog" in an Asian film.

Ross remembered a short story by a Russian border guard a century and a half ago, 'Taman', where Mikhail Lermontov described a border guard's forced billeting in quarters surrounded by low-life smugglers. He often felt he was channeling Lermontov, or experiencing morphic resonance from the Nineteenth century Russian author. The Czarist government exiled him and the rest of potential "trouble-making" authors to the violent and dangerous Caucasus. Alongside their Cossack allies, their duty entailed keeping the dangerous Chechens in check at the Caucasus, once a somewhat natural barrier to illegal, international trespassing from Asia into Russia. Protecting the borders of Czarist Russia failed, and several decades after the deaths of the Romantic Era Russian authors, the country became overpopulated with poor and malcontented Bolsheviks that overthrew the empire. Eventually, a dictator of Asiatic extraction, Stalin, ruled for nearly thirty years with an iron fist. It was long ago when their borders got out of control, but none of the literature Ross had read mentioned anyone complaining and he wondered why that did not alarm him even today.

In Lermontov's story, the traveling protagonist, a naïve junior officer, trusted, or underestimated, the smugglers, and was charmed by a gypsy-like young female member of their band, much to his chagrin and regret.

Ross shook off depressing thoughts of barbarian invasions and declining empires and took a shower. Afterwards he called Rocio on his cell phone.

"I was just about to call you," she said. "I've got some good news."

"I can use some good news. I've been getting depressed by my environment and bad thoughts. I was thinking of asking you what we can do about America's descent into the lowlife."

"It sounds like you've had one of your bad days, Sweetheart. I'm sorry I can't be there to comfort you, but this news should perk you up. My confidential source in the welfare office ran another check on Leah Waters for me."

"And...?"

"Get this: Leah Waters recently made an application for an EBT card right there in Tucson, where you are now."

"Very interesting, and how long ago was that?"

"Not too long ago. Are you sitting down?"

"Yes, right here in my cheap arm chair in my cheap motel room."

"You're not going to believe this: Leah has a follow-up appointment at the Gordita Ponce Welfare office in Tucson tomorrow morning at 9:30 a.m."

"Wonderful! Maybe we can wrap this thing up in a couple of days."

"Persuading her to come home may be the hardest part—or getting her into protective custody so her mother can come and get her. Too bad you can't just arrest her and extradite her to Texas."

"I could get arrested for trying to restrain her, even though I have a temporary co-guardianship. I have to be careful and get her located without alerting her, then get help from the police. In some ways, Arizona is worse than California. Former colleagues in the Border Patrol know how easy it is to make bad headlines here. The major newspapers have become tabloids, and lie, distort, exaggerate and magnify imagined oppression of the downtrodden, which is synonymous arresting anyone that's ripping off the system—especially illegal aliens. The gay, liberal media digs up something negative about the Border Patrol daily to demoralize, weaken and marginalize the agency. Arizona has not much left of decency and a counter to the leftist propaganda, except Sheriff Joe Arpaio, but he's aging and battle-weary. Being a former border guard would add a lot of fuel to the liberal media fire."

"Wow! You sounded as if you had those lines memorized."

"Truth flows naturally."

"I hear that, Sweetie. I'm originally from Sonora, you know, and Tucson is the most common destination for Sonora's worst criminals and fugitives. In both countries the media seems to be anti-law enforcement."

Suddenly, Ross realized his social-condition ranting might be contagious to his wife. He got back to the subject. "I wish I could plan on exactly what to do about Leah, tomorrow, Hon. So much is contingent on others, and in particular, on Leah's behavior, if and when she is restrained. She's had plenty of time to get used to unbridled freedom."

"Well, Dear, I guess you'll just have to play it by ear and see how things go. All the welfare offices open at nine a.m. and I suggest you get there a little early, since applicants for benefits usually congregate outside before the doors open. From her photo, you should be able to spot her, and keep an eye on her while deciding whether to bring the social workers into play."

"You're right, Hon. If I see her, I won't say anything to her, but maybe I'll talk to the office manager tell her that she is a runaway. Since she is apparently making her own application for an EBT card, Leah may be posing as a married or emancipated person. If she's pregnant, she might be considered emancipated in today's insane society, even if the rape was came from statutory. We have to assume our runaway has become street-wise—an elusive coyote like the creep she's hanging out with."

"You'd better get to bed and get some rest, my love, but first call up the desk and request an automated wake-up call to make sure you get to the welfare office before they open."

CHAPTER FIVE

After the phone awakened him, Ross got up, put on clean clothes and caught a city bus to the Gordita Ponce Welfare Office. He got there well before eight a.m., had breakfast, at a nearby small café, and then walked to office, arriving at nine a.m., half an hour before it was to open. Among the early birds, there was no one resembling Leah or Grifty. He made an entry in his journal:

8:30 a.m., outside the Gordita Ponce Welfare Office in Tucson,. Wednesday, October 12

When the office opened, Ross gave a receptionist his calling card and asked her to show him to the director's office so he could report a welfare fraud. When he mentioned the word "fraud," the receptionist's face darkened into a frown. It was obvious that informants in this business were about as welcome as they were in sanctuary cities for illegal aliens. In the topsy-turvy world of the present Administration, informants had become the problem, not the solution.

While following the receptionist, he looked around the waiting area to see if Leah had entered after him. Above the screened-off workstation cubicles, he could see only the tops of the heads of only a few of the workers and their applicants. All applicants appeared to be Hispanic; none was blonde, none remotely resembled Leah Waters.

The receptionist led Ross to an office at the rear of the building, and he waited outside the door while she went in to explain Ross' business. In a few of minutes, she came out of the office and advised Ross that the director would see him now.

The director, in her mid-fifties, was trim and had premature facial wrinkles that seemed frozen in a narrow-eyed, suspicious frown. He reasoned that this job must take a toll on one's personality, and eventually must affect one's physical appearance. Rocio's relative had told her that the most stressful part of the job came from ineligible applicants that did not hesitate to threaten her if she denied an application. It was not unlike the ports of entry and the hostile applicants, often accompanied by arrogant relatives that think all their rights and privileges transfer to their relatives, whether they are eligible or not. Such stressful conflicts were most often diffused by bureaucrats giving applicants what they want and trying to find a rationale to justify capitulation with some obscure, or manufactured, "policy." Such spineless bureaucrats rest assured that they are doing exactly what Washington and all layers of bureaucracy in between want them to do. Capitulation and abandonment of one's duties must be done tacitly, for if a scandal arises, CYA mode kicks in and bureaucrats know that the Government ends up solving such problems with a scapegoat. A border inspector once told Ross that it's not the ones that get past the inspectors, but the ones that you intercept, accompanied by citizen relatives, that run to the consuls, the news media and low-level politicians that trump up all the false charges that cause the problems.

The director told Ross to take a seat opposite her desk. She did not smile or make Ross feel especially welcome; in fact, her demeanor reminded him of management in the border guards. Since the Government had immersed Ross in the intricacies of bureaucracy years ago, he understood their workings. Everyone in management disliked whistle blowers, not because they report malfeasance, but because there was always the possibility that such information would eventually reflect adversely on management, or directly affect their own performance ratings. It was not always possible for management to get the headhunters, also called the Office of the Inspector General, to do their primary task—to find a suitable scapegoat among the lower ranking officials. CYA obtains in every bureaucracy, at every level.

"The receptionist tells me you have some information regarding possible welfare fraud, Mr. Spencer." She spoke with a stark, yet evasive, glare.

"I believe so," said Ross. On her desk, he laid the manila envelope containing Leah Waters' photo, physical description, and other information. "I've stood outside since before the office opened, looking for Leah Waters. I didn't see her come in, although she has an appointment at 8 a.m. She's a runaway."

"But what makes you think she has filed a fraudulent application?"

"She's only seventeen years old."

The director shrugged. "That doesn't necessarily mean fraud. She could be emancipated."

"At age seventeen?"

"Possibly—she could have gotten married, or maybe had a baby and been adjudicated as emancipated by a state agency, or a civil court. There are many ways underage girls—and even boys—can get emancipated while they are still minors, age-wise."

"Could you tell me if she showed up for her interview for food stamps today?"

The woman took a deep, frustrated breath, pulled a lap-top computer over and started typing. In a moment she said, "Leah Waters is here, being interviewed at the present time."

"Really?" Ross removed Leah's photo from its folder and laid it on the director's desk. Along with it, he placed his copy of his court-ordered temporary guardianship of Leah.

The director glanced at Ross' calling card and at both documents, but did not pick any of them up.

Ross continued, "Since I have been designated by her mother—and a judge—as a temporary guardian for Leah Waters, could I speak to her?"

"We'll see, but you need to understand that emancipation would invalidate your temporary custody order." On her desk phone, the woman dialed an extension number and asked for Leah's file.

Through the office window, Ross saw a young caseworker get up from a cubicle, carrying a file. He could see that the young woman the caseworker had been interviewing, presumably the applicant, was not the Leah he was looking for. She was dark-skinned, apparently Hispanic or Native American, wearing a rust-colored shirt. When he had passed by the cubicle earlier, he had noticed she was wearing denim pants.

The caseworker came into the director's office and gave her the file. The director opened it and said to Ross, "This young lady is eighteen, not seventeen. That means she is legally an adult."

"How do you know her age?"

"She has a State of Arizona legal identity card." She showed a copy of it to Ross.

The photo was indeed that of a young, Hispanic or Native American, girl. He said, "It must be fraudulent because this picture doesn't look anything like the Leah Waters I'm looking for."

"Maybe there are two Leah Waters."

"I can't believe that there are two Leah Waters with the same social security number."

"How do you know her social security number?" asked the director with an indignant tone.

"Her mother gave it to me along with a lot of other information."

"Okay, but I meant how did you know what social security number the applicant here is using?"

It was a gotcha question. Ross said, "I have confidential sources."

"It's illegal for anyone in our organization to give out confidential information about our applicants and the dates of their appointments. Who told you she had an appointment today?"

"Again—confidential sources. I'm a private investigator and we have ways and means of finding out such things."

"That is illegal," said the director, turning to sit at her desk.

"So arrest me," said Ross. "But also arrest that young lady over there in the cubicle who apparently has stolen Leah Waters' name and social security number."

"We don't arrest anyone," replied the director in an affected, emotionless, gravelly tone. "We refer cases of fraud—and violations of applicants' privacy—to the civil authorities—to the sheriff's office."

There was a moment of silence while the director and Ross stared at one another. Finally, the director said, "We'll take due note of the information you are providing, assign our own investigator, and if she thinks the case has merit, we'll refer it to the sheriff."

"How long will it take your investigator to make a determination if the case has merit?" Ross asked the director.

"It will take a couple of weeks for our investigator to complete the inquiry, then a couple more weeks for us to make our report. The prosecutor may send it to the grand jury and that will take longer. We may have to re-interview the applicant—and maybe our agency investigator will want to talk to you again, Mr. Spencer, before we bring in the sheriff's investigators."

Ross turned and looked through the office window at the caseworker's cubicle. The young woman was gone. He declared, "I think *your* Leah Waters just took a powder."

The director stood up and craned her neck toward the processing area. She and the caseworker looked at each other with visible concern. "Maybe she went to the restroom," suggested the caseworker. "Or maybe she went out to her car to get papers or something."

Ross rolled his eyes, heaved a sigh of frustration and said to the director, "Well thanks anyway—for nothing." He got up and followed "Leah Waters'" caseworker down the aisle toward her workstation, and listened while she asked another caseworker in the next cubicle if Leah Waters had indicated where she might have gone. She stated, "She said nothing. She just got up and headed for the exit in a big hurry I think she got cold feet. Maybe her application was fraudulent."

"Maybe so," said Ross as sardonically as he could, with a sidelong glance at the caseworker beside him. He strode, almost in a jog, toward the rear exit. He thought, if I can catch up with this imposter, I might get a clue as to where the real Leah Waters is—or what fate has caused her social security card to wind up in the hands of this dark-skinned young woman. Outside the building, he looked east and west. He guessed that she would turn west, toward the parking lot, in order to get off that street and out of sight as quickly as possible. He sprinted to the northwest corner of the building and looked around the corner into the alley between the parking lot and the welfare building. He saw the young woman running east, up Chueco Jerez Alley, then turn west onto another street. Ross ran to that street just in time to see her turn into a narrow alley between two buildings. He continued running, caught up with her and grabbed her by the shoulders. She began to yell for help. "He is chasing me!" she yelled to someone in Spanish.

A young, husky, dark-skinned man with long, straight, black hair stood up between a stack of wooden, loading pallets, next to a loading dock. He wore faded, ragged, denim trousers, a red, plaid shirt, and a beaded, Indian-type headband. The girl ran past him, and stopped a short distance beyond to watch the encounter between Ross and her male companion. The companion stepped out into the middle of the alley, pulled a large knife from inside his waistband and held it menacingly in his right hand. His said nothing, but his lips curled into a menacing sneer, as if daring Ross to come forward. Ross stopped and said in Spanish, "Put down the knife. That girl is under arrest."

The man drew the knife back over his head, lunged at Ross, swinging the knife in a vertical path. Fortunately, the man was drunk or under the influence of drugs, for he was slow and awkward. Ross knocked the knife out of his hand and simultaneously threw a sharp right uppercut to the assailant's left jaw. The man dropped to the ground and rolled over on his face.

The girl began to run again and Ross resumed pursuit. The alley opened into a street with busy auto traffic, but before she reached the street, Ross caught up, grabbed her long, black hair and pushed her up against the wall of an abandoned building. He spun her around, facing him and said in Spanish, "Look, you she-devil, all I want to know is where you got that social security card that you used back at the welfare office."

The woman went into hysterics, looked back up the alley to see if her companion were coming. She struggled to break free, and with more authority, Ross pushed her back against the wall, again, firmly. "Tell me where you got the social security card or I'm going to call the police!"

She whimpered, "You are not the police?"

"No. Just tell me how you got the social security card."

"I bought it!" She quit wrenching her arms and relaxed.

"Where did you buy it?"

"In a flea market."

"Where is the flea market?"

She hesitated for an instant, and then croaked hoarsely, "Portland, Oregon."

Ross loosened his grip on the woman. "Where are you from?"

"Guatemala."

Ross wondered why he cared where she was from. That question must have been a residual reflex from his border guard days. "How long ago did you buy the social security card?"

"Maybe two months. My boyfriend showed me how to buy it."

"Is that guy back there in the alley the boyfriend?"

She hesitated for a moment and answered, "Yes."

76

"What was the name of the Portland flea market where you got the social security card?"

"I don't remember. It was close to downtown and near the freeway."

"Do you know which freeway?"

She shook her head. "I only remember there was a freeway overpass near where we slept."

Ross turned her loose and stepped back. Still speaking Spanish he said, "Well, I appreciate the information. I need to find the girl who really owned the social security card you used to try to make an application. By the way, the welfare department knows that you are a fraud. I'd suggest you go back to Guatemala before you get into serious trouble." He stepped aside, indicating she was free to go back and join her boyfriend. By now, Ross figured that he should have regained consciousness.

Still whimpering, the woman began walking back toward the last place she'd seen her boyfriend. She increased her speed, swinging her arms in an exaggerated arc, and then she broke into a run.

That night, back in his motel room, Ross called Rocio and told her of the day's adventures and misadventures. "We can forget about wrapping up this case for a while," he said. "Now I need to find out how Leah Waters' social security card wound up for sale in a Portland flea market—if that illegal Guatemalan girl was telling the truth. I am inclined to believe her. It sounds plausible, from my experience."

Rocio said, "I can't help thinking about that serial killer, Robert Silveria, who killed dozens of transients in and around the freight yards just to get their I.D.'s, social security cards and EBT cards. Let's hope that she has not met with foul play."

"I understand the worry, Hon, but we are probably attaching too much significance to Leah's social security number. She could have sold the card herself to get money for food."

"Or drugs."

"True. Most transients in the fraud game prefer to carry someone else's social security cards and others' IDs rather than their own to maintain their anonymity and thereby drag a red herring across their trail in case anyone is trying to locate them."

Rocio suggested, "Someone could have stolen it from her while she was sleeping,"

"Possibly. I can attest that tired drifters sleep very soundly—especially when they have a bottle of wine—or some downers—handy. Sound sleep makes them easy targets for pickpockets, especially among their own consorts.

"There is no honor among thieves, as the saying goes."

"Be all that as it may, I need to get on to L.A. and check with Reverend Alfred Tasker at his rescue mission. He's the last one of our contacts known to have seen Leah, and if nothing pans out in L.A., I guess it's on up the West Coast to Portland." He decided to wait to explain the other most recent lead indicating Leah and Grifty may be in Portland. That would be Horseshoe Annie, whose story was now supported by the identity thief.

"I was so hoping that this case would be solved this morning and that you'd be on your way home tomorrow, Amor. I really miss you."

"And I really miss you, Sweetheart. We'll make up for lost time when I do get home."

CHAPTER SIX

Ross got up at five o'clock, went to a nearby restaurant, ate a hearty breakfast, and then started the trek back to the Casa Merced soup kitchen. Walking was not only good exercise, but it seemed to stimulate his brain, and on the way, he began to formulate his plans for the day. He'd top off his breakfast with free coffee and donuts at the soup kitchen then make more efforts to find someone who might give him a clue as to Leah's whereabouts. Before venturing to the West Coast, he wanted to exhaust every chance of stumbling onto Leah Waters in Tucson, or finding someone who might know her. Some of the people at soup kitchens are hangers-on, but many transients come and go; with luck, he still might find someone who knew Leah. It was apparent that some transients along the southern rail routes were already getting to know *Leaping Lorena,* and even more probably knew Grifty in person, or by reputation.

Upon arriving at the Casa Merced, he made a new entry in his journal:

Thursday morning 7 a.m. Re-Visited the Casa Merced Soup Kitchen in Tucson.

His second day at the Casa Merced was proving fruitless, and by noon, he had learned nothing new about Leah. Horseshoe Annie remained the only contact that had actually known her—as *Leaping Lorena.* By late in the afternoon Ross began thinking of hopping a westbound freight train when two hobos he had never seen before took a seat at the table next to his and began talking about the pros and cons of freight hopping, as opposed to hitchhiking on the highway. The larger of the two, a middle-aged man with a grubby beard and broad shoulders, wore grimy, blue-striped coveralls in the older style of railroad engineers. He crammed a donut into his mouth and slurred, "I'll never hitchhike on the highway again after I got stranded in that small town in Texas. There ain't no free soup kitchens in small towns and the people there just want to see street people keep movin' on."

The hobo's companion was slightly built, in his mid-twenties, with short, unkempt hair. He wore a faded, red, plaid shirt and dungarees. He inquired, "So if you get hungry in a small town, what are you gonna do—just go hungry?"

"You do the best you can. I remember a time in another small Texas town when me and another dude I met up with on the road decided to dumpster-dive behind a small mom-and-pop restaurant. We had to climb over a picket fence to get to the dumpster, and someone must have seen us through a back window, for the cops showed up. The cops arrested us for trespassing and we each got thirty days in jail."

"I didn't know dumpster diving was illegal," his partner said.

"The cops said if you crawl over a fence to get to the dumpster, it's trespassing." He leaned back in his chair, smiling triumphantly, holding his cup at arm's reach. "What the Hell, at least we had a solid, jail roof over our heads for a whole month, and we ate pretty well."

"I guess you call that a happy ending," said the smaller hobo with a chuckle.

As the afternoon dragged on, Ross discretely asked a few other transients if they had ever heard of "Leapin' Lorena," but no one had. Horseshoe Annie remained his only source of useful information in Tucson, the drifter he most wanted to avoid. He remembered his frivolous promise to ride to L.A. with her, but if she showed up, he would think up another excuse not to catch-out with her.

A couple of young, male teenage transients took a table to Ross' left and he listened while they drank coffee, ate stale donuts and planned a scam. They had read a book that made it sound very easy to go to a major home improvement store and gather up discarded customers' receipts from the ground, or left in shopping carts in the parking lot. Armed with a receipt of a recent purchase, they'd enter the store as customers, find the shelf with the objects like the one purchased with the receipt, pick up a duplicate, and then, armed with object and receipt, maneuver to the customer service and ask for a "refund" of their money. The underground book they had read made it sound easy, but as an experienced law enforcement agent, Ross would bet that they'd be arrested on their first attempt at that scam. Improved security measures at most stores gave every piece of merchandise its own unique number on the receipt. Moreover, the moment those two entered any big retail store, their dress and looks would attract the attention of Loss Prevention Agents.

Young, wannabe rip-off artists depend upon TV, tabloids and the rumor mill for their "intelligence" gathering. Such articles, mostly fiction, embellish stories to make them interesting and marketable to publishers of the magazines or tabloids. Loud mouth activists misguide such idiots into believing that profiling is illegal, but the shabby dress, unkempt hair and general appearance of these two wannabe scam artists would be a red flag to any half-intelligent LPA. The agents would be standing nearby to take them into custody as soon as they signed for their "refund." Ross chose not to warn them of their folly, for youths nowadays think that they know it all and most likely would not heed his warning. Had he been a real writer, Ross would have stayed close to these two clowns and see how far they got with their planned scam. Instead, he forcibly withdrew from his reverie to the real problems at hand.

After an uneventful day at Casa Merced, Ross studied his street map of Tucson and planned his trip to the BNSF Freight Yards. He walked south on North Third Avenue, knowing that it would lead him to Seventh Street where, he was told, he could find a place to hide while awaiting a westbound freight train. "It's a place where the yard narrows down to one track, the main line, and the westbound trains will be on that track," a hobo had explained.

From his own experience, Ross knew that in Post 9-11-01 days, it is better to wait a few hundred yards beyond the starting point of an outbound train, so that when it goes past, it will not have gained such speed as to making mounting hazardous. Ross, like most veteran hobos, preferred to hop a train that was standing still, preparing to pull out; however, increased security measures in recent years had made catching stopped trains in the middle of freight yards increasingly risky, for there, the bulls are thicker in number. It was a trade-off; swapping stopped trains in the middle of the freight yards for the more dangerous, moving ones to avoid arrest inside the yards. It was a beautiful evening. He felt its last warm rays of the sun on his back as he walked east along North Third Avenue. Grackles alighting for their nightly roost screeched and twittered from atop palm trees. Near North Third Avenue and East Fourteenth Street, a young, full-bodied, Hispanic woman sat with a six-month-old baby, on the porch steps of a modest house. She smiled and waved at him. Her raven hair was pulled back into a ponytail and she wore a black, low-cut blouse that revealed the bold cleavage of capacious bosoms. She said, "I have what you're looking for."

I wish you did, thought Ross, but her business was obviously something other than harboring young, runaway, blonde girls. He ignored her and kept walking.

On the next block stood several old, run-down houses, some of which looked abandoned. He thought he heard a noise coming from a house with a yard overgrown with high weeds. He looked out of the corner of his eye and saw a young man duck behind a front window frame as if to avoid detection. Street people often squat in abandoned houses until evicted. Some even labor under the impression that if they occupy the property for several years, they can apply for, and obtain, title to the property. They cannot obtain "adverse possession," or "squatters' rights," as easily as some think. They must live there for a long time, and the owner must not have taken any action to remove them. However, most squatters are looking only for temporary shelter from the elements, and protection from other street people. A bum is especially lucky if he finds an abandoned home with utilities, or at least the water, still hooked up. Ross had once met a self-educated, old hobo passing through El Paso that had told him about a homeless man who was also a burglar. The burglar checked the newspapers to find homes of tenants on the lam from the law. He could sometimes live there until the mortgage company started foreclosure proceedings, and that might mean months of free tenancy, although usually without running water or other utilities.

As the shadows of evening lengthened and began to engulf South Tucson, Ross stopped beside a railroad tool shed and made an entry in his journal:

October 13, 7:30 p.m. Darkness is coming as I near the Tucson freight yards. The tower lights of the yard are now visible.

The scene evoked mixed feelings: there was the nightmare of that canyon-like freight yard he had told Rocio about; and there was the real monophobia he had experienced upon seeing her drive away, leaving him at midnight in the Alfalfa Freight Yards of El Paso. These yards were spooky at night, but a necessary place of embarkation to explore nearby venues: hobo jungles, soup kitchens, and ultimately, Los Angeles' skid row.

He replaced his journal in his backpack and continued walking south on North Third Avenue, enjoying the twilight walk, observing the neighborhoods. Streetlights were coming on, windows of the few residential houses in the adjacent area began to light up, and the few, security-conscious residents began to pull cords to close window shades. The wind

83

changed direction, lifting the pungent odor of diesel fumes, thinning the air, making breathing more pleasant. Low-base boom boxes in distant neighborhoods sounded like an approaching, yet distant, thunderstorm. He could hear a quarrel between a grown man and a woman, somewhere in the houses to the south. Living near the convenient free transportation of freight yards in a slum probably could drive a normal man to submit to a caprice and roam aimlessly, he thought.

He continued walking east and soon heard the air horns of locomotives. He followed a dirt road southeast a ways, then turned onto East Seventeenth Street, soon finding himself approaching a dead-end. Beyond a barricade, he could see the west end of the Tucson Freight Yards.

Several wild, desert shrubs grew from the base of a chain-link fence that enclosed a yard with unused RVs, and at the east end of East Seventeenth Street was a well-worn car path, deviating to the right side of the street onto the right curb where cars obviously drove around the no trespassing signs, circumventing the vehicular barricade. Since few people read signs, or literature, anymore, he mused perhaps aspiring writers should focus on screen writing for audio-visual productions. The prophetic nature of George Orwell's *1984* is manifesting itself all around us, he thought, and perhaps, it also is in Fahrenheit 451. A pluralistic illiterate society will make outlawing books easier. Who would care?

Ross decided to wait beside a large bush growing from the bottom of a chain link fence near the street curb. After dark, he would make his illegal foray to catch-out. He placed his backpack and bedroll down beside the bush and just as he started to sit down against the fence, he heard a familiar woman's voice. It came from the shadow of another tree he'd just walked past. His eyes strained to see in the darkness, and from beside a large bush, Horseshoe Annie, stood up. She was holding a wine bottle in her right hand.

"*Que milagro!*" she bellowed, hoarsely.

He wondered if she had been following him. "Where did *you* come from, Annie?" He held his voice down, hoping that Annie would take it as a cue and lower her voice, too.

"Ha! You walked right past me. I was sittin' in the shadow of that next large shrub over there, just up from *your* hootch. You ain't the most observant hobo I ever seen." She pulled a pack of cigarettes from her shirt pocket and asked, "Where the hell you been, Jake? I've been lookin' all over for ya."

To Ross' consternation, she lit up the cigarette. So much for security precautions. He cleared his throat and lied, "I got arrested and taken to the police station yesterday. It was a case of mistaken identity, and they let me go this morning."

She set down her wine bottle and stood in front of him, arms crossed, condescendingly. The glowing embers of her cigarette were dangerously close to her left sleeve. "You gotta be more careful, Jake. I'm surprised you didn't see me in my hootch when you walked past. Somebody could waylay you if you're not more careful." She picked up her luggage and moved it next to Ross and her wine bottle. Her pompous attitude, enhanced by booze, was making him begin to think he had overplayed his role as a hobo novitiate.

"Back in Texas, hootch means *booze*," he said, sardonically.

"Well, you ain't in Texas no more. To us hobos, it's a nest—a comfortable place to stay hidden from the bulls until your train pulls out. Make a note of that for your book." She cackled, inhaled, and created another red ball of embers at the end of her cigarette. She spat and blurted, "Anyway, Jake, now that we found each other, we can catch-out to California together, just as we planned."

Ross heaved a sigh of frustration. "Yeah." Before she had reappeared, he had almost forgotten her entirely. Sober, she was bearable; drunk, she was the embodiment of repugnance. He started forming a plan to get away from her. Maybe after they got on the train she'd fall asleep. Winos sleep soundly on freight trains. Then, maybe he would get the opportunity to dismount safely somewhere.

85

Annie sat down next to Ross in the shadow of the shrub, and from her backpack she pulled out two green chili burritos. She handed one to Ross. "Try one of these. They're good, but keep your water jug handy, 'cause they bite back."

Ross was not hungry, but the burritos did smell good. Mostly to not offend Annie, he took it. He peeled back the tinfoil and took a bite. It was delicious, but shortly after the second bite, the spicy burrito started to burn his mouth. He began to hiccup. He unscrewed the cap of his water jug and drank. Annie cackled. "Told you so—they bite back!"

"Tucson chili seems hotter than El Paso's," he said, his voice garbled by food and the napkin with which he wiped his mouth.

Just as Ross was thinking how much Annie's cackle was getting under his skin, she cackled again and said, "Just think, Jake! I'm giving you *volumes* to write about." She bit off almost half of her own burrito, chewed and washed it down with a slug of wine. She wiped her mouth with her shirtsleeve and croaked, "And I ain't even gonna charge ya for *any* of it." She laughed again at her own joke, steadily getting louder.

Ross was beginning to wish he had thought up some pretext other than being a writer to justify his undercover work. Annie seemed to have appointed herself as the chief source of his life-of-a-hobo information. His mind began to fill with "what ifs" and preoccupation. A chronic problem like Annie to worry about was not what he had planned. He hoped that she could hold her liquor well enough not to cause any trouble—as far as had to travel with her. He wished she would lose that bottle, and if the opportune moment came, he resolved to see to it that she did. He also hoped that he would not get diarrhea from the burrito, and the thought caused him to wrap the remainder up and place it inside his backpack. "I'll save it until I'm hungrier," he said.

After more than an hour of waiting, Ross heard the intermittent rumble of a switch engine building up a train. The clashing of cars echoed through the freight yards. Soon the locomotives were a hundred yards to the west. "That train will be leaving in a few minutes," said Annie. "It's over on Track One—the main line west. We need to wait until it starts to pull."

"Obviously," said Ross with a sarcasm that Annie apparently did not even notice.

Annie walked to the end of the chain link fence and looked eastward. She came back to the hootch and said, "The yard lights are pretty dim, but I can see an open boxcar about ten cars back from the last engine. That looks like the best place for us to ride."

As a former border guard, Ross knew more about hoboing than most real hoboes because he had the experience of hundreds to draw from—as well as extended experience hopping freights to dislodge illegal aliens. He had to make a mental note to keep acting dumb so as not to stir up Annie's—or anyone else's—suspicions about his real motives and objectives. An undercover private eye riding the rails could be a death sentence if the wrong people find out and catch you with your back turned. Criminals see them as nothing more than rent-a-cops and professional snitches. He was violating some of his own rules as a private eye: keep acquaintances you meet on the open road casual. His tolerance for Annie, he reasoned, was in appreciation for the information she'd given him about Leah. He could become a hard-ass with her, but she would go whimpering back to her colleagues and tell everyone what an asshole he was. Reputations among hobos spread like wildfire. It was imperative that Ross keep up a congenial facade. Anyway, thanks to Annie, he now knew Leah's street moniker and knew that she had been alive, at least for a while after last seen by Reverend Tasker. If Annie was right, Leah might soon be back in L.A., and that might save him some time and travel.

CHAPTER SEVEN

When their chosen freight train was ready to pull, Ross'
dubious companion remarked, "Look, Jake! Our boxcar is
almost straight across from our hootch!"

"Yeah," grunted Ross, harnessing himself with his backpack and picking up his bedroll. He carried on an inward, silent conversation. This rail trip to L.A. is going to a very long
one, he thought, unless I humanely can get rid of Annie or at
least separate her from her bottle.

The front locomotive unit sounded the highball and Ross
and Annie came onto the edge of the yards. Annie looked east
and west and said, "It looks like the coast is clear, Jake. Let's
do it!" She put on her backpack, held her bedroll and tote bag
in her right hand, and kept the wine bottle in her right hand.
Ross quickly passed Annie, headed for the open boxcar. Then
he heard glass shattering behind. He looked around to see
Annie sprawled on rail-yard slag. Against his better judgment,
he went back and helped her to her feet. "You okay, Annie?"

She brushed the gravel from her hands on the legs of her
jeans and said, "Hell yeah!" Ross stayed with her this time,
his arm under her elbow. "Damn, I had nearly half a bottle of
wine left!" she croaked. She stumbled again, almost fell, and
Ross helped her stay upright, saying with tongue in cheek,
"Too bad about the wine bottle."

The train lurched forward just as the two traveling companions arrived at its rails. Ross and Annie threw their luggage inside the open boxcar. Ross hopped in, turning in mid-
air to a sitting position on the edge of the open doorway. He
grabbed Annie's hand and helped her inside. "I wouldn't try

this if it were going any faster," he observed as he exhaled heavily.

"Why not?"

"Moving boxcars are very dangerous."

"Aw, not really. I've hopped a helluva lot of movin' boxcars."

He was tempted to remind her that he'd just helped her inside, not to mention stay on her feet, but discreetly kept his silence. He was supposed to be the dumb, greenhorn trying to learn enough about hoboing and hitchhiking in order to write a book. He had to remember to let Annie think she's the expert. Annie stuck her horseshoe in the runner of the sliding boxcar door, and they settled near the forward wall of the car. Annie began licking the palms of her hands to alleviate the pain from the scratches where she'd fallen on the slag. He said, "I have some merthiolate antiseptic in my backpack, if you want me to put some on your scratches."

"Hell no! I don't want no monkey blood on my scratches! I know how that stuff burns. I'll be all right."

Ross was thankful that the boxcar they had chosen turned out to be clean. You can get in one with dirt, seeds or other debris and the wind can whip it up into your eyes and make your trip miserable. He started to unroll his sleeping bag while Annie paid close attention.

"Oh well, I see you're doing *that* right, Jake. Always sleep with your head to the forward wall. If you bed to the rear of a boxcar and the train stops suddenly, you'll slide all the way to the forward end and break your neck." She started unrolling her own sleeping bag to the left of his, a little too close, he thought, for comfort. She immediately lay down, using her backpack for a pillow. He was certain he could smell stale sweat on her clothing and sleeping bag.

Ross did not go to bed right away. He walked over to the sliding door, looked out across the desert and enjoyed the lights of the western suburbs and outlying neighborhoods of Tucson. In a while, there were only a few distant lights and mostly darkness across the desert and the stars grew brighter.

In the moonlight, he could see the outline of mountains to the south, toward Mexico. In a while, he walked back to his backpack and removed his small travel thermos. Annie was already sound asleep, snoring loudly. A mixed blessing. Even if he were disposed to sleep, there's no way he could do so with her snoring so loudly. However, he could hear her only when he was nearby, so he decided to move his bedroll over to the east wall of the car. Trains rarely brake suddenly, and considering the torture of Annie's snoring—and just the thought of being close to her—compensated for the indiscretion.

After moving his bunk and gear to the east end of the boxcar, Ross walked back over to the boxcar door, sat down and let his legs dangle. He drank coffee from his thermos, figuring that it would keep him awake for a couple of hours, and in the meantime, he just wanted to relax, sit in the doorway, feel the rumble of the steel wheels and watch the stars and the moonlit landscape glide past. He thought about Rocio and for a brief moment wondered if he should tell her about Annie. He answered himself: Hell no! He was innocent, but he understood a woman's natural suspicions and skepticism when you tell them about how ugly or obnoxious a woman is, or was.

From his shirt pocket, he pulled out his journal, lit it up with a small flashlight, and made a brief entry:

Friday morning, 1 a.m., October 14, moving west from Tucson on a freight train.

He sat in the doorway for about an hour, until after the train passed through Casas Grandes, then went back to his bed. He lay on top of his sleeping bag; his arms folded behind his head for a pillow and sank into deep thought, trying to figure what action to take next to find Leah Waters. He could only plan tentatively, but had to remain flexible for unexpected exigencies. He would continue to make the main soup kitchens and rescue missions along the way to L.A., keeping his eyes and ears open for Leah, or seek information about her. He was becoming resigned to the fact that his next important objective would be the Beacon Light Rescue Mission in L.A. and its manager, Reverend Tasker. He would improvise from there. His thoughts finally drifted into dreams.

While sound asleep, something animate inside his pants awakened Ross with a start. He grabbed it, and as his mind and sight cleared, he realized the invading object was Annie's hand! She had moved her bedroll over next to his, had unzipped his pants, and was groping him.

"What the hell are you *doing*?" demanded Ross tightly gripping her right hand with his and holding it away from him.

"The question *is* what the hell is the matter with *you*? All the men want to ride with me—and they *want* me. Are you *gay*, or *what*?" She angrily jerked her arm from his grip.

Ross picked up his sleeping bag and said, "No, I'm not gay—I'm *what*. Do you realize that some men think about things other than sex?" He picked up his bedroll and moved it to the far corner on the east end of the boxcar.

Annie got up, and muttering petulantly, picked up her own sleeping bag, walked over to the southwest corner of the boxcar and flung it violently on the floor. She said, "Okay, I'll leave you alone—but you better come back to *this* end. You know the danger. If the train stops suddenly, you'll slide back to this end anyway.

"Thanks, but until the train stops, I'll stay on the opposite end from you."

"Suit yourself," she said, lying back down on her sleeping bag. "It's your neck."

Ross lay down, took a deep breath, and wondered when the train would stop for a crew change. None too soon, he thought. Whenever and wherever it stops, he would be getting off to get on the next westbound. He had a bellyful of this aging, obnoxious skank. She was one adventure he wanted to forget quickly. Even if Annie had been younger and still attractive, and he had been eligible, he still would not touch her.

She was probably a human petri dish, growing germ cultures that did not have a name yet. After a few minutes, he could hear Annie resume her loud snoring.

After Annie's assault, Ross did not go back to sleep. He sat on his sleeping bag and placed the backpack against the boxcar wall for back support. After what seemed like hours, the train began to slow and the glow of city lights began to light up the night. He walked over to the door in time to see a railroad sign go past that read "Yuma." Of course! Yuma must be the crew-change city. He decided to hop off, as soon as the train slowed enough—and put distance between himself and Annie, preferably while she was still asleep.

He put on his backpack and grasped his bedroll, careful to make no noise. When the train slowed to about 5 miles per hour, he slipped silently off. About half a mile west, beyond the railroad tracks, across some vacant lots, he could see a few cars traveling north and south. If he could reach that busy, city street, he figured he could find a place to rest until daylight and better get his bearings. He shined his flashlight on his watch. It was 3:30 a.m. Since the Union Pacific is a busy railroad, he knew that he would not have to wait long for another California-bound train. In the meantime, he just needed to find a place to stay out of sight until daylight. He had no guidance, like he'd had in Tucson, when Sandhouse had helped him find a hangout for the homeless and avoid the police. Anyone moving about the streets this time of day would appear suspicious, and he preferred not to have to explain his business to police.

After crossing all the tracks in the freight yard, he noticed the lights of a large business of some type. When he got closer, he saw the silhouettes of two men sitting on a low wall, against a tool shed or some type of small building. There were more men near the entrance. Since the railroad was only a couple hundred yards behind him, he figured they might be hobos. He approached them and explained, "I just got off a westbound UP and I'm trying to find a safe place to stay until daybreak, then catch out again. I'm not familiar with Yuma, or the freight yards, here."

The older of the two men introduced himself as "Jerry," and the younger, "Tony." Jerry replied, "Well, you picked a good place to ask. This whole compound you see here is the Crossroads Mission. You are welcome to hang out here, but it's closed right now." Ross guessed the older hobo to be in his forties, the younger in his mid-twenties. They were both dressed in typical, freight-train travel clothes.

"It's a good place to catch a meal," said Tony, "But the kitchen doesn't open for another hour and a half—until five-thirty a.m."

Jerry said, "You might as well sit here and make yourself comfortable until breakfast."

Ross was not interested in the free meal, only in staying out of trouble and gathering intelligence information about Leah and Grifty. He went to the west end of the bench-like wall, pulled off his backpack and sat next to the two hobos. The three men exchanged small talk. From them, Ross learned that the Crossroads Mission was part of a nation-wide network that provides re-hab services to drug addicts and alcoholics, temporary housing for the poor, free meals and religious guidance. He learned that the mission has a huge soup kitchen there on site, a dormitory, and a thrift store nearby that employs quite a few of their clients.

Ross said, "I'd like to come back someday, but I'm in a hurry this trip. The place is quite impressive—and the practicality of it is surprising—right next to the railroad yards. I suppose quite a few needy hobos have stumbled onto it, like I did."

The older hobo remarked, "Well, I think they put it way out here in the boondocks near the rail yards for a reason."

"Yeah," said Tony. "I think they want to keep us street people out of sight."

Jerry agreed, "There are a lot of tourists in this town, especially during the winter when the snowbirds from the northern states show up in their RVs. Needless to say, we're not considered ornaments to the town."

The conversation soon drifted toward rail riding, and Ross saw an opportunity to ask about Grifty. He explained, "I'd like to find someone that knows a lot about the FTRA and write a story about them someday."

Jerry spoke with a gravelly voice, "I wouldn't fool around with those FTRA guys, if I were you. They operate in the shadows, and you won't get much information from them until they get to know you, and that might take a long time."

"I see," said Ross. "Have you ever heard of one called "'Grifty?'"

Tony said, "I heard of him down in Skid Row in L.A. a couple of years ago, but I never met 'im. I doubt that he gets this far from California. FTRA's stay mostly on the hi-line."

The three men exchanged more small talk for a while, and Ross noticed day breaking in the east. "Well, it's been nice talking to you fellows, but I want to get back on a freight as soon as possible and continue to L.A. Where's the best place to catch out?"

Jerry said, "I ain't no genius, but I'm curious as to why you got off here. Most trains go right on through to L.A. after they change crews. The refrigerated expresses don't even slow down in Yuma."

"I had a bad riding partner that I wanted to get rid of."

"Well, that happens to us all at times," said Jerry, seemingly satisfied with the answer. He added, "At this time of day, it's best to get over to South Gila Street. If you just head west and skirt these freight yards on this side, you'll run right into it. After you get on South Gila, just keep walking north to Giss Parkway. That's usually a good place to catch-out. There's an overpass there and a few bushes on the side of the tracks to hide in. There are two sets of tracks, and you want to get on the north tracks because the westbound trains will be on that one."

Tony warned, "That overpass is pretty close to the downtown bulls' office, but if you get on over there right away, the bulls probably won't be out and about yet. Some of these Yuma cops are pretty rednecky, and you want to avoid them if you can."

Ross thanked the two hobos and started walking toward South Gila Street where the streetlights made him feel conspicuous, carrying the telltale luggage of a freight train rider. He stayed close to the shoulder of the street, even though there was no traffic. The freight yards were still just a stone's throw to his right.

Ross reached the underpass at Giss Parkway, crossed under it and walked about halfway up the levee-like railroad bank to some large bushes. He took off his backpack and laid it and his bedroll under a large cypress tree growing on the slope of the levee. The limbs of Arizona cypress trees grow close to the ground if not pruned regularly and their underbrush makes a good hiding place. He slid under the limbs to await the next westbound freight train.

Suddenly, a white van drove partly up the railroad slope and stopped right near his shade tree. The driver was dressed western and wore a wide-brim western style hat. He wore an oversized brass star over his left breast. His face was sunburned with deep creases in each of his cheeks. Ross guessed he was either a city cop or a railroad agent and started to stand up. "Hold it right there!" the cowboy said, pulling a long-barreled revolver out of a leather side holster. He pointed the gun straight at Ross who raised both hands in the air to show that he was unarmed.

"Get up and show me some I.D.!" demanded the officer.

Ross noticed that the officer wore a nametag inscribed, "McFlazie." He lowered his right hand to his hip pocket, pulled out his billfold, and handed it to McFlazie. The agent perused the driver's license closely and muttered mostly to himself, "Who knows if this is you..."

"It's me. I guess some rail riders use bad ID's and have given us a bad reputation."

"You ain't shittin' they have. Come over here to the van and put your hands behind your back." He put handcuffs on Ross and instructed, "Now, stand there by the van while I check you out on my computer."

Ross stood silent while the agent got back in his vehicle and tapped in some codes on his vehicle's computer. After about five minutes, the man took a deep breath and said, "I'm a railroad agent and it's my duty to inform you that you are trespassing' on railroad property."

Ross said nothing.

"What's your excuse for trespassing?"

"I'm a private investigator working undercover on a case—trying to locate a runaway teenager who got hooked up with a rail-riding gang called the FTRA."

"Ha!" mocked the officer. "I've heard better lies than that. You got any proof?"

"If you look inside the money slot of my billfold, there is a calling card for my agency. The phone is available twenty-four/seven."

The lawman took out the card and looked at it. "El Paso, huh? That's a bad place to be from if you're tryin' to convince me you're not an ordinary railroad bum."

"Like I said, you can call that number and verify what I said."

"I'll just do that."

It was a dedicated, confidential number, and when it rang, Rocio would know that someone was likely checking Ross' credentials. He could hear her respond in the agent's phone, "Investigations."

The agent said, "I'm a railroad agent in Yuma, Arizona. I have a man here who claims he works for your agency. He's out here in Yuma, tryin' to catch a freight train."

"Yes, we have an agent assigned to ride the rails undercover in search of a missing girl," Rocio said. She asked his name, and before answering, he moved several feet away and lowered his voice so that Ross could not hear the conversation.

96

In about a minute, the railroad agent came back to where Ross stood and said, "Well so far your story checks out."

"Can you take off the handcuffs now?"

"Not yet. We're going to take a ride down to the office. If you're really an investigator you've probably heard of AFIS."

"Yes, the Automated Federal Identification System."

"Good for you," said the agent. He called his dispatcher to have a backup meet him at the office.

Ross had never rode in a car with handcuffs on, and now was learning how hundreds of people he had arrested must have felt. There is no way to get comfortable in a vehicle seat with your hands cuffed behind your back. Maybe this is karma.

The agent drove through a maze of streets, turned north up one with a sign reading, "South Third Avenue, and soon came to First Street. At the intersection, he wheeled the SUV into a sally port, stopped at a security card-reading box, slid in his card, and the low gate rolled open. He drove up an incline under a canopy that read "Booking," then drove down. The agent waited outside for a couple of minutes and soon his backup arrived in a regular squad car. With the arresting agent leading, the backup followed behind, escorting Ross inside the building. Near the booking room entrance sat a middle-aged, plump female clerk with a low-cut, white blouse. She sat chewing gum and tapping on a computer keyboard. "Got another hobo, huh, Mac?" she drawled without looking up. She was waiting for a computer printout. McFlazie grunted affirmatively and said, "Well, he was at the Giss Street underpass, apparently waiting for a train. He says he's a private eye, but I'm gonna check him out on AFIS." He put Ross backpack and bedroll in a temporary compartment behind the woman's desk. "If I have to book 'im, I'll be back for this crap," said McFlazie.

They continued through the office to a work station with a small, waist-high table. With the backup officer standing behind, the railroad agent took the handcuffs off and put Ross' two thumbs on a small plate glass while monitoring a small screen. In a couple of minutes, the agent took a deep breath, exhaled and said, "Well, Mister, I guess you're clean."

Unlocking Ross' handcuffs, the lawman said, "I'm cutting you loose, but I can't let you ride the rails out of here. In fact, if I catch you in the freight yards, you'll get 30 days for trespassing. I'm basically a railroad agent, but here in Yuma, we have dual police authority."

The agent escorted Ross' back to the plump female's desk handed him back his gear, and said, "I guess there's no use goin' through your gear, since you have a clean record."

Ross exhaled a silent, "Whew!" Luck was beginning to take a turn in his favor. If McFlazie had found his 9 mm, it would have sunk his ship, since he was not a commissioned officer, even though he had a concealed weapon permit in Texas. Obviously, Yuma was not a good place for a P.I. to get sympathy. He asked the agent, "Where's the intercity bus station?"

The agent gave Ross directions to the bus station and warned, "It may not be open yet."

The entrance opened and in came two more railroad agents, a man and a woman team, escorting a handcuffed, still resisting, obnoxious, drunk woman. Her head was covered with a spit shield. She loudly spewed obscenities at the officers in a voice that sounded familiar. The male agent reported to officer McFlazie, "We caught Annie trespassing on railroad property again."

Sure enough, it was Horseshoe Annie. He ducked his head and looked away, but it was too late. Through the spit screen, Annie recognized him. She screamed, "There he is! That's the man that raped me in the boxcar!"

CHAPTER EIGHT

Ross was stunned speechless by Annie's accusation. The male and female officers in custody of Annie seemed to pay no attention to her. The female officer growled, "You wish, Annie. Shut up!" The officer took off the spit shield and said, "If you spit again, this shield is going to be sewed onto your neck."

Officer McFlazie asked Ross, "Do you know *her*?"

Ross suddenly realized that sometimes discretion was the better part of honesty. "I never saw her in my life," he replied.

"He's *lying*!" screamed Annie. "I can prove it. His name is Jake and he's a writer!"

"Writer, my ass," replied McFlazie. "Annie, why don't you go back to Tucson and check back into the funny farm. We have plenty of work here already."

McFlazie and Ross started toward the building's front entrance. The agent said to Ross, "Well, you're lucky. *We* know Annie. She's been in and out of the funny farm or drug re-hab a dozen times when not in jail. She's been diagnosed paranoid schizophrenic, bi-polar and a few other mental disorders I can't pronounce or remember—and she has a rap sheet a yard long."

Credibility—or lack thereof— is such an important character trait, thought Ross. Thank goodness, Annie had none. He could think of perhaps a dozen epigrams to justify lying to the agent about having never seen Annie. The fact that she thought he was an aspiring writer, while the agent knew he was a private investigator, turned out to be his ace in the hole, for he never had a reason to dissemble before the agent. In cases like Annie, lying was merely fighting fire with fire. One lie offsets another. Did the pre-Socratics, like Heraclitus, not believe in the principle of *coincidentia oppositorium*? Did the Tao not say that in order for a thing to exist, it must have an opposite? Cool. By not uttering the truth, I deprive Annie of the existence of any possible truth to her lie....I suppose it makes sense.

The last thing Ross wanted was to hang around Yuma. As soon as the city judge arrives, he figured that they may let Annie out on bond. He asked McFlazie, "What's the closest route from here to Winterhaven, California?"

"When you go back out the door you came in, keep going west to Fourth Avenue and you'll wind up right at the foot of the Colorado River Bridge. Cross the bridge and you're there."

Ross followed a railed sidewalk out the sally port back to the intersection of First Street and Third Avenue. From there, he could see the Colorado River Bridge, and he almost trotted the block west to Fourth Avenue, which was also the business route of I-8. He turned right onto the bridge, still at a rapid gait, anxious to put distance between himself and the State of Arizona. If Annie keeps repeating that rape lie, someone might believe her and the DA might issue a bench warrant for his arrest. He didn't think that Arizona would ever extradite anyone from California to make him answer a neurotic sociopath's delusional fantasies...or would they? Fellow border patrol agents assigned to Arizona had told him about Arizona's state government having been taken over by liberal politicians, including some prosecutors, hostile to border guards. As a former one, he might be a candidate to become another one of their scapegoats. He'd heard that the word of lunatics and criminals were as good as that of federal officers when it came to their local prosecutors. Sane jurors had been a help in the past, but lately even juries were being encroached upon by activists who lie during the *voir dire* stage of trials to conceal their radicalism and hatred for the *migra*. Before long, hung juries in favor of acquitting agents of trumped up charges, might become minorities. That is the ultimate goal of the irredentists with deep roots in Mexico; those with an obsession for their *reconquista* plan. That landscape had spawned Maricopa County Sheriff, Joe Arpaio. He was trying to shovel back the stormy surf against the tide, but he is getting old and is surrounded by hostile irredentists—and liberals that had recently held jobs in the State—from a couple of U.S. Attorneys to Governor.

Ross paced hurriedly across the Colorado River Bridge, and when he arrived at the north end, a California Highway 95 road sign welcomed him. He breathed a little easier.

He followed State Highway 95 and Business I-8, which bent northwesterly through the small town. He passed a gambling casino on his left and saw a lean, fit young man coming out the front door into the parking lot. He was wearing dungarees, a denim jacket and a baseball cap with a maroon Arizona State logo. Ross asked the young man directions to the Winterhaven bus station. The young man said, "You'll have to go back across the river to Yuma to catch a bus. It doesn't even stop here." He started to unlock his car and said, "I can give you a ride, since I'm headed for Yuma. I nearly lost my ass gambling in the casino last night and now I gotta go back to Yuma and bust what's left of my ass at a construction site."

"No, thanks," replied Ross. For Ross, going back to Yuma was out of the question. Annie and a redneck cop were on the other side of that river. He said, "I don't suppose there is a freight train yard in Winterhaven, is there?"

"Nope, that's in Yuma, too. Good luck—I hope yours is better than mine has been today." The young man wheeled out of the parking lot, headed for Yuma.

From his map study, Ross knew that he could keep walking through Winterhaven and find the Interstate 8 access ramp, and if lucky, not be harassed by local police while thumbing a ride to the next big city, El Centro. There, he knew he could catch a bus. He was getting hungry, so first, he would look for a restaurant.

The westerly curve led him through the center of Winterhaven, and after several blocks up the main drag, he was unable to find even a small restaurant that was open, but he did find a small supermarket. Inside, he bought two fresh apples, a pint carton of chocolate milk and a large, fried burrito.

He took his small manila bag of groceries and walked a block north looking for a quiet, private place to eat. He noticed a dead-end, unpaved street leading west off the state highway. There were no houses or businesses nearby, and at the end of the dirt road was a nice, palm tree. The location seemed to offer a modicum of privacy. Perfect, thought Ross. Nearby, there were also some high bushes, offering privacy, in case nature called.

Although not a Zen, Ross decided to try meditation before lunch to try to put the events of the day into some kind of perspective. It worked for Kerouac, didn't it? He pulled off his backpack and bedroll and assumed a cross-legged zazen position. After a few moments of meditation, Ross felt stable enough to call Rocio. She answered on the third ring, probably the first she heard, considering the maze of cell-tower relay circuits while in roaming mode. He took a deep breath and in a pleasant voice said, "Hi, Hon!"

"Did everything go well?" she asked.

"Yeah, that railroad agent you talked to on the phone brought me to the office to check me out on AFIS. I got lucky. He didn't check my baggage and find my weapon. I'm on my way west again. Actually, I'm already in California."

"Thank goodness," she said.

"You were perfect dear—you sounded real professional on the phone—I could hear your voice on the agent's phone."

"Well, I *am* a professional, *aren't* I?"

"Indeed you are."

"Where in California are you—and how did you get there so fast?"

"I'm in Winterhaven. All I had to do was walk north on one of the main streets in Yuma, cross the Colorado River, and here I am, out of Arizona and in California. I thought about waiting for a bus in Yuma, but I wanted to get out of Arizona before I get in trouble again."

"I hear that."

Remembering crazy Annie's accusation, he told himself, you haven't heard the half of it, Sweetheart. To his wife, he said, "I guess you remember the stories I told you about Arizona's criminal lawyers trumping up charges on border guards, about their being in cahoots with the media, and trying to railroad, or permanently discredit them."

"I remember. That was back when they had that liberal activist as a federal prosecutor—and another as a federal judge."

"Well, I'm not a border guard anymore, but I still get a nervous stomach just thinking about some things that happened to some friends of mine stationed there. I didn't feel any safer in Arizona than the scores of my colleagues that got prosecuted."

"We're both glad you're out of Arizona, Hon, and we both know why. Winterhaven is a pretty name. What is it like?"

"Winterhaven is just a small town with a couple of on-ramps to the Interstate. It looks dead, economically, except for a couple of small gambling casinos. Yuma is a big city in comparison. There are no train yards near this town, so thumbing seems the only way to go. I haven't hitchhiked on the highways since I was in the Army, so we'll see how it that works. "

"Well, you be careful, my love. Use that sixth sense of yours, and don't accept a ride that gives you bad vibes."

Ross and Rocio chatted for a few more minutes and then he ate his lunch. Just as he was finishing lunch, a young man in his early twenties with long hair and dirty ragged, denim pants stumbled toward him. "Hey, bro, got a joint?" he pleaded. He was holding his stomach as if in pain.

Ross smiled and politely answered, "Nope, I don't use it."

As the unkempt young man, apparently another drifter, came closer, Ross sensed no danger. The chap walked unsteadily and appeared ill. When he got under the shade of the palm, he half way collapsed, leaning against the trunk of the tree.

"You all right?" asked Ross.

The man exhaled loudly and said, "I guess I'll live. I haven't eaten in about twenty-four hours. I've been walkin..."

Ross gave him one of his apples. "Try this."

The man clumsily took the apple and took a bite of it.

"You better chew it well, bro. Your stomach has to be delicate if you haven't eaten anything in twenty-four hours. You could get some bad stomach cramps if you eat too fast."

The young man began to chew more slowly and started gagging. He spat up the mouthful of apple.

Ross had about half of his pint of chocolate milk left. He handed it to the young man. "Here. Start with this, then eat the apple."

The man eagerly took the chocolate milk and gulped the remainder of it down. In a few minutes, he closed his eyes and appeared about to go to sleep.

"They have a nice transient shelter in Yuma where you can get a free meal," advised Ross. He handed the young man his fried burrito.

"I know about it. I've been there a couple of years ago, but I haven't been to Yuma this trip yet. After I rest some, I'll go over there. I've been walkin' across the desert north of here."

"Why?"

"I got mugged by three guys in a pickup truck. They took all my money and all my belongings. I had a backpack and bedroll."

"How'd you get tied up with those guys?"

"They picked me up hitchikin' about ten miles east of Yuma, yesterday. I rode in the bed of the pickup." He took a bite of burrito, chewed for a moment, and continued, "They didn't speak much English—I think they were illegal aliens. Anyway, they said they'd take me all the way to San Diego. A few miles west of here, they turned off on a dirt road and drove through the desert. I yelled, and they said they were going to pick up a stash of weed out in the desert. After about a mile, I yelled again and they kept goin'. They were goin' too fast for me to jump out, and besides, there was no place in the desert to get away from them. About five miles further into the desert, they stopped, stripped off my clothes and searched everything I had for money. I had a baggy of marijuana and they took that, and they took nearly a hundred dollars I'd earned in Tucson workin' for a yard maintenance business."

The man stopped talking and took another deep breath. He wiped his brow with the sleeve of his badly soiled, denim shirt. He took another bite of burrito, chewed for a moment and continued talking with his mouth still full. "The bastards took everything I had except the clothes on my back."

"Why'd you come over here?" asked Ross.

"A couple of years ago, I was hitching on my way to L.A., and I tried sleeping under the river bridge, but there were two many drunks and bad actors under there. I got away from them and walked all the way out here. I slept under this tree and no one bothered me. I figured as soon as I could rest up, I'd try to make it to the shelter in Yuma." He swallowed more burrito, and then took another bite of the apple.

Ross got up, strapped on his backpack and bedroll. "Well, I'm on my way to California, Be careful and stay a good distance away from the railroad tracks in Yuma. I got picked up by a bull there. He detained and fingerprinted me."

"Thanks. I'll take the roundabout way. I got a warrant out for me in Texas and I can't afford to get pinched."

"A warrant?"

"Yeah—nonpayment of child support."

Ross gave the unfortunate man ten dollars and said, "Peace out, bro." He walked back to Second Avenue in Winterhaven, backtracked to the grocery store, bought another fried burrito, two more apples, two energy bars and a pint of mineral water. He headed west, and after about a mile, came to an I-8 onramp. He laid his backpack and bedroll behind a weed near the shoulder of the highway, remembering tales from older, experienced hitchhikers. You stand a better chance of getting a ride if you have little or no baggage. Jack Kerouac said cut it down to the bare minimum, then cut that down to half, or something like that. Traffic zipped on past on I-8 at the speed limit, plus. He figured he might be there for a while, so he peeled the tinfoil off the burrito and began discretely eating between thumbing of westbound cars.

He stood at the on-ramp for about two hours, until the western horizon began to turn red, and began thinking that he should start looking for a safe place to spend the night, perhaps a culvert under the Interstate. Suddenly, a middle-aged couple stopped and Ross got into the back seat of new, black Lexus with Louisiana license plates.

"We don't ordinarily pick up hitchhikers," said the woman, a dumpy, pasty-faced blonde-haired woman that wore a pinafore dress with brass-buckled shoulder straps. "But when I saw you, I said to Spike, 'Let's give that guy a ride. He looks like a decent sort.'"

Spike was a, middle-aged, slender man of average height. He wore a dark suit and a white shirt without a necktie. He had salt and pepper hair, combed straight back, and seemed to smile perennially showing deep creases in his cheeks.

The blonde woman introduced herself. "I'm Jana and this is my significant other—Spike." Jana had bright, red lipstick, too much eye shadow and false eyelashes.

Ross told them, "Call me Jake."

As Spike sped down the highway at a rate at least ten miles above the speed limit, the woman turned sideways in her seat, pulled up her skirt, and through the backrest partition, Ross could the top of her left thigh. She kept up a steady banter, directed always at Ross. He nodded politely occasionally but did not necessarily agree with anything she said. In fact, in spite of all her talk, she seemed to say nothing but banal clichés.

The man said very little, but cast an occasional, studious glance at Ross in the rear view mirror, making him feel uneasy. Ross inconspicuously opened the top pocket of his backpack where he kept his 9 mm, but he did not take it out. He kept it where he could get it quickly, if needed.

The blonde frump kept up her whimsical discourse all the way to the outskirts of El Centro, California, which they reached at about ten p.m. Her husband said, "Babe, what do you think about staying here for the night. We can still be in L.A. for the convention by noon tomorrow."

"That sounds good to me Baby Doll."

Ross declared, "You can just let me out anywhere here on the shoulder and I can manage from there."

Neither the man nor the woman said anything. Instead of stopping to let Ross out at the street curb, the man drove the Lexus under a canopy in front of the business office of an upscale motel. He stopped, turned to Ross and said, "Jake, why don't you just spend the night here—as our guest. We'll rent a suite. Then tomorrow we can take you all the way to L.A. with us."

Before Ross could answer, the female piped up and said, "The convention we're going to is for swingers. Are you cool with swingers?"

Ross, busy arranging the straps on his backpack, said, "I've heard of 'em."

Without hesitation, the woman continued, "We pair off, usually, with other couples, but Spike doesn't mind if I solo with a man. He likes to watch, right Spike?"

Spike smiled, nodded, and said, "You guys wait here in the car and I'll go get the accommodations."

"Ixnay!" said Ross. "Count me out. This is where I get off." He opened the door to the Lexus, pulled his backpack and bedroll out, and said, "Thanks for the ride."

He walked west, along the shoulder of the highway, headed toward the middle of El Centro. The woman got out, hustled up even with him, thrust her bosom against his right arm, and said, "You never know what you're missing until you've tried swinging, Jake." Ross picked up the pace, making it difficult for her to keep up, totally ignoring her words. Finally, the woman stumbled over a rock, almost fell and muttered a frustrated obscenity about gays, implying Ross was one, and with a disappointed scowl, went back to Spike.

Ross muttered to himself, "Just when I thought I'd seen or heard of everything, I get picked up by a couple of perverts."

He walked about a mile and arrived at the intercity bus station. He bought a ticket to L.A. and waited only twenty minutes for his bus. Before he got on the bus, he put his billfold in his left front pants pocket. While checking buses in the Border Patrol, he'd come across more than one tired traveler who'd gone to sleep on a bus who had awakened to find his billfold missing. He figured it almost impossible for a pickpocket to steal a billfold from the front pocket of a sitting man, unless he is very drugged-out. Some thieves must ride on buses, especially late at night, he thought, just for that purpose.

There were only about ten other passengers aboard, two of them women, each with two children near the front. Ross chose a seat on the left side next to the window more than halfway toward the back of the bus. That way, whimpering babies that need a diaper change would annoy him less. He spurned the overhead luggage rack; put his backpack under his feet and his bedroll in the seat to his right. There were plenty of vacant seats remaining on the bus, and he figured that the bedroll would discourage anyone from wanting to sit to his right. He soon fell sound asleep.

CHAPTER NINE

Ross awakened when the intercity bus pulled into the downtown Los Angeles station. While still seated, he made an entry in his journal.

Saturday, 9 a.m., October 15: Arrived in L.A.

He put his journal back in his shirt pocket, retrieved his backpack and bedroll and got off the bus. He bought a city map of L.A. and headed toward Decatur Street; there he walked east to Seventh. The roar of city traffic pounded his ears and the pungent air stung his nostrils. He'd served briefly in L.A. on a Border Patrol detail, and the noise and pollution are things you do not soon forget. He looked up at a sun that struggled to beam through a hazy sky. He took a deep breath, bracing himself for submersion into this maelstrom of humanity. He had read how L.A. had declined in the years since his last visit. Misguided, liberal, political agendas exploited the worst aspects of migrating humanity. Most illegal aliens from the banana republics had more freedom in the slums than they had legally in their home countries. It was a newfound freedom not understood, but for the criminals among them, one that, instinct told them, the city was ripe for exploitation and abuse; thence, they occupy their share of police blotters.

Ross walked on, fighting off trepidation that spoke to his inner sense of survival, forewarning of hazards ahead. He had never met Leah Waters, but he shuddered to think how brutally this environment can, and does, quickly subdue and suborn the innocent and inexperienced. Young, naïve girls are practically defenseless against the Rasputin-like pimps and other predators.

His paper map was big and bulky. He decided to sit on the curb and pull up an Internet map of L.A. on his note pad. Just then, he saw a young wino sitting against the north side of the Greyhound maintenance building on 7th Street, his legs sprawled on the sidewalk. The derelict wore dirty, denim trousers with genuine holes in the knees and a denim jacket, unneeded in this balmy weather. He had long, stringy, dish-water blonde hair and several-days growth of beard. Beside him, was an empty, green wine bottle, ill-concealed by a twisted, wrinkled, manila-colored paper bag. Ross asked, "Say bro, could you direct me to the Beacon Light Rescue Mission?"

The wino looked up at Ross with addled, bloodshot eyes. He pointed west, burped, and with moist, purple, distorted lips, slurred, "Go that way for about ten... fifteen blocks...and you'll see San Julian Street. Turn right and go two blocks up the street, you'll see it on the left. It's 501 San Julian. You can't miss it because a lot of people live on that street and I *do* mean *on* the street."

"Thanks, bro. You seem quite familiar with downtown."

"I stayed at the Beacon Light one time...back when I was sober...it was my last home."

Before Ross could step away, the wino said, "Could you spare a couple bucks. I ain't ate nothin' for a couple of days."

Ross knew that was a lie, for on Skid Row there are free soup kitchens on almost every block that serve full meals. This young drunkard probably hung out near the bus station in order to spot strangers, knowing that anyone who had to ask directions in L.A. was a favorable target to hit up for a handout, and greenhorn enough to believe the blatant lie. That was probably why so many bums hang our near bus stations. Ross dug in his billfold, figuring that if he gave him five, instead of two bucks, maybe that will spare him begging from four more people. The young sot took the five-dollar bill without a word of thanks. Maybe he thought he had earned it by supplying information, or maybe he just had a typical, modern, socialist-oriented entitlement complex. Yes, Reverend Tasker—you have plenty of work to do here—but do charity and sermons really help these people? On the other hand, a sermon on self-reliance would definitely be politically incorrect in this venue; beggars and thieves probably consider themselves self-reliant. Relativism is a useful philosophy when you have to compartmentalize bad behavior. Oh well, altruism is what makes Skid Row evangelists' engines run, and Ross had no intention of debating the issue with Tasker, nor even with himself, at the moment. He had to focus on finding Leah.

Ross followed the young wino's instructions, and by the time he arrived at San Julian Street, it was mid-morning. The wino had been right. Many people *were* literally living on this street. Rag pickers pushing grocery carts were too many to count. The carts contained dumpster-dived junk most of which was worthless, not to satisfy any human need, but to satisfy an obsessive, compulsive disorder to acquire material things, even worthless things.

Some of the homeless living on San Julian Street had constructed small, makeshift; lean-to canopies against the sides of buildings and walls to shelter them from the elements. The congested sidewalk, and perhaps a degree of paranoia, or claustrophobia, induced some of the denizens to walk in the middle of the street, as if they were in a strip mall. A few babbled to themselves incessantly; others walked, or staggered, along with dubious destinations. Apparently cranked out on meth, or some other drug, many were in the early stages of premature, drug-induced dementia. Painted on the wall of the south side of the street was a large, official-looking sign that read:

Skid Row City Limit
Population: Too many

The denizens were mostly domestic, but Ross' professional experience enabled him to discern plenty of illegal aliens. As Ross saw it, the human condition on Skid Row is a microcosm of the future of America. You can find the well-educated down here along with the mentally ill, but there is a general mood of resignation, despair and self-blame.

The bottom rung of the economic ladder, where many middle-class Americans used to start work, was largely no longer available. The politicians in Washington had decided that the bottom rung were jobs that Americans did not want. The corrupt politicians had used that as a rationale for opening up the borders to the peons from the third world; to people whose concept of "success" included plans for obtaining a big part of their economic sustenance from American welfare, whether here legally or illegally. Their main ambition is to wait for the day when can vote and have a say in selecting the leaders who promise making easier their pathway to the Horn of Plenty, and make easier the pathways of relatives to follow.

Bad decisions may be only a small part of the flaws that put our native-born street people in this rut. Big brother tells the losers that social injustice and prejudice caused their plight, but the real answer to the problem of unemployment is visible in people all around them—people spending money from mysterious sources in small restaurants and other stores, while still wearing the strange clothing brought with them from third world countries.

Ross continued up San Julian and noted that once elegant buildings on Skid Row now display renovated facades, but adjacent vacant lots strip aside the façade and display the sides of the buildings, pocked with broken, hollow red-clay bricks from a century ago.

Ross picked up the pace, and at the end of the block, beheld the Beacon Light Mission— just as the young wino had said—at the corner of Fifth and San Julian. Gaudy lavender and yellow paint ornamented the building, perhaps to offset the gloomy street scene. The mission offered temporary lodging to selected clientele and across the street stood a place where anybody could get a free, hot meal, the Jehovah Jireh Soup Kitchen.

Ross trudged up the steps of the building, and just inside the entrance, saw an office with a teller-type window. The window framed a slender young man with long hair and an eye patch that half covered a stern, suspicious stare. Above the window was a sign that read, "Information." The one-eyed volunteer was one of those "home guards" that live and work in the Skid Row rescue missions. Chosen from among successful rehabs, their experience qualifies them to be tough on occasion, a necessary trait, considering the type of humanity with whom the business deals. They have a ringside seat to Los Angeles' underbelly. Ross introduced himself to the young man and said that he was looking for Reverend Tasker.

"Reverend Alfred Tasker? His office is up on the fourth floor. Do you have an appointment?"

"He's expecting me, but we hadn't set a specific date and time. If you tell him Ross Spencer is here, and he'll know who you're talking about."

The home guard stammered nervously on the phone and related to someone that a Ross Spencer had requested to see him. In a moment, the young man seemed relieved and a little surprised. He looked back at Ross with his single eye and declared, "The reverend is coming down for lunch. He said to wait for him here."

While waiting for Reverend Tasker, Ross surveyed his surroundings. The large foyer had a high ceiling, causing an echo. At the far west end, he could see a middle-aged woman wearing a pink kitchen apron, indicating that she was a server. She brought a bag of trash out into the foyer and handed it to a young black man. He took it and headed for a rear door of the building.

A smiling, tall, slender, balding, middle-aged man wearing casual business clothes without necktie came out of the elevator and walked toward Ross. He wore black, plastic-framed glasses with thick lens. He extended his hand to Ross and said, "I'm Reverend Alfred Tasker, and I'm guessing you're Ross Spencer."

"You guessed right."

"Have you had dinner, yet?"

"No, Sir."

"Then, I'll invite you to dine with me and I'll bring you up to date on what I've heard that might interest you."

The two men walked down the steps, out of the rescue mission and onto the sidewalk. Reverend Tasker turned left, toward Fifth Street, and Ross noticed from the corner of his right eye a shuffling among the young men that loitered under the arched doorway of the Jehovah-Jireh Soup Kitchen, across the street. One or more of them apparently forced their way to the rear of the knot, as if to avoid being seen. Ross dismissed it as probably one or more troublemakers that Reverend Tasker had likely run out of his mission, or one or more who had hoped that by staying out of sight for a while, he would get another chance to lodge at the Beacon. Unfortunately, homesteading, would-be transients tend to grow roots in a favorite place. Hiding their identity is not as easy as it is for the interstate drifters that scam the welfare system. The Home Guards get to know them by sight and reputation, their names being less relevant, since so many carried false identity documents.

Ross and the reverend rounded the corner onto Fifth Street and passed a row of fancy green and gold-trimmed sidewalk toilets, placed there by the city for the homeless. The stench of human waste penetrated his nostrils, and Ross noted an apparent laxity in servicing the privies. Urine, mixed with other human waste, seeped from overflowing containers onto the sidewalk and trickled into the gutter. Taking care of the homeless is obviously politically popular, almost everywhere nowadays, and so is window dressing it with all kinds of fancy facilities, especially during election campaigns. However, after installing such facilities, politicians seldom arrange for effective, perpetual funding to service them.

They walked west, and near the end of the block, on the left side of the street, Reverend Tasker led Ross through the door of a small café. It had one counter for ordering and another for picking up orders. After ordering hamburgers, fries and Cokes, the two men took a table to wait for their orders.

Alfred Tasker said, "I have a picture of Leah pinned to the wall inside the front office next to the entrance. Sister Rachel sent it to me in hopes it would help me find Leah. The employees that work the front admissions window of our mission know all the regular customers, and many of those that drift from one mission to the other. One of them, Bruce Smith, remembers having seen Leah, and is keeping a watchful eye in hopes that she will re-appear. Smith tells me that he thinks she left with her beau, known on the street as *Grifty*. From what he overheard Grifty say to a companion, Smith got the impression that the pair may have left for Eugene, Oregon, but that was some time ago. Grifty could have returned to L.A., or be almost anywhere."

Ross placed a soda straw in his Coke, stirred the ice, and said, "The transients get around, don't they?"

"Yes, they do. The experienced hobos know the schedules and make good time on the trains. Since Grifty has never tried to register for lodging at our mission, we do not have a name for him. Smith reported that he vaguely remembers that Grifty, and the girl believed to be Leah, came here only once or twice for a free meal. We do not keep records on participants of our nutritional program. Neither do any of the other rescue missions, and we know that most of our beneficiaries also patronize nearly all of the other missions in downtown L.A., from time to time. We share information when a wanted person is being sought. Some of the denizens of Skid Row have money to buy meals in restaurants, but prefer to spend it on alcohol or drugs."

"From what I've heard about him, Reverend, I'd say that Grifty probably has at least a dozen stolen IDs and stolen EBT cards. I'd guess he has a pretty expensive drug habit."

"We always ask for IDs from beneficiaries that check in here to billet, but we hear the same old story so often. They often say 'I just got rolled,' but as a former law enforcement officer, I suppose you are used to aliases and the way some play confidence games to gain advantage."

Ross nodded. "Homeless wandering is absolutely sometimes a refuge for criminals. Drifters are not always what they appear to be, and most criminals, especially those on the lam, are not too uppity to lie low on Skid Row awhile. I can understand your security measures. Hobo jungles near railroad freight yards are also good places to hide out for a few days. Police mostly leave management of Skid Row to people like you, Reverend."

Tasker nodded. He spoke smoothly and effortlessly, like the usual cleric, and did not waste many words. He continued, "We have to frequently remind ourselves that not all of them are indeed innocent victims of circumstances beyond their control, you know, down on their luck. Others are victims of their own bad decisions, not infrequently *criminal* decisions. We work with other agencies in various types of rehabilitation of those that have strayed from the straight and narrow, and we have to be vigilant for the hardened criminals that are always trying to outsmart us and use our resources for a temporary refuge. You cannot rehabilitate that type. We dispatch them in a hurry. We have more success helping recovering alcoholics and drug addicts to re-adjust to society, you know, provide them with a temporary place to stay to keep them out of the gutter before we refer them to professional rehabilitation institutions. We give them some counseling and moral support—as long as they obey our rules and stay fixed on definitive goals for rehabilitation."

Ross pondered the cleric's words. Some drunks and deadbeats are by definition petty criminals and never were on the straight and narrow. That was where he differed in opinion and optimism from men like Reverend Tasker. However, he no longer argued with anyone over human frailties. Those fruitless arguments are for college liberal arts classrooms, but he doubted that nowadays there were many confrontational opinions in college classrooms to detract from the liberal view, unless a student wants to be a pariah.

Ross was beginning to get a bit antsy and doubtful of Reverend Tasker's usefulness as a source of information. He said, "Well, Reverend, from what you tell me, it looks like my next step might be hanging around the various downtown rescue missions and soup kitchens here in L.A. for a few days. Maybe I'll get lucky—maybe run into someone that knows something—or perhaps run into Leah herself—or Grifty. If no solid leads develop here, maybe I'll take a freight train up the west coast to Portland, where he's been seen recently."

Reverend Tasker took a swallow of Coke and said, "I was just getting around to that. Maybe your next step should be couch-surfing." He peeled back wax paper and took a big bite of hamburger.

"Couch...what?"

After chewing for what seemed like a full minute, the cleric washed down the hamburger with Coke and explained, "One of our mission associates and volunteers, Regina Borrego, lives out in Muscoy, a town north of greater San Bernardino. She is a widow and sometimes a couch surfer host for young travelers of good moral character. She called me late yesterday and said that a young man named Lorenzo Castillo, had contacted her on the Internet about staying there. She remembered having seen his name in our rescue mission newsletter as a person of interest in the disappearance of Leah Waters. She ran a background check to see if he is the same person of interest by that name mentioned in our bulletin. She learned that Castillo is a parolee. She would like to help us, although understandably concerned, living alone as she is, about hosting an ex-convict. She told Castillo she'd let him know today, pending a possible cancelation by another guest. She used the delay to call me. She had no pending cancelations, of course, but little white lies are acceptable if they can be reconciled with a noble, Christian end."

"Then he *is* the Lorenzo Castillo who is a friend of Grifty?"

Tasker nodded.

"Would I ever like to talk to *him!*"

"I figured you would, and I told Ms. Borrego that. She said that if you were there, she would not be afraid to host him. How would you like to be a couch surfer for a couple of nights?"

Russ said anxiously, "I'm not completely up to snuff on this couch surfing. How does it work?"

"Couch surfer hosts, or hostesses, are volunteers who give young travelers a place to crash, take a bath and get a free meal. Most of the hosts are outgoing, liberal thinkers who like to meet people from different backgrounds and cultures, excluding dangerous criminals, of course. Regina Borrego is very liberal, but a good Christian lady, I can assure you."

"I'm very interested in being her guest—and having a chance to meet Castillo—but with all due respect to Ms. Borrego, couch surfer hosting seems like a dangerous practice."

"It could be, if their network were not discreet in screening their applicants. Since she said she had two male dormitory bunks available, I told her I'd call her back as soon as you got here. We both want to make sure that she would not have Castillo in the house, unless you were there also as a guest. I was confident you would want to seize the opportunity to meet and talk with Castillo."

"It sounds like a great opportunity that might lead to information about Leah."

Reverend Tasker checked his wristwatch. "You should try to get out there as soon as possible because she said Castillo was supposed to show up around dark, this evening. I'd personally take you out there, but I have an important meeting to attend later this afternoon. There's an intercity bus leaving for San Bernardino in about 45 minutes. It's about an hour's trip from here."

"You are very efficient, Reverend. You should have been a cop."

Tasker wagged his head slightly to the side with a wry smile, "Oh, no, not me—but I do get an occasional opportunity to cooperate with law enforcement. While working on Skid Row I have learned to be more observant and to remember more details about suspects. We frequently get alert bulletins from law enforcement agencies. If information got out that we cooperate with the law, some in the Christian world might condemn me. Some of my brethren see only good in everybody. Me? I also see Satan in some people, and I am more circumspect than some fellow Christians might appreciate. Many of our guests are just one step ahead of the law and if word got out that we are informants, it would hamper our mission."

"Not to mention endanger your life. "

Tasker seemed to ignore Ross' dark observation, and continued, "To save a soul in distress, we need to first make them feel safe and wanted..."

CHAPTER TEN

The bus ride from Los Angeles to San Bernardino gave Ross a chance to call Rocio and bring her up to speed on the latest. Then he phoned Regina Borrego, and she told him that Reverend Tasker had already reported to her that he was en route.

On the trip to San Bernardino, the hazy San Gabriel Mountains to the east offered an exiguous contrast with the frantic freeway. He figured that I-10 East must have nearly a dozen traffic lanes, all jammed with Saturday shoppers and workers, now anxious to get home, break out the beer and watch football games.

When the bus pulled into the San Bernardino terminal, Ross went to the passenger waiting area, called a taxi, then sat down and brought his journal up to date:

Saturday, October 15, 6 p.m.: Arrived in San Bernardino by bus. Taking taxi to Regina Borrego residence.

Regina Borrego's home was a modest, one story dwelling in a quiet side street, just off busier Gray Street. It had no garage, only a carport, sheltering an older, red sedan. Plastic garbage cans of various sizes and colors lined the street curb, waiting for collection. Holding his sleeping bag and backpack in one hand, Ross rang the doorbell. A plump, middle-aged Hispanic woman appeared in the doorway, smiling broadly. She wore gray, tight-fitting vertical-striped pants and the plunging neckline of her tank top revealed the cleavage of a well-endowed bosom. She eyed him admiringly, and with a musical lilt in her voice, said, "You must be Mr. Spencer. I'm glad to see you."

Ross removed his hat, nodded politely, smiled charmingly, and said, "Ross Spencer, at your service Ma'am. Reverend Tasker recommended me."

They exchanged mundane pleasantries and Ross explained, "On the road, I am Jake—Jake McFadden and I'm doing research about homeless people."

She smiled and nodded. "I'll remember....Jake. Reverend Tasker told me all about your business. Due to the mission bulletin, I was already familiar with the story of the missing girl you are trying to find." She invited Ross inside and escorted him through the living room into to the men's guest room at the south end of the home. The room was not very large, but it accommodated two Army-type bunks quite well. She showed Ross the closet, and in it, Ross placed his backpack and bedroll.

"I hope you'll be comfortable here, Mr. Spencer."

"I'm sure I will, Ms. Borrego."

On the west side of the bedroom was a short hallway leading to the bathroom. Near the doorframe was posted a computer-printed notice announcing *Rules for Guests:*

Guests will share the closet. No alcohol or drugs allowed on the premises. No loud noise, no playing of musical instruments, no loud talking, and no radios or quarreling. Bedroom lights are out at eleven p.m. TV privileges are in the living room only and end at 10:30 p.m. No talking on phones after 10:30 p.m. Remember, most guests want to get some sleep. Please respect them. The host serves meals in the dining room at exactly 8 a.m., 12 noon and 8 p.m. The host provides one set of clean linen for each guest.

Being an X Gen, Ross figured that the rules were neither too many, nor too harsh; but he figured that most couch surfers were likely to be Millennials, and not too fond of rules.

Regina Borrego stood by with arms crossed, watching Ross explore his surroundings. There was a bible on a nightstand between the two bunk beds. A framed, eight-by-twelve inch image of Jesus in the Garden of Gethsemane hung on the wall, centered just above and between the heads of the bunk beds. A chair with its back to the wall faced each bunk bed. The room had two windows, both near the northeast corner of the room.

"You seem to have very good manners, Mr. Spencer. I can't remember the last time a gentleman removed his hat for me. Where are you from?"

"West Texas. You live in a nice town, here, Ms. Borrego."

"It's not really a town."

"What do you mean?"

"It's a called a 'census-designated place,'" she indicated quotation marks with her index and middle fingers on both hands. "Our population is counted in the census separately from San Bernardino, but we are under the same city government."

"It must be confusing to the mail carriers."

"Not really. We get our mail by street address and zip code."

The woman continued showing Ross around. "The bathroom is in here," she said, opening a door on the west side of the bedroom. "Inside, you notice the bathroom has two doors. The men and women guests share it. The women's bedroom is on the other side of the bathroom. When you use the bathroom, remember to latch both doors for privacy, and when you leave, be sure to unlatch both. There are notices on the doors to remind you as you leave the bathroom."

She then led him back through the living room to the laundry room and showed him how to operate the washer and dryer. "Use what detergent and other things you need," she said, pointing to a shelf containing those necessities.

"I can hardly believe that you are so generous and that you do not charge anything for all this service," said Ross.

Regina Borrego laughed and said, "It's my hobby. I get a small stipend from the mission in L.A., but mostly I pay for everything myself. Since my husband passed, it gets very lonely in the house. My only daughter married three years ago and is now in Germany with her husband, who is in the Army. I enjoy having guests and listening to their stories. Of course, I invite all of them to attend our Mission in downtown L.A."

"I noticed quite a few railroad yards in the San Bernardino area," observed Ross.

"Yes—and the railroads still bring a few travelers to San Bernardino, but not near as many when I was growing up here." She laughed and added, "Most of my freight-train-riding guests are glad to travel the rest of the way to L. A. by hitching rides, or go with me when I drive in that direction. Some go on up the Valley, toward Fresno."

Although the home was nothing fancy, Ross could see how useful it could be as a place for a sojourner with limited funds to crash for a day or two.

"My guests are often very entertaining," said Ms. Borrego. "Young Europeans are among the more frequent users of the couch surfing, and they are so polite and considerate..."

Ross said, "I understand you will be having another guest tonight."

"Yes, Mr. Lorenzo Castillo. He is from Texas, too. Reverend Tasker told me you wanted to meet him."

"When will he be arriving?"

"I just got a text message from him a few minutes before you arrived. He expects to be here within the next hour. You have time to bathe and freshen up before he gets here, if you wish. You will have the bathroom all to yourself until then. Our female guest is taking a bus tour and says she will be back about 8 p.m. She will be leaving me in the morning. She is a very quiet, college student from Montana."

"I'm sure she is nice. Your place seems very cozy, Ms. Borrego."

She smiled with gratitude and pointed to the list of house rules. "As the rules state, supper will be served at eight o'clock. Breakfast is at eight a.m., and there will be sandwiches for lunch at twelve noon. I will be in the living room, or kitchen, if you need anything. My guests are always welcome to watch TV in the living room until lights go out at 10:30. My desktop computer is also available when I am not using it. I retire at about 10:30, after the late news on TV." She handed Ross a house key. "I give most of my customers a key to my house so that they can come and go in case if I have to go out to run an errand. Don't tell Lorenzo you have it, and of course use it only in the rare case that I won't be here when you want to get back in the house."

After a shower, Ross changed into a pair of Bermuda shorts and put on a blue-striped polo shirt. He did not shave. After putting his shoes back on, he heard the doorbell ring. He walked back into the living room, assuming correctly that the visitor was Lorenzo Castillo. "I'm Lorenzo Castillo," the young man said. "I'm the one that called about couch surfing here."

Regina Borrego invited him in and introduced him to Ross: "This is Jake McFadden, our other male guest."

Lorenzo Castillo extended a doubled up fist toward Ross and said, "Hey, wazzup, Bro." They bumped knuckles and Regina Borrego said, "I just went over the rules with Mr. McFadden, and he can tell you about them. There is a list of them on the wall next to the bathroom door. Mr. McFadden will explain about the bathroom door. Men and women share it. You must remember to lock both doors when inside, and unlock both when you leave. Your bunk will be the one on the left as you go inside the male dormitory room."

Castillo contemplated Ross with dark, slightly bloodshot eyes, peering suspiciously from beneath the turned-down brim of a brown, Milan hat. He obviously did not intend to remove the hat from his head inside the house, and Ross wondered if he slept in it. He followed Ross into the dormitory and contemplated the list of rules on the wall. "Say, bro, I lost my readin' glasses. Could you read the rules to me?"

Ross quickly read the rules to Lorenzo, and afterwards, Lorenzo began to inspect the area, looking under the bunk, in the bathroom and on the walls as if searching for something. The new couch surfer was a short man, perhaps five-feet-six, swarthy with strong, broad shoulders. He wore black tennis shoes, a blue and white horizontal-striped polo shirt, and brown, Koolin Out shorts that reached his shins and clung precariously to a waistline that was discernible only due to a wide, black leather belt. His dark hair was beginning to curl around his ears, indicating his recent liberation from the grooming rules of probation. He wore a gold ring in his left ear lobe, signaling his heterosexuality. He carried a small, canvas handbag in his left hand, along with a rolled-up blue sleeping bag with a flashlight embedded in the center.

Ross knew that Lorenzo did not mean to be rude, but his scowling tone and general demeanor could be intimidating to unfamiliar observers. Ross already knew that the young man with apparent barrio upbringing somehow had managed to catch only one minor, dealer-level marijuana case since attaining majority age. Had it not been at Reverend Tasker's request, he knew that there is no way Regina Borrego would have considered him as a guest.

His dark, wide-set, eyes flitted about the room, and then settled upon Ross. "Pretty cool place to stay, huh, bro?"

"Yes it is. I'm going to enjoy a good night's rest. I slept in a boxcar yesterday."

"Where you from, bro?"

"Originally from a small town called "Royalty, Texas, near Odessa."

"You a long way from home, bro."

"Yes I am—West Texas. I decided to take a semester off to do some research on hitchhiking, and write a story about the subject." Ross hoped he would not slip up in Lorenzo's presence and forget a detail of the image he was establishing with the man. Criminals are more skilled at lying than he, but interrogating cops usually cross them up easily. They are by nature suspicious of strangers. It was easy to underestimate someone like Lorenzo.

"West Texas. Cool. You a homie, bro. I used to live in El Paso, but I prefer Califa. I tried college out here, but I got bored."

"That's very interesting, Lorenzo." Ross did not have to feign interest in Lorenzo. He maintained flattering eye contact, knowing that this man had a big ego. He had to encourage him to continue talking about himself, hoping he'd eventually arrive at the subject of his friend, Grifty.

Lorenzo said, "I'll use my two nights of free room and board here with the couch surfer host, then find a place to camp, maybe in Lytle Creek. It takes a few weeks to renew an EBT car when you let 'em expire. It's even harder when you are homeless and have no address, but here in Califa they go ahead and give it to you anyway, they just want to make you beg for it for a few days. If you draw 'em a map and show 'em a bridge or a tree you sleep under, tell 'em that's your resident address, they'll accept it and give you a card."

"You say your EBT card expired?"

"Yep, my Califa card expired when I was workin' at the Kwiko Taco in El Paso. I wasn't eligible for Texas benefits because I earned too much money workin' and had only myself to support. Now that I'm not workin', I'm eligible again. If you ain't got a job, Califa is better than Texas. As they say on the border, *más seguro*. That means *more welfare*," he said with a wry smile.

"So you're having trouble finding steady employment?"

"Yeah—if you've been in the joint for drugs, like me, and if you're homeless, it's harder to find a job. I caught a case here in Califa and they let me transfer my parole to El Paso where my mom used to live. She was sick, but passed away, so when I finished my parole, I'm back out here."

"Sorry about your mom."

"In Texas, I was stayin' at a halfway house with free rent, and that made it easy to work at the fast-food places. The managers could call up the halfway house staff and check my

126

residence, or they could call my parole officer. Now that I'm off parole, nobody respectable here knows me or recommends me. A parole officer makes a good recommendation—know what I'm sayin', bro?"

"As a student, I'm used to scratching for my bread. I'm sure you'll make it too, Lorenzo."

"Yeah, I just need to get set up again. I got connections with homies around here that know all the ropes."

"It's always good to have connections." Ross could have expanded upon that, warning him to select carefully his connections, but that would wait—there is a time and place for everything.

Lorenzo sighed and sat down on the edge of his bunk. "Sit down for a moment, bro," he said, pointing to Ross' bunk. "I'll let you in on some secrets of surviving on the road."

"Secrets of the road! I'd like that very much." Ross sat facing Lorenzo, his hands on his thighs, listening attentively. His companion reached over and touched Ross on the knee, lowering his voice. "You asked why I don't ask for anyone's help: it's because the Man doesn't approve of me gettin' more than one EBT card, or me using more than one name, bro. But the Man ain't lookin' over my shoulder anymore. I plan to get more cards."

Ross smiled to conceal his amazement at Lorenzo's candor, crassness and contempt for welfare laws. However, he found it flattering to have so quickly gained Lorenzo's confidence. "Yours sounds like you have a Catch-22 situation, Lorenzo"

"A catch what?"

"Catch 22. It's just describes a situation where you get entrapped into the system's rules and regulations..."

"Well, I hate rules and regulations. But as long as I am homeless, I qualify for one EBT card—and if I get more of 'em and play my EBT cards right, I can have a lot of money. It beats hell out of workin' for a livin', bro."

"Nice pun, that playing your EBT cards right."

"What's a pun?"

"It's just a comment on your clever way of talking about playing your cards right." Ross wished he could keep his colloquialisms at Lorenzo's level.

"Well that's the way everybody livin' on the streets says it, when it comes to takin' advantage of the system."

"What if you get caught with more than one EBT card? Couldn't you get into a lot of trouble for that?"

He waved his hand forward at Ross and answered curtly. "Naw. Y'know when I was in the joint I learned how the smart ones get by with it and how the dumb ones get caught. Nearly all of these so-called homeless people do it. For the junkies, it's a way to feed their drug habits without havin' to rob and kill people. I aim to get some money together and get into the business of sellin' that more expensive stuff, man. I ain't gonna fool with that *mota*, like before I went to *la pinta*. If I get locked up again, I want it to be for somethin' worth the time I'll do." He leaned backward, watching Ross' reaction to what he was saying, bracing himself with his hands against his bunk. Satisfied that Ross was impressed, Lorenzo continued. "Welfare fraud ain't near as bad as catchin a case for holding up a convenience store. For welfare fraud, I might catch a year, a year and half. But knockin' off a convenience store for three, maybe four hunnerd bucks, could get me life behind bars, since I have a prior conviction." He stopped and leered suspiciously at Ross. "You sure you ain't some kind of cop, Jake?"

Ross laughed. "Nope. Why do you ask?"

Lorenzo rolled his big, brown, bloodshot eyes first toward one window, then towards the other, as if expecting someone to be outside, eavesdropping. He returned his intent stare upon Ross. "Well, the way you talk about gettin' in trouble and all that. Hell man, the future belongs to the risk taker—I heard that from this cool dude I met in jail."

Ross chuckled, bumped knuckles with Lorenzo and said, "Bro, I'm just a dumb college student trying to learn about the real world, and maybe write a book someday. Do I look like a cop?"

Lorenzo studied him suspiciously and after a moment of hesitation, said, "Naw, not really. You're too damn smart to be a cop. I think you're really a smart dude, Jake. I think maybe you really *are* gonna write a book someday. Most of these guys you hear say they're gonna write a book are losers, man—crack heads and meth freaks who ain't ever gonna do chit except try to score some more crack or meth."

Ross lowered his voice, touched his lips and motioned toward the kitchen with his eyes. "Watch your language, Lorenzo. Ms. Borrego might hear you. We don't want to get tossed out of here."

Lorenzo nodded and went to the bathroom, got a few sheets of toilet paper and blew his nose loudly and flushed the paper down the commode. He stepped back inside the dormitory room, craned his neck, and looked again at the rules posted on the wall. Without looking at Ross, Lorenzo continued, "Yeah, man I see a lot of those cranked-out dudes. I used to see one hangin' around a rescue mission in L.A., carrying a long yellow note pad and writin' on it with pencils he stole from the library. Everybody was suspicious of 'im because he was always writin' things down. He didn't have no friends."

"I find that interesting, Lorenzo."

"Just don't ever use my name when you write all that stuff, bro. And I'll tell you something that might keep you from getting' your ass kicked. Don't ever write while you down there in Skid Row around those soup kitchens where all the bums hang out. They'll sucker punch you or pick a fight with you when they see you writin' things down. They're all...what's that word I'm tryin' to think of...para-something."

"Paranoid?"

"Yeah, *that's* it."

"I find that interesting too, Lorenzo. You really do have a lot of experiences I could benefit from."

"Remember my stories, but forget my name when you write, dude."

"Check." He bumped knuckles again. "Don't worry, Lorenzo. To be a success as a writer, it is important that I have the confidence of my sources of information."

Moving his eyes closer to the list of rules posted on the wall, Lorenzo's eyes squinted and his brow furrowed as if struggling to understand them. "If I broke a rule, you wouldn't rat me out, would you...Jake?"

Ross laughed and said, "Well as long as you don't endanger somebody's health or life, I'm pretty easy to get along with." He quickly changed the subject, "Have you been here in San Berdoo before, Lorenzo?"

"Yeah, it's a good place to camp out and to get a few freebies, you know. They got a couple of good soup kitchens downtown. I spent some time over in Lytle Creek Wash a couple years ago. Me and my homie pitched a tent over there."

"That sounds interesting. Maybe I could include that in my writing. Maybe you can show me the place." Ross wanted to be alone with Lorenzo figuring that he'd open up more if there were no danger of anyone eavesdropping.

"Yeah, a few dudes pitch tents over there in the dry creek bed because of the wide open spaces. Nobody lives there permanently because once in a while the wash fills with water and you don't want to be there when that happens."

"Not hard to figure why. Maybe we can go over there and check the place out together and you could show me around. Maybe I'll pitch a tent there myself someday."

"Well, I've got nothin' goin' tomorrow mornin', how about you?"

"Sounds good, bro."

Regina Borrego knocked, and then walked into the room with a small waste can, freshly lined with a plastic bag with the logo of a discount store. She said, "If you gentlemen get rich writing your memoirs let me know. I might try my hand at it someday—and you can advise me how to do it."

Ross chuckled and said, "You probably *could* write better stories—I mean you must have heard a lot of stories as a couch surfer host."

"Yes, I could tell you a few stories."

Ross hoped he would have time to listen to some of them someday, but currently, writing was role-playing, and he must not let his undercover role be a distraction. He laughed again and remarked, "Well, Ms. Borrego, I'm not counting on writing being my ticket to riches. At least not yet."

CHAPTER ELEVEN

After a hearty breakfast, prepared by their host, Ross and Lorenzo got ready to hike to Lytle Creek Wash. Ross pulled out his journal to make an entry. With Lorenzo looking over his shoulder, he wrote:

Sunday Morning, 9 a.m., October 16, left with couch surfer companion to explore Lytle Creek in Muscoy.

He held the notebook so Lorenzo could see without craning his neck, pointed to the entry with his pen and said, "See, Lorenzo? I didn't use your name."

Lorenzo moved his head back and forth as if reading the entry. Ross began to suspect that Lorenzo could read very little, if any. He doubted that he ever used any kind of glasses; much less reading glasses, as he had claimed earlier. For that reason, he did not really worry about Lorenzo asking to see the rest of his journal. Lorenzo uttered his approval of Ross' new journal entry with, "Yeah, Okay, that's good, bro."

The two hikers walked south on Gray Street until they came to a dead-end, blocked by a six-foot high vertical, steel bar fence. "That fence at the end of the street reminds me of jail," said Lorenzo.

The steel barricade connected to a run-down chain-link fence on either side of the street. On the right side, there was a metal, corner pole. Pedestrians had pushed it aside from its original position, where the chain link fence had once been connected to the iron bar fence. Trash littered the ground near a sign that read, *No Dumping*. Lorenzo squeezed through the v-shaped gap on the right side, between the short stretch of iron fence and the bent-over chain-link corner post, and entered a vacant area. Ross followed.

They walked west along a winding footpath through low brush toward a high railroad embankment that appeared to function also as a river levee. The two climbed the embankment, and stood for a moment on the railroad tracks, gazing at the wide span of Lytle Creek Wash. On the opposite side of the half-mile-wide creek, beyond another levee, they could see the roof tops of a residential area. "That's North Rialto, over there where you see the tops of those houses," said Lorenzo. "I used to have a *ruca* that lived over there."

"I'll bet she was pretty."

"Yeah, but she got on dope and left town. I don't know where she is now."

Across the creek bed were chalky-colored rivulets running north and south in the gravel. There was a narrow span of low brush between the railroad and the edge of the creek. Ross observed, "Obviously they get some heavy runoffs from rains up in the mountains north of here. I wonder where all the water goes when it rains."

"It runs into the Santa Ana River," said Lorenzo. "The banks of the Santa Ana is another good place to pitch a pup tent when you're hiking' through this part of Califa"

Lorenzo started down the embankment and said, "C'mon, bro, let's see if the big bush where me and my homie camped is still there, or maybe got washed away. I think I may see it from here." Lorenzo pointed toward the edge of the underbrush of the creek. A few feet from the railroad right-of-way was a cluster of low bushes. "Right there—beside that bush. That's where we pitched our tent."

There was broken glass and a couple of beat up beer cans stuck in the lower limbs of the bush. Lorenzo picked up a beer can lodged in the branches of the bush, looked at it and declared, "This was one of our beer cans. You ever drink hot beer, bro?"

Ross laughed. "Not recently, you're lucky to have a good, dependable friend with whom to camp, Lorenzo."

"Well, he used to be a homie, but in the last couple of years he got on meth and really went downhill. He has really gotten sorry. He even robs other drunks that he rides trains with. I mean I ain't no saint myself, but I don't do the things he does. Man, he likes to get young girls hooked on meth, and when he gets tired of them, he pimps them off for more money to buy more meth. He talked a young *ruca* in El Paso into comin' out here with 'im. Yesterday, I ran into another homie of mine at a San Berdoo soup kitchen, and he told me a lot of the latest stuff about old Grifty. The next time I see 'im. I don't know whether I'll bump knuckles with 'im or kick his ass."

"Did you say his name is *Grifty*?"

"Yeah...that's his moniker. You met 'im?"

"Oh, no, I was just admiring the moniker. It has an interesting ring to it. The monikers of all these dudes interest me. I'm making a list of 'em to put in my book. What's the moniker of your homie—the one downtown?"

"The homie I met downtown? *Switchrail*. Go downtown with me and I'll introduce you to him and my other homies."

"That's not cool for this...Grifty...to get these young girls hooked on junk."

"Yeah, man Switchrail told me that Grifty talked about taking that girl to TJ as soon as he gets back from Fresno and sell her to a rich Mexican pimp he knows down there. That pimp runs a hotel and whorehouse and Grifty thinks he can pick up some cool cash for her."

Loud alarm bells rang inside Ross' head. "I wonder why a man would do such a thing."

"Hell, who knows. Switchrail said he mentioned that her coke and meth habits were gettin' too expensive for Grifty."

Ross' heart sank. "So you think Grifty and the girl are in Fresno now?"

"Maybe. When Grifty goes up there to renew an EBT card, he camps out on the river with the migrant laborers and picks up a little cash sellin' 'em *mota*. It's safe because the cops don't even bother with transients anymore."

"He sounds like an interesting fellow. I'd like to meet him."

"Well, he's interestin' all right. But I got no interest in what he does."

"So you think I might find Grifty in the labor camps on the river?"

Lorenzo leered suspiciously at Ross. He coughed, spat, and said, "Man, you got a thing for that Grifty. He ain't worth writin' two words about. I mean he taught me how to beat the system with EBT cards and a lot of chit, but I draw the line on gettin young chicks addicted to junk and sellin' 'em to TJ pimps."

Ross nodded and said, "As a writer, I am interested in everybody—even those guys that seem to put girls under a spell. Take Charles Manson for example. I read that young girls surrounded him and did everything he asked them to do. He's a little midget of a guy that never was good looking...now he's rotting in prison."

"So you think wild-ass dudes make good people to write about, huh?"

"Yeah, you might put it that way."

Lorenzo frowned and looked off in the distance. Holding a thumb to his right nostril, he snorted, blew his nose on the ground, and frowned again. "Y'know Jake, I have a problem understandin' you—and the dudes that *impress* you."

Ross chuckled and said, "I've heard that if you want to make out with the women, just become an outlaw. Me? I can't stand jails, so I guess I'll try to make a living writing, or doing something else quiet and easy and just take what girls come my way. Selling dope is too risky a crime, not to mention enticing San Quentin quail—underage girls—to leave home and live like vagabonds. That sort of thing can get you twenty years in the big house."

"You got that right, bro, I'm tellin' ya, the joint was full of dudes like Grifty. Hell, you can describe him on half a page."

Ross shrugged. "I think I could write more about this Grifty guy than just half a page. By the way, you said that when Grifty comes back from Fresno he may go to TJ—by *TJ* you meant...?"

"Tijuana. *Mexico*, dude. Now ain't that about as low as you can get, I mean takin' a teenage American girl and sellin' her to a Mexican pimp."

Hoping against hope that Grifty's girl might not be Leah, Ross asked Lorenzo, "Is his girl *pretty*?"

"Yeah, man—*very* pretty—and a *real* blonde. I saw her a couple of times in the *taqueria* where I used to work in El Paso, but I never learned her real name. Switchrail said that Grifty calls her *Leaping Linda* or somethin' like that."

Ross' heart sank. That approximated the "Leapin' Lorena," that Horseshoe Annie had called Leah when she saw her picture. Names can be corrupted when passed along by hearsay. He felt he needed to keep Lorenzo talking about the Kwiko Taco. "That *taquería* you worked at in El Paso was a pretty neat place, wasn't it?"

"Yeah, did you ever eat there?"

"I think I ate there a long time ago, but I went there *only* to eat—after school was out one day."

"You got a good memory, bro. You know, bro, I think maybe *la mota* ruined mine. I used to smoke a dozen of those joints a day. Or do you think maybe it's just because when you got mostly bad memories like me, a dude just *wants* to forget?"

Ross figured that Lorenzo's inference that marijuana ruined his memory was rhetorical and steered him back to the topic. "Most of those high school girls are, well, too young to legally consent, you know, San Quentin quail."

"Yeah, I know, but Grifty don't give a chit. I guess he's got a charmed life. He claims he never spent more than a month in jail at a time, but you can't believe anything that dude says. Even some *dudes* hang around him just to listen to his bull chit. They don't really believe any of it, but they still like to listen to 'im and laugh at his stories. Now that's a story teller for you. If he could write, he could make millions, but like me, he dropped out of school."

"He sounds like the kind of guy I'm lookin' for. You don't have to *like* a guy to *write* about him, you know. Maybe by writing about him, I can captivate the same type of audience that he does and maybe make money at it."

Lorenzo looked confused again. "Whatever, bro."

Ross struggled to keep his personal feelings inside. "I guess some girls *want* to be controlled by someone cool, someone other than their parents."

"Yeah! Ain't that weird, bro? Y'know somethin', me and you think a lot alike."

"Yeah...Hey, bro, do you mind if we do a selfie together."

"Why not, dude. Where do you want me to stand?"

"Right where you are is fine." Ross moved beside Lorenzo, and holding his cell at arm's length, clicked. Satisfied with the screen image, he quickly saved the photo to memory and returned the camera to its belt holder.

Lorenzo had ratcheted-up in Ross a new sense of urgency in finding Leah. He needed to find her before Grifty could sell her, like so much used merchandise.

"Lorenzo, why would Grifty take that little blonde fox to TJ to sell? I mean if he was going to do something like that, why go to Mexico? There must be a market for that here in the U.S., too."

"Yeah, but *young blonde* girls bring a big price from those pimps down across the border. It's the..." Lorenzo halted, swinging his little finger and thumb, extended away from the center of his hand, and then continued, "You know...it's the *variety*. Those horny machos across the border want variety, and it's safer to do those things in Mexico. Down there, nobody asks a girls' age. Grifty don't have to worry about gettin' sent up for a long stretch for doin'—or sellin'—San Quentin quail. Besides, Grifty says that pimp he knows down there is in tight with the Tijuana cops."

"She could still come back across the border and complain against him here in the U.S. It could be a federal case."

Lorenzo shrugged. "Hey, bro, he must have figured after he sells her, she'd never get out of Mexico, at least not alive. Don't you read those news stories about all those mass graves they dig up of young *panocha* down there across the border?

137

Mexican pimps keep a close watch on their investments. Grifty knows what he's doin', bro. He's sold em down there before."

"It still sounds like dangerous business."

"Yeah, and when the pimps dump them, they get pissed, especially if they're pregnant. Those *rucas* want to get even and cause a lot of problems."

"Heaven has no rage like love that's turned to hate."

Lorenzo stared blankly at Ross for a moment and declared, "If you mean they go crazy, you right, bro. Tryin' to get even is what gets 'em killed. Breakin' off with a ruca is always a lot harder than hookin' up with 'em, unless you're cool at the game, like Grifty. Hell, once he gets 'em hooked on meth, they'll do anything for their next fix. The pimps down in Mexico do the same thing. Meth and coke is cheap in Mexico and dope is about all the hookers down there work for—besides room and meals at those whorehouse bars. When the pimps get tired of 'em, they are lucky if he just kicks 'em out on the street. I hear they live three or four to a small room barely big enough for one cot. They work and sleep in shifts—if they get any sleep. Crank keeps 'em goin' 24/7. It's the worst kind of addiction." Lorenzo pulled out a cigarette packet from a shirt pocket. "Here, bro, this *mota* is the only safe junk. Take one."

The packet contained three neatly rolled marijuana joints. Ross pulled a joint from pack and said, "If you don't mind, I'll keep it until I need something to help me sleep." He placed the joint in his shirt pocket to keep it for disposal, as soon as he was out of Lorenzo's sight.

"Suit yourself, bro." Lorenzo lit up, inhaled deeply and exhaled slowly. He held the joint near his face, studied it, frowned and said, "It was a dude in *la pinta* that told me these reefers can make me lose my memory."

"Say, Lorenzo, where in TJ would I go to find ...uh..."

"Young *gringa panocha*?"

"Yeah."

"Over around *Coahuila Street*—and *Constitución*."

"*Coahuila* Street, huh?"

"Yeah, it's up in north TJ—the *Zona Norte*— close to the border. You know, the red light zone, where prostitution is legal. Switchrail was the first one to tell me about the *Zona Norte*. We went down there together once."

Ross nodded. "Every Mexican border city has its *zona de tolerancia*. Juarez has one, and it was a hangout for single men looking for cheap female company—girls that would hop in bed with them for a few bucks. I guess TJ is just like Juarez. Some bars had rental rooms next door, or upstairs that they advertise as cheap hotels, but I don't remember seeing many American girls hustling in Juarez."

Lorenzo continued, "I haven't been down to TJ since me and Switchrail went. When I got out of jail, my probation officer restricted my travel. There are a several bars and hotels down there that specialize in American girls, if that's what you want. Grifty used to hang out in one of those places near the corner of *Calle Coahuila* and *Constitución*."

"Grifty sounds like an expert on TJ. What bars do you think old Grifty would recommend to find that *gringa* stuff?"

"Well, Grifty used to make 'em all—but for white stuff, I'd say try the Chicago first. They say you can find any color you want there. If you don't find what you want there, go to Adelita's or the Skandall." Lorenzo took a deep, wheezing draw on his joint, coughed, and continued, "To each his own, bro, but Mexican *panocha* is good enough for me, and besides, they ain't worn-out hags like those *gringa* meth freaks. Hell, bro, after they get cranked out on that meth, they look twenty years older. I mean you can find 'em ready and willing to roll, if you know what I mean, even in hamburger joints on this side of the border, like the one where I worked in El Paso. Take my advice, bro. If you go to TJ, the brown stuff is cleaner than blonde stoners." Lorenzo gazed at Ross with his penetrating, brown eyes. He said, "You really don't plan to go way down there just for *gringa panocha*, do you, bro?"

"No, I was just curious. I like to see new things that I haven't seen before. It gives me something to write about."

"Well, just remember that you can find anything you want around *Calle Coahuila* and *Constitución*. Drugs, white girls, Asian girls—black girls—anything you want. You can also find any kind of smuggler you want—people, drugs—for any kind of contraband you wanta get across the border." He took another draw from the joint, spat, and abruptly threw it to the ground as if were an insect. He angrily smashed it with the sole of his shoe, and said, "Man, this *mota* don't do it for me, today. I feel like I got a hangover. I gotta go downtown, find my homie and score some bennies. Let's get outta here, bro." He lifted his Milan hat, wiped away inexplicable perspiration with his shirt sleeve, pressed his forefingers to his temples and grimaced in pain.

They started walking back toward the railroad and Ross warned, "Maybe we could just go back to Regina's and get some coffee—I hear those bennies could get you addicted."

"Yeah, I know, bro, but coffee don't give me a good kick. Coffee and reefers ain't what I need right now."

"I'd hate to see you get sent back to the joint, bro."

"Ha! Don't worry. The cops know I'm not a dealer, just a small time user. It's all there on my record. If the cops catch me with two or three pills, here in Califa they'd just give me a citation."

"Maybe you should go downtown or someplace for a while before you go back to Regina Borrego's home, Lorenzo. If you come back to the dormitory after smoking dope, Regina Borrego will smell it and kick you out."

"I know, bro. Clean women can smell *mota* on you a mile away. I ain't lookin' for no trouble. I just wanna get my gear, check out, and head downtown."

"Where will you stay, Lorenzo? I'd like to stay in touch. We seem to hit it off, and you could help me with my book."

"Hell, who knows where I'll sleep tonight, bro—maybe on cardboard, in an alley. Hell, after I down a benny or two, I may not wanna sleep."

"You could get picked up by cops by hanging around on the streets late at night."

"I got some homies downtown that I ain't seen for a while and some of 'em are dealin' in that small stuff. One of 'em hangs out around the bus station. I'll sleep where he does. Maybe I won't even sleep for a while. I got a few bucks, and if I get sleepy, I might crash in a flop house."

Ross did not doubt that Lorenzo would find a street dealer. When he had first arrived in San Bernardino on the bus, he had observed some sleazy looking characters in that neighborhood. He offered to give back to Lorenzo the joint he had in his shirt pocket.

"Naw, you keep that, bro. Right now, all I want is a benny. Hey, why dontcha come along? I could introduce you to some interestin' people in downtown San Berdoo—some people that could tell you some stories for your book. Who knows, we might even find old Grifty down there."

Right now, Ross' instincts were pointing toward Fresno as the best place to come across Grifty and Leah. That's where Lorenzo had said that he had recently gone to renew an EBT card. If Ross decided to catch a bus to Fresno tomorrow, he'd take time to check out downtown San Bernardino, walk through a few hobo jungles, see what he could find out about Grifty, if anything, and maybe see Lorenzo down there, too. If Grifty is in San Bernardino, he'll probably be with Lorenzo— or Lorenzo will know where he is. Discretion told him it was best not to hang out in public with Lorenzo, not in the ex-con's present emotional state, lest both of them get arrested.

He told Lorenzo, "It's tempting, bro, but I need to go back to the dormitory, borrow Regina's computer and record a lot of stuff I've been learning the past few days before I get too far behind. Maybe tomorrow morning I'll catch you downtown and we can have a beer together." He pulled out a USB flash drive from his left pant's pocket and showed it to Lorenzo. "I record everything I remember right here, bro. When I get back to Texas, I can print it all out. Besides that, I have another night's free rent at Regina's and I need to save my money."

"Just remember not to put my name on that thing, bro—or in your book."

CHAPTER TWELVE

Ross and Lorenzo were back at Regina's home by mid-morning. Regina had left a note on the front door to tell them that she had gone to take her female guest to the bus station and that she would be back in half an hour.

Ross opened the door with the key the host had given him earlier, and Lorenzo asked, "Why didn't she give *me* a key?"

"I guess she gives only one key to each pair of guests." Ross was not sure Lorenzo accepted that explanation, but he said nothing more and went to the dormitory room to retrieve his sleeping bag and backpack. "See ya later, dude," he said curtly. "If ya decide to come downtown San Berdoo this afternoon, look me up and I'll buy you a beer."

When she returned, Ross told the host that he was thinking of going to Fresno by bus because Lorenzo had indicated that Grifty might be there, or soon headed there, to renew an EBT card. "I'll try to catch a bus out of here tomorrow afternoon, but before I leave, I want to check out some hobo jungles in San Bernardino and see if I can find out anything useful. Grifty has been here recently and there ought to be some transients around that know something about hi."

He sat down on the living room couch and spread some of his maps on a coffee table. Regina Borrego came in from the kitchen with two cups of freshly brewed coffee and said, "Why don't you use my computer, Mr. Spencer? All the satellite map software is installed and I have a color printer. They are frequently in demand by my couch surfers."

"Do you have Google Earth?"

"Yes."

"Great! That way I can get a street level view of some of the places I need to explore." Today, he noticed that she was wearing a black dress and blouse and he could not ignore the plunging neckline.

"Your computer will save me some shoe leather, Ms. Borrego. If I wind up in Fresno, I'll need detail. Computer satellite imagery could save me an enormous amount of walking around San Bernardino. Satellite images can tell me where the hobo jungles are likely to be."

"Can they, really? How do they do that?"

"I look for footpaths near railroads and likely hobo camps. When you are used to seeing them, they stand out."

She brought Ross her laptop and went back for the small printer. She set both down on the coffee table and said, "My female guest got up and left early this morning. We have the house all to ourselves today."

She sat down next to him, a little closer than Ross thought appropriate, and he detected the fragrance of fresh perfume. He determined not to be distracted, and downloaded a satellite map site of the BNSF train yards in downtown San Bernardino.

A few blocks from the train yards, he marked the Intercity Bus Station where he had arrived in San Bernardino. It was a good place to get his bearings, and from there he could branch out to the nearby hobo camps, shelters for the homeless, soup kitchens and other places where Grifty might be, or where he might get information about him, thinking himself too unlucky to find him in the San Bernardino area. Getting information from drifters was the key. He marked a public library a couple blocks east of the bus station. It had benches in front, and the image showed some people lounging under palm trees on the front lawn. Libraries are often popular places for the homeless to hang out between meals.

Regina soon got bored watching Ross do research and went to the kitchen.

A couple blocks east of the library Ross noted a homeless shelter that looked like a good location to check out. A long block south of the bus station was a Salvation Army services center, which also might be worth exploring.

When he finished checking out satellite and street level views of San Bernardino, Ross finished off his cup of coffee and dialed up the bus station to check the schedule to Fresno. He tentatively chose a run scheduled to leave San Bernardino at two p.m. the next day. That should give him time enough scope out the downtown area.

The next morning, Ross bade farewell to Regina Borrego and asked for directions to the closest bus stop to downtown San Bernardino. She insisted on giving him a ride.

"Oh, no, you've done too much already, Ms. Borrego." Ross already felt guilty for exploiting Regina Borrego's generosity.

"I want to find Leah as much as you do, Mr. Spencer. The members of our missionary organization feel like Mrs. Rachel Waters and Leah are part of our family."

Unable to argue that point, Ross accepted her offer of a ride. He printed out all the maps he thought might be useful and then touched home base with Rocio on his cell. Satisfied that everything on the home front was tranquil, he grabbed his backpack and bedroll and got into Regina's compact Ford on the passenger side. He made a new entry in his journal.

Monday, October 17, 8:00 a.m. After breakfast, leaving the Muscoy couch surfer home with host Regina Borrego driving her car, headed for the intercity bus station.

At Ross' request, Regina Borrego stopped her car along the curb at Mt. Vernon Avenue, near its intersection with 5th Street, a little before 8:30 a.m. He removed Regina Borrego's spare house key from his key ring and handed it back to her. "According to my maps, there might be a hobo camp under that overpass up ahead, and this should be a good starting point," he declared. He got out, strapped on his backpack and grabbed his bedroll. "Thanks for everything, Ms. Borrego."

His host's eyes were sad and she said, "Stay in touch, Ross. Email me to let me know how the hunt goes." Her abrupt switch to the familiar form of address took him slightly aback, and he said, "I will...Regina." He knew it would be a difficult promise to keep, but he determined he would contact her on occasion. Who knows, maybe another case might bring him back here someday, but he knew the possibility was remote.

He got out, started walking up the sidewalk toward 5th Street. Regina Borrego sat there in her car, for a moment, watching him, and in a moment, she made a U-turn and headed back north.

He again worried a little about his former host, sensing her loneliness and the boredom that induced her to become a couch-surfing host. In that position, she could be vulnerable to rogue couch surfers. In spite of Reverend Tasker's assurance, he instinctively discerned the hazards to such hosting. Security checks are like padlocks, effective only with the honest. It further worried him that he had no time to try to convince her of the hazards of her hobby, but on the other hand, she had been enormously useful to him on this assignment.

He crossed Mt. Vernon Avenue, stepped on the curb of 5th Street, and turned left, starting up the incline of an overpass that spanned part of the railroad tracks of a large freight yard, and North-South I-215, as well. The sky was leaden, the air heavy, and he was surprised to begin labored breathing. The automobile traffic on the freeway exchange, along with the locomotives in the main BNSF yards to the east, added a muffled cacophony to the air. Beyond the overpass, to the east, he could see the San Bernardino Mountains. Their peaks were snow-capped from an early season snow and they shined like a beacon of majestic contrast with the teeming city.

To his left, he saw the small, neat park that he had noted on the Internet map. In the center of the park was a serpentine sidewalk, winding roughly parallel with the curb of 5th Street. He visually corroborated the image he'd seen on the Internet with the BNSF Yards—the many gantry cranes used to load and unload containerized cargo, the freight cars and trucks. Switch engines roared and idled, moving forward and backward to build trains. He had never seen such a large yard of containerized cargo. Further to the southeast, through a thin haze, he could barely make out the Union Pacific Yards, which he had marked on Regina Borrego's computer printout. Those yards joined the BNSF yards to the Union Pacific yards at the top of a wishbone-like formation.

Near the apex of the overpass, he reached a metal, security fence, came to a halt, and studied his position. To his left, was a well-worn footpath leading down the slope of the overpass, and from the satellite image he had surmised that the path down the slope led to a hobo camp under the 5th Street overpass. He left the sidewalk and followed the footpath down the slope toward the bottom of the overpass.

The area under the overpass was surprisingly clean, unlike the terrain under the Delta Street overpass in El Paso. It bore a resemblance to a hobo jungle. There were a few empty beer cans lying around, a few food wrappers, some human waste and other debris, but he suspected that it was no longer a regular catching-out place. Ross quickly saw what had made the hobo jungle obsolete: A high chain link fence, one he had not seen on the satellite image. It kept would-be train hoppers from crossing from the west end of the overpass to enter upon railroad property. Here, the railroad yards had several sets of railroad tracks that made a tangential turn north, under the overpass, then ran parallel with the southbound traffic lanes of I-215, but in the opposite direction.

From a geographical standpoint, Ross gathered that this no doubt had once been an ideal location for hobos to catch-out. He looked to the east and saw more reasons why it was no longer attractive to hoboes. A seven-foot-high chain-link fence separated the non-railroad property from the north and southbound tracks of the BNSF yards as far as the eye could see. The fence was silent testimony to how 9-11 had changed the social landscape of America, hampering a mode of life for those afflicted with wanderlust, especially for those who loved the freedom and ease with which they once could travel by freight train; and even hitchhiking is no longer so easy. As jails become overcrowded, more felons that are dangerous are

147

released prematurely, and former carefree wanderers are saying that motorists are becoming more wary and more reluctant to pick up strangers today than a couple decades ago.

Either the city, or the railroad, had placed large boulders on the ground at close intervals under the overpass, and on a small vacant lot just north of it, tall palm trees swayed in the gentle breeze. The chain link fence had three strands of barbwire atop as further insurance against intruders. Hobos he'd met in the El Paso train yards had recounted stories about the old days, about the ease of hoping freight trains out of San Bernardino to Bakersfield and Fresno. His research in preparation for this trip had lessened the shock of what he saw in these yards: more evidence that the days of safe and leisurely train hopping were gone forever. Homeland Security, in response to threats of terrorism, and to a lesser extent, the deeds of serial killers and transient railroad gangs, especially the FTRA, had changed all that. He lamented nostalgically that his opportunity to experience illegal train hopping came at this late point and deprived him of all the thrills of the not-too-distant past when he still had authority to enter freight yards and mount moving freight trains to dislodge illegal riders; those from across the border. He had recently learned that even the Border Patrol now rarely hopped onto moving freight trains, but then the Border Patrol does very little in the area of enforcement of immigration laws anymore, as our nation's leaders engage in its dangerous experiment with open borders and unlimited immigration.

Looking at the high, chain link fence, Ross verified what he already knew, but was reluctant to concede: Nowadays, only the most seasoned and bold hobos successfully catch trains on a regular basis, and they had to work around the new security measures and be willing to go to jail for criminal trespass. Grifty, by all appearances, was of that ilk.

Ross sat down on one of the boulders to relax and re-think his plans. Catching out by freight north from San Bernardino was looking less and less like a viable option. He decided to look for hidden hobo jungles further north, along the tracks.

Parallel with the tracks was a narrow, alley-like street between the railroad fence and residences. He had learned from hobos that trains pulling out of freight yards in congested cities often move slow enough to catch for a mile or two beyond their yards. Moving boxcars were the most dangerous because there was nothing to grab hold of except the floor of the car. Moving hopper cars were safer, up to about seven miles per hour, because they have a ladder that you can grasp and climb to their "porches."

The morning was growing short and he would soon have to decide whether catching a freight train to Fresno, or taking an intercity bus, was the best choice. He hoped to find some hobos to talk to, possible sources of intelligence information. He had little time to beat the bushes of the hobo jungles around the BNSF freight yards before the next bus left for Fresno, and little time left to decide the best course.

Just as he started folding his map, Ross heard a husky man's voice say, "Hey, you! You're on railroad property! Move along!" The voice belonged to a bareheaded, graying, bald man in a green khaki uniform. His paunch hung over a gun belt that had a revolver attached. The cop repeated, "Move along!" He made a stabbing motion with his left hand, pointing northward, away from the freight yards. Ross doubted that the boulder he was sitting on was actually on railroad property, for it was near the base of the west end of the overpass. Notwithstanding, he knew that his backpack and bedroll left no doubt in the railroad agent's mind as to his intentions, so he decided not to argue. He replaced all his maps inside the backpack, strapped it on, slung the strap of his bedroll over his right shoulder, and marched northward.

A short distance from the overpass he came to the beginning of the narrow street and a street sign on the corner that bore the names, Avenue I and West 6th Street. There was no east 6th Street here because the street ended at the chain link fence, and then bent 90 degrees north to become Avenue I. The chain link fence seemed to stretch for at least half a mile and he guessed probably did not end until it reached a place so far out of the freight yards that outbound trains, at that point, would be traveling too fast to hop.

There was a Mom and Pop grocery at the intersection. Signs painted on the storefront window indicated that a hungry man could buy a burrito inside, and as he walked north on the sidewalk he saw a liquor sales sign painted on the side of the store. He guessed that, at one time, the grocer might have had considerable trade in beer and burritos from freight train hoppers.

Ross continued north, up I Street, which was narrow, and more like an alley because it had garbage containers on the west side, next to the fences of one-story residences. A short distance further east, beyond the railroad tracks, and parallel to them, Interstate 215 was busy with north and southbound vehicular traffic. Scaling the security fence into the railroad lines could be daunting for an easily discouraged and non-athletic freight train hopper. However, in spite of the security measures against train hoppers, there was evidence that some very athletic hobos had indeed climbed over the fence. Several of the barbwire-supporting line arms, usually pointing upward and outward at a 45-degree angle, had been bent downward by trespassers and seemed to give a nod to the daring risk taker.

Ross continued walking north on I street, and after another block he noticed that I Street was blocked by a fenced-in vacant lot. A few spare railroad ties and a small, grey steel shed inside the fenced-in property suggested that it belonged to the railroad. Near the end of I Street, he saw a young man appearing to be in his late thirties sitting against a stucco fence, his legs on the sidewalk, pointing toward the street. He wore new jeans, a blue baseball cap and his backpack leaned against the fence beside him. He looked up from keyboarding on a mini-computer, and with an amiable smile said to Ross, "Looks like you intend to catch-out."

"It crossed my mind."

The man, who sported a neatly-trimmed black beard, chuckled and said, "Well good luck. Train hoppers are a vanishing breed around here."

"Do you mind if I sit and visit for a minute?"

The young man pointed to a clean space without weeds to his right and said, "Be my guest. I'm Robert. For some reason, my friends call me *Bob*."

"I'm Ross." That's a nice tablet you have there. You must be a writer."

"I dabble in it."

"Do you have a hobo nickname?"

"No," replied Bob, "You have to earn those cognomens from your rail-riding acquaintances. I guess I didn't stick around long enough in the business to earn one. I used to ride the freight trains often, during summer vacation, when I was a teenager. Recently, I decided to write about my experiences. Your plain old Hobo used to fascinate me. Now the *vanishing* hobos have my attention. They represent a change in our social condition—and I'm looking at the subject from a sociological viewpoint. Conventional writers on hobos are a dime a dozen on the blogs, and you meet a few of those types out here in the hobo jungles, and in the rescue missions. Those types are trying to relive stories they've read or heard of the way things were twenty, thirty years ago. The condition of the erstwhile hobo definitely needs to be updated. Homeland Security and stepped up trespassing enforcement have intrinsically changed the hobo."

"Your observations coincide with mine, Bob. It seems nowadays you must be willing to risk going to jail to engage in the practice of train hopping. That must seriously discourage people who fear starting a criminal record. They say cities are commissioning railroad agents almost everywhere as policemen, and they can now file their own criminal cases in city and state courts."

Bob leaned back, took a deep breath and said, "Yes, you heard right, and that has had an effect on the changes in the hobo. The city police commissions for railroad agents have the effect of extending their jurisdiction beyond the freight yards to the adjacent city streets. They can legally stop, frisk, ID and check backgrounds of hobos in the *vicinity* of freight yards. That makes would-be hobos subject to being stopped, questioned, and identified on city streets *near* railroad property. Trespassing on railroad property is a more serious offense than it was twenty years ago, and more rigorously enforced than when I was in high school. 9-11-01 changed everything. Due to security crackdowns, many former hobos have given up riding the rails and become highway hitchhikers. However, crime being what it is in the country today, it's getting harder and harder to find someone who will pick up a stranger on the highway. Highway tramps are not usually meticulous about dress or hygiene, and they do not exactly adorn the highway. They are more likely to get a ride with minority ethnic motorists than with the old, wealthy, altruistic couple in the Cadillac. Middle class motorists used to pick them up for company and to satisfy their curiosity about life on the other side of the tracks. It' was part of the old American custom of slumming, for, you see, I think there is a little hobo in all Americans. It's like going to Mexico nowadays as compared to twenty years ago—self preservation instincts override curiosity. You know, Ross, there are a lot more rogues running around on the streets today than there are in the overcrowded jails. By contrast when I was in Germany a couple of summers ago, I noticed that even respectable women hitchhike alone without fear." Bob picked up a pebble and flicked it toward the railroad's chain link fence. His voice trailed off and he looked northward with a nostalgic gaze. "I am feeling the demise of the hobo, the hitchhiker, the tramp. Welfare and Government regulations have forced once happy wanderers into herds of welfare parasites."

"You are obviously well educated and you seem to be channeling my very thoughts, Bob. I envy you. You have had a ton of experience in the subject, having done this since high school."

"That was nearly twenty years ago, but I never dropped out of school. I consider my experiences on the open road more enriching than most anything I ever learned in a class room—even at the graduate college level. After college, I considered the Peace Corps, but that just puts one in the position of dispensing our Government's handouts—sort of like issuing rations to Indians in the late Nineteenth Century. People are not unlike stray dogs—feed them and they become dependent upon you." He halted his monologue and abruptly looked up at Ross with a quizzical leer and said, "Well, Ross, you pretty much know my life, and you're not much younger than I, so tell me your view on American bummery."

Ross knew that at times in his business one must occasionally take risks, and Bob looked like an individual in whom it might pay to confide. "Well, obviously you're much more learned on the subject from a sociological viewpoint, Bob, and I can't argue with anything you've said. In fact, when you complete your work, I'd like to read it. However, my present objective is very different from yours. My real name is Ross Spencer. I'm a private investigator looking for a missing teenager believed to be riding the rails with a guy who....well, *enticed* her. He's supposed to be an FTRA member."

"The hell, you say."

"Since you are familiar with transient and rail riding haunts, I'd like to show you some pictures to see if you might have seen her, or her charmer."

The man shrugged. "What the hell—Why not?" He set his computer on the grass beside him.

Ross pulled out the pictures of Leah and Grifty, told him their monikers, and showed them to Bob. The researcher studied them for a moment and said, "Yep, I recall running into those two around the Union Rescue Mission in downtown L.A. about a month ago."

"Did you get to know them well?"

"No, just casually, but I recall that one day when a group of transients were waiting outside the Union Mission for a free meal. I stood around listening to dialogue between them to

153

see what I could learn about today's homeless element. I didn't need the *free* meal, mind you, but soup kitchen dining rooms are also wonderful places to pick up gossip and ideas. That Grifty was not the type of person with whom I'd hang out. It took just a few seconds for me to size him up. He was a know-it-all windbag and braggart whose lack of a good education quickly became apparent. However, that girl with him looked at him as if he were the reincarnation of Socrates and Adonis wrapped up in the same package. I thought he looked like a bad clone of Mick Jagger, without Jagger's intellect, of course."

"Yeah, those types have a certain charm for certain members of the opposite sex, especially defenseless adolescents. Did he, or the girl, give you any idea as to their travel plans?"

"I remember the fellow talking about going to Las Vegas to renew a SNAP Card. Another guy told me that he was going to Fresno for the same reason. Yet another guy said Grifty was leaving for Tijuana the next day. Guys like Grifty are so flaky you can't believe anything they say."

Ross rubbed his chin pensively. "All that's interesting, Bob. I'll have to mull over that a bit. I'm trying to choose the best course of action and save as many wild goose chases as possible." The uneasy memory of Lorenzo telling about Grifty planning to take a girl, most likely Leah, down to Tijuana to sell to a brothel, came back to haunt him. That was a worst-case scenario. Bob's information seemed to make a trip to Tijuana more urgent due to the possible dire consequences in store for Leah.

Ross got up to leave and exchanged calling cards with his newfound friend.

"Good luck on finding the girl, Ross, and if I see or hear anything about her, I'll contact you."

Ross strode back south on Avenue I, feeling a small victory. He now had an ally ready and willing to help. He walked back up the sloping, hobo trail onto the west end of the 5th Street Overpass. Walking along the sidewalk of the overpass and increasing his elevation, he enjoyed the panorama of the city skyline and the distant horizon. Except for a slightly brown haze in the distance, the sky was still clear. To the east, the snow-capped San Bernardino Mountains still looked clear and enticing. Someday those mountains might make a good hiking trip with Rocio, he thought.

Nearing the apex of the overpass, Ross stopped, placed his journal on the handrail of the bridge and made a new entry:

Monday, October 17, 1 p.m.: left freight yards for bus station. Made an interesting contact on I Street. Reconsidering trip to Fresno.

At the east end of the 5th Street overpass, Ross continued past North H Street, passed a Salvation Army mission and cut northeast, across a vacant lot to the sidewalk of North G Street. About a hundred yards to the north, a man caught Ross' attention. Crossing North G, a slender man with a long stride headed west toward the intercity bus station. He seemed to be wearing faded jeans, a T-shirt with an unreadable logo, and a faded red, baseball-type cap. Ross' pulse quickened. Could he be so lucky? Could that be *him*? He stopped behind a large palm tree, took out his binoculars, and focused it on the man. He was apparently unaccompanied and the closer view was even more convincing that he was looking at Grifty. The man sauntered across the bus station parking lot and entered the intercity bus terminal. Ross quickly placed his binoculars back in his backpack and broke into a jog toward the bus station. If the guy turned out to be Grifty, he did not know exactly what he would do, other than keep tabs on him as long as possible, try to start up a conversation, win his confidence and hang out with him for a while. Outlaws like attention, and when they think you admire them, all but the most paranoid loosen up to dialogue. People will sometimes shock you as to how candid they can be about their personal lives, even to border guards, once they see them as no threat to their way of life.

When Ross was within fifty yards of the bus station, a police car entered the front parking lot. The driver pulled into a parking space, and the two cops sat inside the vehicle while the driver, a corporal, talked on his two-way. Now might be a good time to ask them for help, he thought. As Ross got closer, the two officers abruptly got out of car and walked over to the south side of the bus station, and the object of their attention became apparent. A grubby-looking man of the homeless type sat half -hidden in the bushes, his back resting against the bus station wall. Ross stood by anxiously while the cops pulled the man to his feet, frisked him, and asked him for ID. From the derelict's hand, the journeyman officer removed a twisted, paper bag containing a wine bottle and poured the remaining contents on the ground.

Ross became aware that the man he suspected of being Grifty might disappear if he delayed any longer. He decided to check out the bus station and get back to the officers before they left. Just then, a husky, young security guard in a black uniform came out the front door and approached the two officers. Ross stopped at the entrance, peered through the glass door into the terminal lobby, at the same time trying to keep an eye on the officers and the security guard. There were only a small number of passengers in the waiting area. The Grifty look-alike was nowhere in sight. Ross decided to check the men's room and found it unoccupied. He walked briskly over to the north doors leading outside to the passenger loading area, looked up and down West 6th Street and saw no one.

Ross hurried back out the east entrance of the terminal, and returned to where the two cops now stood talking with the security guard. The security guard was accusing the derelict of trespassing, panhandling and harassing bus passengers. At the request of the security guard, the corporal issued the panhandler a trespass warning and gave a copy to the security guard. Upon the command of the corporal, the derelict started ambling unsteadily south on G Street, headed for the freight yards, or perhaps for the Salvation Army mission.

"Today, he's just panhandling," complained the security guard. "Yesterday we go a complaint that he tried to sell some crisscross to a teenager in the waiting area."

The officers started to leave, and Ross advanced toward them. He showed his credentials to the cops and the security guard. Addressing the security guard, he asked, "Sir, did you see what happened to that guy with the faded baseball cap that walked in the front door just before these officers pulled in?"

"Interesting that you should ask," said the security guard. "The dude had just asked about the bus schedule to San Diego when these two officers pulled into the parking lot. The sleaze-ball made a hasty exit through the north side-door, though the passenger loading area, into the bus parking lot."

"He must have really lit a shuck as soon as he got outside," said Ross. "I checked the lobby, the men's room and then the passenger loading area and there was no one there." From his shirt pocket, Ross pulled out the folded computer-generated composite of Grifty and showed it to the security guard. "Did the guy look anything like this drawing?"

The two cops moved closer to also observe the drawing.

"Yes sir. That sure looks a lot like him," said the security guard. "He had that same embroidered image of a marijuana leaf on his baseball cap—just like your drawing."

"Did he give any indication whether he'd be back to catch the bus to San Diego?"

"No, he just asked when the next bus left for San Diego, and as soon as I told him, he looked around, saw these two officers pulling into the parking lot. He boogied out the north passenger-loading door and I think he hauled ass west. He sure was spooked by these two officers as if he were up to no good."

The corporal asked Ross, "Exactly why are you looking for this guy? Maybe we can help you find him."

"He enticed a seventeen-year-old high school girl to run off with him to California. As a private investigator, her mother hired me to find the girl and take her back to her custody in El Paso. I have co-custody by court order."

The security guard said, "I think you can rule out his catching the next bus to San Diego at 7:15. That dirt bag is probably still running."

The corporal said to Ross, "Well, good luck, Mr. Spencer, but even if you find him, seventeen-year-old chicks in California are more or less fair game, unless there is a big difference in their ages—except for extenuating circumstances. It's kind of like immigration laws. There are a lot of gray areas. Contributing to the delinquency of a minor is seldom prosecuted when a girl, or boy, reaches age seventeen."

Ross heaved a sigh of frustration and declared, "He is believed by the girl's mother to be a member of the FTRA, that notorious, violent gang of freight train hoppers."

"We are aware of them," said the corporal. "They've left a body or two in the freight yards around here."

"I know this is not top priority with you fellows, but the same guy is also believed to be engaged in multiple welfare fraud with stolen or forged identity cards from several states. I don't know his real name, but his street name seems to be *Grifty*." Ross pulled a copy of the Grifty's composite from his backpack and gave it, along with a copy of Leah's picture and a copy of her fingerprints, to the corporal. "You can keep these copies of the composite and picture, if you wish."

The corporal took the copies and said, "We'll turn in this picture and the fingerprints of the girl to the missing persons department—and report the guy to the bunko squad about his suspected welfare fraud. They'll see if he fits the description of anyone that they may be looking for." The corporal started to leave, and then hesitated. He turned and said, "We're not too busy right now, and if you want, we'll take you on a ride-along with us around the area to see if we can spot the suspect and check him out. Judging from that marijuana leaf image on his hat, I'd say he may have warrants, or may even have a joint or two on him. If we can find a reason to arrest him, we can take him down to the station, fingerprint him and find out who he really is—or at least find out what his favorite alias is."

Ross willingly relented. "I suggest your letting me sit in the back caged area, handcuffed, posing as an arrestee to keep from blowing my cover if you catch up to him and get a chance to question him. If you don't arrest him, maybe you could set me free with him and try to become friends with him." Ross used his crooked fingers to illustrate quotation marks for the word, "friends."

"I get your drift," said the corporal. He opened the trunk compartment and Ross put in his gear. The corporal handed Ross a set of cuffs and said, "Put these on real loose, Mr. Spencer, so you can get them off in a hurry if you need to."

The corporal drove out of the parking lot and turned left onto West 6th Street. "I thought that the FTRA was pretty much out of business, since they caught that Robert Silveria Jr.," the journeyman said. "Silveria was supposed to be a ringleader and on the death squad of the gang. He was investigated here for a murder in the Union Pacific freight yards, and he was convicted of multiple counts of murder up in Oregon. I hear he's serving a life sentence. A lot of hobo murders are never reported because of their transient lifestyles. Their companions know how to make murders look like accidents by throwing bodies on the railroad tracks so an outbound train will mangle them beyond recognition. I'd say that young girl that ran off with this Grifty character is in a world of danger, not to mention catching a case for...well...you know what I mean."

The officer was trying to soften his words, but Ross understood. He meant prostitution or trafficking in drugs, charges that could exacerbate her case and maybe keep her if California for prosecution. Ross shuddered at the thought, but he knew it was true. Once a young girl gets hooked on narcotics, she'll do anything for a fix.

With Ross handcuffed in the back seat, the corporal drove the squad car west on West 6th Avenue onto North H Street and said, "When he ran out of the terminal he most likely ran west, since he knew we were on the east side of the terminal. He may have run into those apartments over there." The apartment complex covered nearly half of the block southeast of the intersection H and G streets. "If he did, it's like looking for a needle in a haystack, and considering the neighborhood, you're not likely to get any help from witnesses."

Ross replied, "I'm more worried that the girl, Leah, was *not* with him, than I'd be if she *had been* with him. I'm wondering where she is."

The squad car radio crackled with the dispatcher's voice, giving the officers an assignment to check on a family fight several blocks away. "Well, good luck, Mr. Spencer," said the corporal. They took back their handcuffs and let Ross out in the alley behind the bus station. "Let us know if anything develops, Partner. We gave it the best shot we could."

Ross thanked the two officers and gave the corporal his calling card, his personal cell phone number, and asked them to contact him if they got any information. In reciprocity, he added, "If I can ever help you guys with anything, give me a ring." He knew he would probably never cross paths with these officers again, but it was worth the effort, and the card was a professional courtesy.

When the patrol officers left, Ross sighed in frustration, went back to the bus terminal passenger waiting area and sat on a passenger seat. He wracked his brain. Where is Leah? After collecting his thoughts for a moment, Ross got up, bought a Coke from a vending machine, and sat back down. He would have to ponder his next move with patience. He called Rocio on his cell to bring her up to speed on events. Maybe she could help suggest the next course of action.

Rocio listened as Ross explained the latest occurrences. She said, "I'm thinking about what you once told me about illegal aliens crossing the border, Hon."

"Go on."

"Well, as you said, once they make up their minds to cross illegally, they'll go ahead and carry out their plans, even if they suspect the Border Patrol may be that distant car they see in the shadows, but can't be sure."

"I get you. Then you think Grifty will continue his plan to head for San Diego—and then to Tijuana with Leah—maybe to sell her?"

"I think it would be a possible scenario. When he realizes that those cops were not after him, it's possible that he'll be back to the terminal, and buy the ticket for San Diego. I think he may wait a day or so, until he thinks it's safe, then go back and catch that bus—or maybe he'll go to another bus station. He might choose a different bus station, thinking that the management might tip off the cops."

"You may be right, Hon. He might have left Leah at a rescue mission, or at a library, or some other place, planning to go back for her. Remember, he came to the bus station only to check the bus schedule—he was probably not ready to leave San Bernardino yet. It's guesswork, whatever course we decide upon, but I think your idea would be the best. I'm going to rent a car and head down to Tijuana. I'll need a car with a good-size trunk, if I can't talk her into voluntarily coming back across the border with me. I may not even risk trying to get her back voluntarily."

"Then the hand and feet restraints will come into play—and the duct tape, right?"

"Right. Mouth tape might be a better name for it, in this case. I've got to do some deep research on Tijuana. If this turns out to be an abduction type of rescue, then I need to find an ideal spot to lure her, if I can."

"The end justifies the means. By the way, what are you going to do with your 9 mm?"

"Good question." Ross thought for a moment and said, "I'll guess I'll drive the rental care back to the couch surfer hostess and ask her to keep it for me for a few days. I'll have to leave my P.I. credentials with her too. When I cross the border I'll just have my driver's license for identity—along with my passport."

"What about your backpack? You certainly don't want that to get seized—or stolen."

"I'll take it with me to Mexico. I need it to keep those pictures of Leah and Grifty, in case I find someone worth asking about them—and to use the backpack as part of my disguise. Young tourists from all over the world have backpacks, and a few do go to Mexico. There'll be nothing in my backpack that the Mexican police would not expect from your ordinary, single, American, male tourist. That's also where I keep the restraints and tape, but I can think up a lie to justify having them if asked."

"Make sure you eat regular meals, my Love. I know that when you get engrossed in a case you sometimes forget your body's nutritional needs. I want you back home, healthy."

CHAPTER THIRTEEN

After renting a Ford sedan, late in the afternoon Ross returned to Regina Borrego's home. She was happy to see him again, though disappointed that he had not returned to be her guest. She eagerly agreed to keep his gun and credentials in her office safe for a few days. He assured her that he expected to return in a few days, but he left her instructions on how to mail the gun to his wife —through an El Paso gun dealer—in case of an emergency. He did not specify what kind of emergency, but Regina knew that nowadays trips into Mexico were fraught with risks for ordinary tourists, not to mention those in Ross' profession. He gave her his agency's phone number with instructions to get further instructions from Rocio. Back in his rental car, he made a new entry into his journal:

Monday October 17: 3:30 p.m.: Left Regina Borrego's home for the second time, this time in a rental car, headed for Tijuana, Mexico.

Ideas beginning to shape in Ross' head reaffirmed a need for further map study of Tijuana. He declined to ask Regina Borrego for use of her computer again. The more time he spent there, she seemed more disappointed each time he left.

After driving through San Bernardino and Colton, Ross stopped at a truck stop in Riverside, bought a map of San Diego, and found a vacant booth in the dining area. He ordered coffee and a meal. He sipped coffee and studied the map intensely. I-15 would lead him to San Diego where he would catch I-5 straight to the border. He needed to find a public library to get computer satellite images of the areas of Tijuana

163

that he considered most important. He remembered from Lorenzo's stories, and from other stories, he'd heard all along the border, that the intersection of *Coahuila* Street and *Constitución* Avenue were pretty close to ground zero for vice of all kinds in Tijuana. Upon arrival there, he would need to find a place to park his car near a large cantina and then find a decent hotel from which to observe pedestrians on the streets when not pounding the sidewalks, searching.

From the phone book, he got the address of the closest Riverside public library, looked up the address on his road map, and headed there. It was a branch on Madison Street, not far off the Interstate. On the way, he ruminated about the information he had accumulated so far and tried to reassure himself that this venture south into Mexico was the best option, at least for the present. Lorenzo had been a source of some information that he could corroborate, or reject as worthless, by studying street level images through geographic imaging services. He realized that, ultimately, he would have to rely mostly upon his sixth sense and he hoped that it would be in top form. It was more his sixth sense than logic that influenced his choice to go to Tijuana.

Initially, he figured to concentrate his search in bars in the area of the intersection of *Coahuila* Street and *Constitución* Avenue. He acceded to himself that Lorenzo is a cunning, street-level criminal, but he had no reason to lie to his new homie, "Jake," about the center for vice in Tijuana.

Ross reached into the recesses of his memory and recalled from personal experience the reputation of the *Coahuila* and *Constitución* area of Tijuana. Back when Border Patrolmen wrote complete reports, including intelligence information, he had questioned smuggled aliens as to their travel arrangements, trying to identify any familiar principals or any kind of pattern that might help those involved in the investigation of smuggling activities. It had been a long time ago, but he remembered that the Intersection Lorenzo talked about was also a contact area for smugglers and their customers.

From witnesses he had interrogated in his Government career, smugglers often hatched their plans in the sleazy cantinas on *Calle Coahuila*. Sometimes the smugglers would bring along illegal aliens to act as lures to draw out the Border Patrol from concealed stakeouts before they risked bringing in their more valuable contraband. Others paid their smuggling fees as human "mules," hauling contraband in backpacks.

He folded up his map of Southern California, got up from his booth, and stopped by the truck stop's curio shop. He purchased a maroon baseball cap with a USC logo. He was not a USC fan, but the cap was a common ornament for residents of the region. He got back in his car and headed for the library.

Driving, like napping, was an inducement for Ross to ruminate about essentials of the moment. The cap, in addition to his backpack, should induce witnesses to mutter, "Jerk," under their breaths, unless they were ardent USC fans. Most everyone looks at people and pigeonholes them into one category or another. Everyone is a bigot to one degree or another and good private investigators exploit that human frailty in abundant proportions. After people tuck away their stereotyped images into the recesses of their brain, they focus their attention elsewhere—perhaps upon something less boring, like a sexy female walking past in a mini skirt.

If conversations were necessary to elicit information in Tijuana, Ross' accoutrement would support an oral claim to being a candidate for a doctoral degree in Spanish. His presence in Tijuana would configure with getting a little practice speaking Spanish, as well as gathering information for his doctoral dissertation about international relations along the U.S.-Mexican border. That identity might be useful to kick-start a conversation that could lead to helpful information in his true mission. In his careers on the border, he'd seen scholars of the border condition in all stages of their education, and invariably they seemed more oblivious to reality in the later stages than in the earlier, so asking dumb questions and giving dumb answers to others' questions came with the territory. If career failure became inescapably obvious to those types, there was always liberal politics or teaching to fall back on. In Ross' present objectives, he figured his chosen temporary role of an advanced liberal arts student was a useful camouflage.

At the Casa Blanca branch of the Riverside public library, Ross began another laborious task of gathering intelligence information, but he wanted to finish up in time to be in Tijuana by the beginning of full-flourished nightlife. Libraries were a valuable asset to any investigator, especially one going into a foreign country. From experience, he knew that in cartel-controlled Mexico, the fewer questions he had to ask, the better his chances of not arousing suspicion, and the better his chances of returning to the U.S. inside his rental car instead of inside a pine box. He had read many Juarez newspapers. Having his headless body dangle by its feet on a rope from a Mexican overpass was a real, possible consequence if cartels suspected him of being from a rival cartel, much less a P.I.

On the computer map, Tijuana's intersection of *Coahuila* Street with *Avenida Constitución* looked like the place Lorenzo had described. It was in the *Zona Norte* of Tijuana where American tourists, mostly males, look for fast female company. Mexican cops and taxi drivers often refer to such areas of Mexican border cities as the *Zona de Tolerancia*, or tolerance zone, where prostitutes can ply their trade without worry of arrest, even though prostitution is actually illegal in all Mexican cities. Such areas enjoy the protection of the most powerful drug cartels.

Street-level computer images of the area showed bars, gentlemen clubs, dance halls and the ubiquitous, yellow cabs, evidence that this intersection was a good place to look for prostitutes. He mused that neither Mexican cops, nor their government, nor horny, perverted male tourists seem to have a frame of reference for the Mann Act, better known as the White Slave Act. He feared that Leah might be, or soon become, a victim of the crime that is seldom successfully prosecuted.

Ross read on one Internet blog that, in order to allay the fears of Americans, and bring back the enormous *Zona Rosa* clientele that Tijuana had enjoyed in the pre-cartel war days, police had announced that they had installed "nearly a hundred" security surveillance cameras on the streets in the most tourist-frequented places of the city. Ross surmised that in a city the size of Tijuana, a hundred security cameras are not very many, and the Mexico-wise know that dummy cameras, bought for pennies on the dollar, are just as effective as real ones to allay the concerns of tourists, and dummies require little maintenance and no monitoring.

Ross came across the blog of a self-described expert on the Tijuana nightlife. Much of what he said was consistent with what Lorenzo had told him about the best places to find American hookers. The blogger also said that one could buy almost any kind of drug at almost any of the small stores squeezed in between the night clubs and bars around *Coahuila* and *Constitución*. That triggered a thought about how he might get a stubborn Leah back across the border, if he could find her. The answer was knockout drops. The thought was repugnant, but in the private investigator business, like Rocio had said, the ends justified the means. He knew that one can buy such drugs as Spanish fly and Rohypnol on the black market from many different places in the red light zones of border cities, and Rohypnol might have a use other than its common reputation as the "date rape" drug. A sleeping Leah could facilitate getting her bound and gagged, then transported back across the border in the trunk compartment of his car. He was confident in finding the drug, but logistics was a problem. He went back to surfing the streets of Tijuana on the computer for ideas on how and where to perform those feats.

Ross saw something on a street level Internet map that interested him. Near the intersection of *Coahuila* and *Constitución* was a parking area with a towering neon sign that read "Molino Rojo." He looked it up as a cantina on a Tijuana blog written by some knowledgeable playboy, and found that the *Molino Rojo Cantina* had closed some twenty years ago, and all that remained was the parking lot, advertised by the elegant, elevated sign with flashy electric lighting. The parking lot was right across the street from the Chicago Club, one of the places Lorenzo had mentioned where one might find American girls working as prostitutes. He regretted that he had not had time to evaluate the reliability of Lorenzo as an information source, but time was of the essence and he had to do something fast if Leah is in danger of being sold to a Mexican pimp. Even if he got to TJ first, and Leah was not already working in the Chicago Club, it would still make a good base for his operations.

His mind worked at warp speed. Wherever he might find Leah, if she was working in Tijuana, he'd lure her to the Chicago, across the street from where his rental car would remain parked. From there, he would have to improvise a way to get her into the trunk of the car. Ross began to visualize arranging a "date" with Leah, wherever he might find her. The head bartender of Mexican border bars usually also functions as head pimp and supervisor of all the hookers that were permitted to cadge drinks on the premises. Some of the prostitutes are often free lancers, and others have an agreement with the bar. In either case, he'd need to pay the bartender a bribe to buy "outside time" with a "date." Normally, the prostitutes were restricted to entertaining their tricks only in the rooms on the premises, or in hotels owned by the same establishment, usually next door, or on an upper floor of the bar. If a hooker sneaks out of a bar where she is allowed to hustle, without her date paying the release money, she would be barred not only from that place, but word would get around quickly, and she would be banned from all cantinas, and soon find herself a street walker. That was a best case scenario. In a worst case scenario, Leah would wind up in a shallow grave, or body dump, for disobedient girls out in the desert. Bartender releases granted hookers were usually for only an hour, but for extra money, the time could be extended.

On the street level map, Ross noted a uniformed security guard sitting at a stand at the entrance to the Molino Rojo parking lot. That guard, or attendant, meant another bribe. Upon entry, he'd mention to the security guard that he was looking for his girlfriend and that she drank too much, and that the guard should not be shocked if his girlfriend were unconscious from drink when the two of them returned to his car. Also upon entry to the parking lot, he'd try to choose a parking spot near the rear, in the shadow of a tree, or between two large vehicles so his bind-and-gag activities before leaving would, preferably, go unobserved by the security guard.

Before exiting the cantina with Leah, he'd pay the bartender the going fee for "outside time" of an hour. The timing for administering knockout drops was critical. It had to be done no more than ten minutes before they exited the Chicago Club to travel to his nonexistent Tijuana beach "suite." He'd prefer to get her into the cab of his car before she passed out, then when she did pass out, he'd bind her, tape her mouth, and surreptitiously put her in the trunk compartment. If by chance the security guard saw any of this, it would cost him another bribe, but that was of little concern. Everything in Mexico has its price, and he was good at guessing the price of just about anything.

Ross had never used a Mickey Finn before, but he knew it demanded skill. While drinking with his "date," Leah, they would sit at a table in a dark corner of the cantina. He'd order exactly the same drink as she, and drink it at the same speed as she drank hers. Getting the drops in her drink was even more delicate. He figured that before they left the cantina for his "beach house," she was most likely to need to go to the women's room, and if she did not go voluntarily, he would suggest that she go, since it was a long drive out to the beach. If that did not get her out of sight for a moment, then maybe he'd find a smudge on the back of her neck that needed attention. As a last resort, he'd pay some dude a hundred dollars on the sly to invite her to dance, and insist that she accept the invitation. At the opportune moment, he'd slip the Mickey into his own drink, stir it, and then switch drinks with her.

He mentally rehearsed the plan several times as he drove south toward the border, worrying about Murphy's Law, or another old cliché, "the best laid plans of mice and men often go awry." However, one *has* to make plans when engaged in bringing a rebellious runaway teen back across the border to the U.S. side. He did not anticipate any trouble from the American port inspectors, since he was armed with the court order of co-custody. If they send him to secondary inspections for a vehicular search, he'd obey politely, and then ask to speak to a supervisor, and then tell him/her about the contents of his car's trunk compartment. He had documents at the ready and phone numbers of everyone that could corroborate his story, including the parent and the San Bernardino police officers whom he'd talked to at the bus station. From experience in the border patrol, he knew that inspectors at the ports of entry were usually cooperative with private investigators and bounty hunters. At all costs, he must not seek, nor receive, any publicity. If his mission and his identity were ever discovered by Mexican authorities, they would execute a warrant for him, or request his extradition to Mexico. They might even put a bounty on his head. Under present laws, the U.S. would send him back to Mexico to maintain good relations. Getting a Mexican warrant dismissed can be expensive.

However, if faced with a Mexican warrant, Ross knew the drill, for he had arrested fugitives from Mexico, and those who had money already had several copies of an *amparo* when Mexican authorities learned their whereabouts in the U.S. The *amparo* is a Kings X that makes them immune from any further action by the Mexican justice system. The drill begins with a Mexican attorney, hired by the defendant, meeting the defendant on the American side of the border. There, perhaps in a motel room, he would prepare the petition, have the defendant sign it before a notary, then take it back to Mexico, along with some thirty to fifty thousand dollars of the defendant's money. About forty percent goes to the attorney, and the rest to the court where the presiding judge will invariably find in a preliminary hearing that there is no probable cause to pursue the charges in the warrant any further. The cost of an *amparo* is usually directly proportional to the amount of publicity given the defendant's "dirty deed" by the Mexican media, factoring in the depth of the defendant's pockets. Media attention can be as severe in Mexico as it has been in Arizona where they seem to emulate Mexican tabloids. Most of the newspapers are nothing more than tabloids, and the local TV stations fit in the same category as their Mexican counterparts; but in the culture of a country where truth has less impact than drama, emotions and ballyhoo, tabloid journalism can influence the cost of an *amparo*.

A Mexican fugitive with an *amparo* will usually have someone to pose as an anonymous informant, call the Mexican police, and give them the name of a hotel where the fugitive was staying. The fugitive will be gone, but the night stand will be a copy of the *amparo*. When the Mexican police read it, the *amparo* immediately takes the wind from their sails. The key is to get the *amparo* before being arrested; afterwards, the charges can be dismissed only in a court trial, and that seldom happens. Adverse publicity and laying out fifty grand for an *amparo* were two things that Ross wanted to avoid.

Ross studied several blogs on Tijuana to learn as much as he could about the nightlife, and tried to narrow down the most likely places to find American prostitutes. In a Mexican border city, nightlife is synonymous with indulgence in pay-for sex, alcohol and drugs. On another web site, he noted that one of the bars in the *Coahuila-Constitución* area catered to Arabs, another to Japanese. He was particularly interested in those because he knew that tourists and students from those countries are attracted to blonde, American girls. The same blog mentioned "20,000 little stores" in Tijuana that sold ten-dollar packets of crystal meth. Any store that sells crystal meth, probably has other drugs, namely Rohypnol.

CHAPTER FOURTEEN

Satisfied with his cyber-investigative efforts, Ross left the library, got into his rental car and brought his journal up to date.

Monday October 17, 4:30 p.m. Left Riverside library, resumed trip to Mexico.

After reading all those blogs, a higher sense of urgency pervaded Ross' mind. Venturing into an unfamiliar border town made precise planning more difficult. He still mulled over options and alternative strategies, knowing that he likely would implement none of them after he became more familiar with Tijuana. Nevertheless, the mental exercise kept him focused, for when he was devising strategies, he was more relaxed. Improvising strategies and options from maps are of limited value. Tijuana is a big city—a big Mexican city.

The hazy skies over southern California began to darken, and by the time Ross reached the I-15 junction with I-215, black clouds had begun to roll in from the southwest. Rain is not rare in northern Mexico in mid-October; nevertheless, Ross had hoped that the balmy weather he had enjoyed thus far on this assignment would endure until he could get things wrapped up in Mexico. When he reached the city of Temecula, large raindrops began to splatter against the windshield, and when he reached Escondido, the rain-soaked freeway became more crowded. There were far more cars headed south toward Mexico than traveling north because at this time of the day most of the southbound cars carried commuters returning to Mexico after a day's work in southern California. The cartel drug wars had not significantly altered that aspect of border life. Ironically, thousands of Mexicans are successfully filing applications for asylum in the U.S. under the convoluted policies of the present Administration, while thousands of American citizens are on their way to exploit economic opportunities in border industries.

Ross wondered whether Congress would ever be held accountable for their reckless disregard for the purposes of legal immigration and the way asylum laws were being abused. So were all laws designed to maintain balanced quotas of immigrants to the U.S., He sometimes felt guilty that he had left that rat race for private enterprise, knowing that the job needed heroic dedication and patriotism. However, common sense and his instinct for self-preservation—physical and mental—eventually prevailed. Ross fell into the category of a common, ordinary, Anglo-Saxon American—one that would be a good candidate for a scape goat, when the Government needed one.

Immigration "law enforcement" has become another oxymoron and only duped citizens can see a rainbow over the manure pile. Ross had long ago resolved to not feel guilty about having a job that exploited opportunities created by the Government's reckless abandonment of its responsibilities under Article IV, Part 4 of the Constitution. When Government fails, private enterprise sometimes steps in, but the enormity of the consequences made him feel that his part in cleaning up Armageddon's aftermath was infinitesimally small and insignificant. The worst consequences of the Great Surrender of our sovereignty is yet to come, and change will be subtle, at first, and one day Americans will wake up to see the abject changes in our values, language, laws and foreign policies. They will all seem imported to the elder citizens, and unnoticeable to the younger generation. Some anointed minority writer will no doubt receive a Nobel Prize for "discovering" a phenomenon that has been visible to esoteric circles for several decades.

Traffic slowed to a crawl as he entered San Diego, and soon Ross found himself in line waiting for inspection by Mexican Customs and Immigration authorities. He got his passport out of his backpack and left it unzipped on the passenger side of the front seat for easy inspection by the Mexican border guards. Inspection was under a large canopy handling a dozen lanes of traffic. Soon, he faced a Mexican customs inspector who had a glass, left eye. With his good eye, he perused Ross' car suspiciously and asked *"Que lleva?"*

"Nada." answered Ross with a congenial smile. *"Nada* was the correct answer if you had no contraband, and a smile was always an essential. Any hint of contempt for the Mexican officers' authority would be met with suspicion, hostility and even worse contempt, if you happen to be an American.

The guard took his passport, perused it briefly, and peered into the back seat of Ross' car. Ross began to suspect that the agent's vision was not good in his right eye either. The officer handed back the passport, and with a motion by his white-gloved hand, muttered *"Sigue."* Ross replied, *"Gracias,"* and proceeded into Mexico.

Ross had not anticipated any trouble at the checkpoint. He had been through the drill hundreds of times in Juarez, but he still heaved a sigh of relief. You never know if you might remind the guard of the *vato* that left his daughter pregnant before high-tailing it north across the border to disappear among millions of other illegal aliens in L.A., or some other teeming American city.

Ross laid his internet map on the console, trying to follow the streets he'd highlighted to get to the intersection of *Coahuila* and *Constitución*. Mexican streets signs are not tourist friendly to begin with, and the heavy rain had reduced visibility. He turned his wipers on maximum speed, got on Mexico Highway One and followed a stream of cars around a large traffic circle. He exited northward off *Calle Segundo y Juarez*, and after a few blocks it led him to the intersection with east and west running *Coahuila* Street. He turned left and began to see gaudy-painted hookers dressed in skimpy dresses standing in bar doorways, part of their job description to lure male tourists into their bar. Some looked foolish, holding newspapers and other objects over their heads when they could avoid getting wet by simply retreating into the bar. Knots of young men, Hispanic and American stood gawking, evaluating the crop of girls available at that bar, those passing by on the sidewalk, and those standing in the competitors' doorways nearby.

Soon, Ross found the intersection of *Coahuila* and *Constitución*, and just north of it, the *Molino Rojo* parking lot sign, across from the Chicago Club. He drove into the parking lot, found a parking space on the opposite side of a Chevrolet Avalanche truck with California license plates. Perfect, thought Ross, as long as the driver of this truck doesn't move it, I am concealed from the street. He put his backpack in the trunk compartment and walked back up to the security guard and attendant. He told the attendant that he expected to stay parked there for two days, but he paid for three in advance. In Spanish, he repeated the litany that he had committed to memory about looking for his girlfriend that drank too much, that she often passed out when she drank too much, and that she might be a little tipsy when they came back to the car. He handed the attendant a folded up ten dollar bill as a tip. The attendant took the bill, nodded vigorously, saying that he understood his problem with a girl that drank too much and that he saw that situation often. The guard quickly stuffed the bill in his front pants pocket.

Now, Ross needed to find the drug that would ensure that his "girl," Leah, would indeed be tipsy and maybe even unconscious when he was escorting her to his rental car. Mexican taxi drivers are the most knowledgeable source of information for finding anything connected with border vice. He saw one of the yellow vehicles parked on the curb on *Avenida Constitución*, near the intersection with *Calle Coahuila*. He pulled his USC cap down tight, trotted down to it, and opened the rear passenger door and got in out of the rain.

"Where to?" asked the driver.

"Where can I find some Rohypnol?"

The driver said, "Many places. I have a friend that will sell you some."

"Then let's go see your friend."

The friend was at a small café that specialized in tacos made with charcoaled beef, which Ross suspected was just a front for illegal drug dealing. The taxi driver walked over to the counter and called over his friend who wore a white cook's hat. He was a short, middle-aged man with a large head and several gold teeth. The driver and cook talked in abated voices across the counter for a moment and then the cab driver told Ross to follow them to rear of the establishment. At the rear of the room was a short hallway at the end of which was a tiny office. The cook sat on a rickety side-type chair behind his desk. The chair had twisted wire braces to keep the legs from separating from the sockets. The cook said to Ross in Spanish, "So you want to buy Rohypnol?"

"Yes."

The cook opened the center drawer of his desk and pulled out an amber-colored plastic bottle that apparently had once held an American prescription medicine. "There are six pills in this bottle. Is that enough?"

"Pills? Don't you have it in liquid form?"

"No. Only pills."

Ross thought about how much harder it would be to add a pill, even if crushed, to a mixed drink and get it to dissolve quickly enough so that Leah would not notice. "I really need something in liquid form."

The cook and the cab driver discussed the problem for a moment, and then the cook reached back into the desk drawer. He pulled out a small, plastic bottle that had the label of a popular brand of American eye drops. "This is better than Rohypnol," he said, handing the bottle to Ross to examine. It was half full of a clear liquid.

"It looks like eye drops."

"Yes, but that is a disguise."

"What *is* it?"

"Ketamine."

"Ketamine?" Ross had heard of ketamine, but was not thoroughly familiar with it. He looked questioningly at the cab driver and the cab driver assured Ross that if he wanted to put someone to sleep, ketamine was as good, if not better, than Rohypnol.

The cook injected his own reassurance. "Doctor's give it to people to put them to sleep before surgery."

"How much?"

"Fifty dollars," said the cook.

Ross paid the cook, placed the small bottle in his shirt pocket, returned to the cab with the driver and requested to go to the Chicago Club.

Ross got out of the cab paid the driver his regular fee plus a twenty dollar tip.

A couple of scantily dressed girls stood under the stoop of the Chicago Club, along with several young Hispanic males who were just watching the rain and the few pedestrians that ventured out in the rain. A young man came out of the Club accompanied by a garishly painted Mexican girl. The couple entered the door of a hotel next door, just to the left of the Chicago Club, and began climbing a staircase.

If Leah is inside the Chicago, Ross had to find a way to make her his drinking companion. If she were not here, he would have to find her and bring her here so that after he got her sedated, he would have to get her only from the club to the parking lot across the street. The Chicago Club might be just the first of perhaps several bars he would check out. The thought that she might not be in any of them crossed his mind and gave him a sinking feeling in the pit of his stomach. He remembered an old Army cliché: If in the heat of battle and unsure of the next step, do *something*, even if it is wrong. He'd also learned a similar strategy in open field running as a halfback in high school football: Keep moving and changing course, or risk getting blind-sided.

Inside the large, dark, main room of the Chicago Club were two pole dancers near the center of the dancing area. There were tables in rows around the perimeter all the way to the walls to facilitate sharing a drink with the female entertainers—and planning subsequent moves. A few male customers were sitting at the tables with female companions, no doubt negotiating for sex.

Ross stood near the entrance of the Chicago for a couple of minutes, until his eyes became accustomed to the darkness. Most of the light was afforded by neon signs attached to a mirror behind the bar that advertised Carta Blanca and XX brands of Mexican beer. The music was a low base beat to which the pole dancers applied suggestive moves, as if the brass poles were phalli. There were about thirty skimpily-dressed, unaccompanied girls sitting either at the tables or at the bar, ready to entertain lonely or horny male customers. Ross strained his eyes but could not see a single patron that could qualify as "blonde." The females that had paired off with males at the tables kept bartenders busy re-filling tiny glasses with a suspicious "purple fluid," in tiny shot glasses, and each time the bartender delivered a girl a drink, he rewarded her with a wooden chip called a *ficha*.

Ross was familiar with the scene and it was not unlike that at the bars in the tolerance zone of Juarez. He and a fellow soldier from Fort Bliss had been sucked into the "purple drink" scam. The watered down wine cost three dollars a shot, and the girls drank the contents of the tiny glasses at a rate of one about every fifteen seconds. The soldiers quickly did the math and realized that their entire paycheck could be spent for the company of these girls, called *ficheras*, in just a couple of minutes, after which the girls commonly called, *ficheras,* would move on to another sucker. At the end of their shifts, the girls could exchange the *fichas* for cash.

However, Ross was interested only in a certain young blonde girl, and after carefully surveying the dance floor once again, he was satisfied that there were no blondes in the place at all, and it was time to move on to another bar that Lorenzo had said allowed American hookers to hustle in them. One of them, Adelita's, he remembered, was just a short walk, half a block east, on *Avenida Constitución*.

A knot of young men loitered around the entrance of Adelita's. Ross guessed that the guys standing around outside the entrance had already perused the girls inside, and decided to check out the street walkers. That did not bode well for the quality of the girls inside. He hesitated near the entrance and decided to strike up a conversation to see if he could gather some intelligence information. He approached a hatless young man with short, curly blonde hair and remarked, "I suppose this many guys standing around outside, culling the streetwalkers, must mean the hookers inside are not so hot. You lookin' for some light-haired stuff?"

"Not necessarily. I'm just out here to get away from the cigarette smoke and get some fresh air. I don't like smoke."

"How is the crop inside? Any blonde American girls?"

"Just a couple of old fat skanks of the type that like *beaners*."

"Then I can understand why these guys out here are gawking at the street walkers."

"They won't see much in the way of street walkers on this street. The cops make the street hookers stay off the main streets like *Coahuila* and *Constitución*. Those types sort of gravitate over to *Segundo de Coahuila* where you seldom see a cop."

"Maybe the street walkers give 'em a little *panocha* for lookin' the other way."

"Maybe. Over there on *Segundo,* they say a new hooker in town can make a few bucks until she can get a job in a cantina. That street is more like an alley than a street. They say it's a good place to get a dose because the girls that walk the streets haven't been to the health department to be tested and certified STD-free."

"I see. By the way, I'm Jake. I'm a writer looking around down here in TJ for a story."

"Willy, here. I'm a security guard in San Diego. I'm working on my associate's degree and expect to finish up next

179

spring. Then, I guess I'll go on and work on a four-year degree in physical education."

"You seem to know your way around here in TJ."

"It's cheap entertainment for a single stud. By the way, if you want to nail a street walker, look for one that's new in town. They're cheaper than the girls in the bars, and being new in town, may not yet have an STD. However, I figure that picking up one of them is like playing Russian roulette with your health."

"Where *is Segundo de Coahuila*?"

Willy stepped out closer to the curb and pointed north.

"See that hotel down on the corner? That's the Garcia Hotel and Segundo is just around the corner, half a block south of it, off *Constitución*. You're not really thinkin' about pickin' up one of *those* hookers, I hope."

"No, but I'm a writer, you know. Writers are curious about everything."

Ross excused himself from Willy and left him to take a look around inside Adelita's.

There were more girls in Adelita's Club than in the Chicago. When his eyes became accustomed to darkness, he went to the john and walked around as much as possible without becoming conspicuous. There were a few American tweakers among the hustlers, but obviously no Leah or Grifty inside the establishment. He was getting tired and decided to go and check out the Garcia Hotel as a place to stay.

The entrance to the Garcia Hotel was at the east end, next to the entrance of another bar that sported the name "Pla Bo" on a sign over the entrance. The silhouettes of two rabbit's ears substituted for the two "y's," of Playboy. Obviously, the bar was not in the class of anything Hugh Hefner would own, so the substitution was probably to discourage an international lawsuit for copyright infringement. Several young men loitered around on the sidewalk in front of the entrance to the bar, indicating that the pickings inside may not have been as great as the sign above the entrance seemed to promise.

Ross opened the gray, wooden door, which had been painted different colors several times. He walked up a narrow flight of squeaky, wooden stairs to the second floor. There was a small lobby with a counter in one corner, and a squat, middle-aged Mexican woman wearing an apron emerged from a vacant room. The noise Ross had made walking up the stairs substituted for a desk bell to alert her of a visitor. Apparently, the cleaning lady also functioned as the manager. Ross could see several room keys inside a pocket of her apron. In a shrill voice, she asked if she could help him. Ross asked her if the corner room was vacant.

She shook her head and declared, "No. It is occupied. Another young man rented the room about an hour ago."

"Could I talk to him? I'd like to rent *that* room and I might offer him—and *you*—something to get the room."

The woman began to shake her head, but when Ross pulled a twenty from his billfold and offered it, she hesitated for an instant, then grasped the bill and said, "Let me go talk to him." She started down the hall toward the room, hesitated, and looked up at Ross' face with a mischievous leer and whispered, "If he doesn't want to give up the room, I'll tell him he was placed there by mistake and that you had a reservation."

She knocked on the door of room 22 and announced in her high-pitched voice that management was calling.

A young, Hispanic man appeared in the doorway. He wore stylish black slacks and sported a neatly trimmed Frank Zappa style moustache and beard. The woman spoke to him in Spanish, explaining that she had rented the room to him by mistake and that Ross had a reservation and wanted the room. She added that Ross was willing to pay him something for the inconvenience of moving to another room.

The young man glanced back and forth at Ross and the woman. His dark eyes rested upon Ross and he asked, "How much?" Ross' sixth sense told him the young man was probably a middle-management drug dealer.

"Would forty do it?" asked Ross.

"Make it fifty."

"Done."

Ross forked over the fifty, and when the young man retired into the room to get his things, he gave the woman another fifty dollars, in addition to the original forty dollars, for a single night's lodging. "I may want it longer, but I'll let you know before check-out time tomorrow," he told her. The woman never mentioned registering, nor did she even ask Ross his name. In about five minutes, the young man vacated the room, carrying a small suitcase. He handed his room key to Ross and took a key from the manager for a room two doors east, down the hallway. The housekeeper went in, inspected Ross' room, and even though the young man apparently had not lain on the bed, she said she'd be back shortly with clean linen.

After Ross took a shower and changed clothes, he sat on a chair, looking north up *Avenida Constitucion*, toward the Chicago Club, and alternately glancing east and west on *Calle Coahuila*. He reasoned that, sitting, he could get a good view of pedestrians going all four directions within a hundred feet of the intersection. He then went out of the room, down the hall a short distance and exited onto the balcony. If he needed a better view, he could go down the hall and exit to the balcony. To his surprise, "Frank Zappa" was sitting on the balcony in a folding chair, seemingly also surveying the area, perhaps waiting for a trafficking contact. They nodded recognition, but neither seemed in a mood to start a conversation, due to the likely contrasting aspects in their missions.

Ross went back to his room and took out the small binoculars from his backpack, backed his chair away from the corner window to stay out of sight, and started surveillance. Street lights were coming on, adding a little light to the streets, and now he figured he could see well enough with the binoculars to identify Leah or Grifty at least a block away on *Constitución*, and a shorter distance east and west on *Coahuila*. He was good at seeing through disguises, if the two happened to use them, but he mentally dismissed disguises as unlikely;

182

Leah and Grifty had no reason to know a private investigator was on their trail.

While maintaining surveillance on the streets below, Ross dialed Rocio on his cellular. He updated her on the latest, and she assured him, "All is well on the home front, as the saying goes."

After a brief chat with his better half, Ross breathed a sigh of satisfaction and again picked up his binoculars. He continued watching the streets until a few minutes after ten p.m., getting more bored—and lonesome—by the minute. He smirked inwardly at the image many people have of private investigators. Hollywood has created an image of them with lives filled with action and drama. Surveillance scenes in movies are very brief, quickly followed by more action, a la Phillip Marlowe, Mike Hammer or Joe Friday. In reality, PI's like border guards, spend more time on surveillance than in action, and almost as much time bogged down in paperwork.

Ross had always found people-watching an interesting pastime, but soon the present scene before him—young men loitering around bars, bent on engaging in vice or crime of one kind or another—turned him off, psychologically. He remembered what Willy had told him about *Segundo Callejon de Coahuila*, just a block to the south of where he sat, where streetwalkers, plied their trade. According to Willy, there would most likely be some newly arrived hustlers there. If Leah is, or has been in TJ, she would be a newcomer. It was another long shot, but if she is not there, but has been there, other hookers might remember seeing her, and it would not hurt at all to make a few contacts among the street hookers for future use. Streetwalkers also have pimps.

He put away the binoculars and noted his wristwatch. He walked over to the dresser and made an entry into his journal:

Monday October 17 10:15 p.m. Began foot patrol to check out Segundo Callejon de Coahuila.

Using the word, "patrol," in his journal triggered ominous memories. He had long ago compartmentalized the word into a dark recess of his mind reserved for unhappy memories, and he was surprised that he had just used it in his journal.

Ross skipped back down the stairs without the use of the handrail and strode energetically into the street. Loud music blared from La Gloria Bar and he hoped it would not keep him awake later, when he turned in. The knot of young men outside the Pla Bo Club had shrunk in size and Ross wondered if they had gone somewhere else, or perhaps the quality of the girls inside the bar had improved. He strode on toward *Segundo*.

He hesitated on the corner of *Segundo Callejon* for a moment. The street lighting came from short, decorative poles, about half of which were not working, making the street very dim under the shadows of palm trees that lined both sides of the street. It was a narrow, one-way street, and vehicular traffic consisted almost entirely of taxicabs.

Ross began strolling at a more leisurely pace, taking in the sights. *Las Charritas* stood on the corner to his left. He began to visualize Grifty, palming off Leah to a pimp, or Grifty personally filling dual roles for a day or two to make a little extra cash. He shook off that sordid, homosexual image of Grifty and tried to focus on the street scene. He could not enjoy sightseeing, unless Rocio were sharing it with him. At the present, he had a job to do and he had to focus on that. He remembered when he had been amused at being hustled by prostitutes on the streets of border towns, but he had outgrown that mode of false-flattering entertainment at about the same time he had outgrown the Army—and long before his border guard experience.

Few prostitutes stood in the shadows of the palm trees on the alley-street, waiting for a bold trick that did not worry about STDs. In all border cities, the city health department inspects weekly those girls that work in the bars of the *zona de tolerancia*. Those that did not keep their health cards up to date were subject to fines, jail terms and being run out of town by pimps or cops, or both.

He was nearing the end of the block-long street when he saw a short, blonde girl standing under a palm on the southeast corner of the next street, *Niños Heroes* that ran north and south. His pulse rate jumped. The girl seemed to try to keep the trunk of her palm tree between her and Ross. As he got closer, his heart sank. He saw that she had olive skin, dark eyes—and *dyed* hair. She wore a short skirt and a low-cut white blouse. He nodded a greeting and smiled at her. She immediately propositioned him in broken, vulgar English, "You wanna date?" She restlessly moved her arms, jerking her head about, the signs of a meth addict. He asked if business was good. She nodded and said, *"Si."* No prostitute with any experience at all is going to reveal that business is bad, or that she is desperate for money to get her next fix. It was a meaningless conversation starter. He invited her to a small Chinese restaurant at end of the alley, on *Niños Heroes* Street. She politely declined.

"This won't cost you. I'll pay for your meal and pay you thirty dollars to dine with me."

Her narrowed eyes bespoke her suspicions. Obviously, nobody had done all that for her without expecting something sexual in exchange, or used it as a ruse for some diabolical scheme. He assured her that all he wanted was her company and that he would make sure that she did not lose money by leaving her post with him for a little while. She cast doubt aside, linked her right arm in his left and accompanied him.

The alley opened up into *Niños Heroes* Street and Ross' companion hesitated and looked both ways, up and down the street.

"Who are you looking for?" he asked her in Spanish.

"La Sanidad."

Of course. The health department. He was a little surprised at her candor. Being an unregistered prostitute, she would be fined. If she could not pay the fine, she would be jailed—if investigated by officers from the health department.

Satisfied that there were no health officers around, she started walking with him to the restaurant.

"My name is Jake," said Ross.

"Lucila," said the girl.

Ross knew there was little chance that was her real name, but it did not matter. Any kind of name would do as long as she was consistent; he needed a way to ask for her in case he had a future use for her as a source of information. The only thing that really matters in the world of the *Zona Norte* is the gringo dollar. All of these guys you see standing around in front of the bars, ogling the hookers as they walk past, never need to use such an attribute as good looks—if they indeed had any. In fact, the *Zona Norte* habit, regardless of these guys physical appearance, made them less likely to experience anything with a woman, ever, other than a physical relationship. That habit-forming practice in its own way is more degenerative than alcoholism or even a drug habit. It permanently affects one's values and habits and perforce affects an addict's method of approach as well as the type of woman willing to accept his "unsophisticated" advances.

They took a table near the front entrance of the restaurant and a waiter brought menus. After turning in their orders and ordering B and B aperitifs, Ross pulled from his pocket the photo of Leah and asked Lucila if she had seen this person.

She held it, studied it, and said, "She is very pretty."

"Do you think you have seen her?"

She shook her head and handed him back the picture.

Ross knew that she probably had not been here long enough to know anyone outside the area in which she hustled. Moreover, it was probably too early for Leah to be here anyway, but he needed to lay the groundwork to find her as soon as possible to protect her from the consequences of such a life—usually a very short life. It had been just another shot in the dark; one that so far had missed. Returning the photo to his shirt pocket, he said, "If you see her, follow her and see where she works, where she stands. I will give you a hundred dollars for that information. I'll buy you dinner again tomorrow night when you are not busy."

She nodded vigorously, reaching for her glass of B&B. "Of course." In a moment, with the drink in her hand she frowned and asked, "Are you going to stay here long?"

"I may be here a couple of weeks."

They carried on a conversation about worldly subjects and Ross got to know a little about her background. She had been raised on a small farm in Sonora where poverty is common in the world that she knew.

She sipped liqueur and looked blankly at the table, perhaps struggling to reconcile her good luck in finding Ross with the stark reality of her hopeless situation. She was young but was inured to disappointment. Romantic heartbreak was a concept long hidden in the recesses of a mind that grew up on a farm in central Sonora, less than a hundred miles from where his wife was born. She told of stealing a bag of corn with a girlfriend and the two using that money to buy bus tickets to Tijuana. The girlfriend had a little extra money she had been saving, had already bought her health certificate, and was now working in a nearby bar. Ross wished that he could give her some hope of romance, or extended friendship, but that would be dishonest and impossible. The scene evoked sordid images of the style of a GI, far from home, in a strange land where exploitation of a foreign girl's natural curiosity about Americans enticed them into un-meaningful relationships. It evoked images of GIs disappointing and abandoning them; images of the cavalier attitudes engendered by sudden freedom from the vinculum of the community. The scene evoked echoes of cavalier laughter and GI clichés: *Love 'em and leave 'em,* or *hit and run, man,* and other callous jokes commonly heard in Army barracks.

Young men on the prowl in cities like Tijuana were much worse than overseas GIs that take advantage of foreign girls. Ross shuddered at the lessons in human cruelty and callousness that waited in ambush for this young girl, adrift in the border tempest.

After their shared meal, Ross left Lucila in the shadow of the same palm tree where he had found her. Walking back to his hotel room he wondered briefly what her next trick would be like, but he already knew the answer. Just look at the clueless guys hanging around the entrances to the ubiquitous, cheap bars of the *Zona Norte*.

Back in his hotel room, Ross made another entry in his journal:

Monday October 17. 11:55 p.m.: No new leads to finding Leah. Returned to hotel room, took a shower and went to bed to get some badly needed rest.

CHAPTER FIFTEEN

Ross got up early the next morning and went for breakfast at a nearby restaurant on *Coahuila* Street. After starting on his coffee, he bought a newspaper from a paperboy and began reading it while waiting for his order of scrambled eggs and chorizo. His phone rang, and expecting Rocio, he was surprised that the phone's screen showed the source as Regina Borrego.

"Ross, I think you better get back here as soon as possible," she said in solemn tone.

"What's going on?"

"Early this morning they found a body of a young girl under an overpass near the Union Pacific yards. I downloaded the Sheriff-Coroner case number from the newspaper and saw the face, and...well....I've never seen anything but her picture, but the description..." She began to choke up.

"I suppose they haven't identified her yet?"

"No, not yet, but they said she was a blonde in her late teens and said she had a tattoo of a marijuana leaf on her right shoulder."

"Well, I am in Tijuana because I had a hunch that Grifty may have brought Leah here. I'll leave for San Bernardino immediately, but since this is Tuesday morning I can imagine the miles of commuter cars waiting in line to get into the U.S."

"Give me a call as soon as you get close and we can meet at the office of the Sheriff-Coroner in San Bernardino. I talked to the Coroner Watch Commander and told him that the description of the body she had seen on TV seemed to match that of Leah and that you could help identify her. Let's hope the body they found is *not* Leah...but I am so worried..."

Ross was worried, too. What Regina was telling him brought back mental flashes of the scene at the San Bernardino intercity bus terminal where he had spotted whom he was almost certain was Grifty, mysteriously unaccompanied by any female, when the sleaze ball had dodged the cops. This latest information might bode ill as to why Leah was not with Grifty at that time. Ross got his things together, and made an entry in his journal:

Tuesday morning, October 18. 745 a.m. Got call from Regina Borrego about a dead body being found in the San Bernardino Union Pacific Freight Yards. She thought it might be Leah. Preparing to leave Tijuana immediately for San Bernardino.

He checked out of the hotel, and when he came out of the hotel door, he saw a man that jolted his senses. It appeared to be Lorenzo, stumbling drunkenly, south, across *Avenida Constitución*. He was about fifty yards to the north, but he was in fact *certain* it was Lorenzo, still wearing a Milan hat, a polo shirt and those long shorts.

"Hey, Lorenzo!" shouted Ross.

Lorenzo stepped up onto the south curb of *Constitución* stopped, tottered precariously on the edge, and jerked his head in the direction of Ross.

"It's me! Jake!" shouted Ross, starting toward his former couch-surfing partner. Lorenzo continued his gaze, swaying drunkenly on the edge of the curb until Ross reached him. He pointed at Ross and slurred, "Hey, you...?"

Ross approached Lorenzo and said, "I'm Jake. I was your couch surfer partner in Muscoy. Remember? We went to Lytle Creek together."

Lorenzo tossed his head back in an awkward gesture of recognition and said, "Sure, I remember. *Jake.* What you doin' in TJ, bro? You come down here to check out the *panocha*?" He and Ross bumped knuckles.

190

"Just checking out *everything*." I'm kind of disappointed in the city. They say the good looking *viejas* are now in L.A., since the President pulled back the Border Patrol and essentially left the border wide open."

"You got that right, bro. There ain't nothin' left in TJ but *gorditas* and skanks." He swayed and put his hand on Ross' left shoulder for support.

Ross added, "I was just getting ready to drive back to San Berdoo."

Lorenzo looked at Ross quizzically. "Did you say you were gonna *drive* to San Berdoo, bro?"

"Yep. I have a rental car."

"Take me with ya, bro. I need to get out of here. I got in a fight in a bar with a *puta* that tried to steal my wallet, and the Mexican cops are givin' me a hard time. They gave me just thirty minutes to get out of TJ, and the last thing I want is to go to a Mexican jail."

Ross could hardly believe his good luck. He wanted very much to ask him about Grifty, but the time was not right. He was sure that the San Bernardino police also would want to talk to Lorenzo—if the body Regina had called him about turned out to be Leah—since Lorenzo was a known associate of Grifty—the man who would have to know a lot about her death.

"Of course I'll give you a ride, bro," Ross assured him. "You had enough of TJ, huh?"

"Yeah. Where's your car man? I been drinkin' all night and I ain't' slept in two days. I can barely stand up."

"My car is right up *Constitución*, across from the Chicago Club. Come on, let's get outta here."

While in the line of cars at the POE, waiting for inspection, Ross managed to keep Lorenzo alert by talking to him and shaking him occasionally. He had to be awake for inspectors to talk to him. In the meantime, he brought his journal up to date

Tuesday, October 18, 8:10 a.m. Expect to be though U.S. Customs in about fifteen more minutes, en route to San Bernardino to meet with Regina Borrego. Lorenzo in tow.

Lorenzo squirmed about restlessly and said, "You got a cigarette, bro? I need a smoke."

From a conditioned reflex, Ross started to say "No," that he did not use them, and then remembered those in in his backpack. "I have some in my backpack." When traffic stopped again, Ross got out and pulled the cigarettes from his backpack. He took advantage of the opportunity to pour the ketamine on the ground, and then he walked over to a trash container on the sidewalk and tossed in the container. He got back in the car and handed the smokes to Lorenzo who grasped them with a shaky hand.

Lorenzo lit up with the car's lighter and said, "This morning I made a decision to go completely straight, Jake. I don't wanna go back to the joint again, man. That place sucks. I'm goin' straight startin' today—and tomorrow I'm gonna look for a job. If I have to bus tables in a fast food place, that's okay for a while. I tried to work on my GED, right after I got out of the joint—but they wanted me to take that reading course...what do you call it..."

"Was it called remedial reading?"

"Yeah, that's the one. I'm gonna take it, learn to read good and start workin' on a GED."

"I'm proud for you, bro."

Ross lowered Lorenzo's window from the control on his own door to allow Lorenzo's cigarette smoke to go out *his* window and not flow across to his side.

Lorenzo flicked some ashes from his cigarette out the window, cleared his throat and said, "I want to ask you for some advice, bro."

"I'll try to help you, if I can."

"I'm in deep chit, bro."

"How's that?"

"Sunday night—you remember when I left the couch surfing house—well, I met up with Grifty in downtown San Berdoo. He was with this young *ruca* from El Paso that he calls Linda, the one I told you about. The three of us scored some meth and whiskey, and around midnight we all three went down to the UP yards in Colton, way down there below I-10, to find a place to crash. Linda was really antsy, if you know what I'm sayin'. She said she hadn't slept in a week. To make her sleep, Grifty gave her a trank. She washed it down with a swallow of whiskey. I warned both of them that downers and whiskey don't mix, but they ignored me. Anyway, I woke up about daylight Monday morning and I looked at the other two. Grifty was snoring loudly, but Linda had turned blue. I woke up Grifty, and we tried to wake Linda, but couldn't. I gave her mouth-to-mouth, but I couldn't get her to breathe. I listened, but I couldn't hear no heartbeat. I called 911 and Grifty said he was goin' up to I-10 and Pepper Avenue to show the ambulance how to get to Linda. I waited next to Linda for about half an hour. I heard an ambulance come down that way, but none ever showed up down in the yards. I made a pay-phone call so I they could not read my address on my cell, and they said that no one had met the ambulance on I-10 so they thought it was a prank call. I gave them the location again and waited up on I-10 at Pepper until the ambulance got there. I showed them where Linda was, but I was sure she was dead and I didn't go back. I panicked because it looked like Grifty had hauled ass and left me holdin' the bag. I jumped on a freight train headed east and wound up in San Diego. Then I walked over here because I needed a drink. I needed a drink real bad."

"I can see you've had a few."

"I had a *bunch* of drinks, and when that whore tried to pick my pocket in that bar, I threatened to kick her ass. They bartender called the cops and gave me a warning to get out of town. Then I met you, but right now those Mexican cops are the least of my worry."

"I see."

Lorenzo took a deep draw on the cigarette and blew a large cloud of smoke out the window. He continued, "I never heard of anybody leavin' a friend dead in a freight yard...." Lorenzo took another deep draw on the cigarette and coughed. "What do you think I should do, bro?"

Ross was deep in gloomy thought. He was struggling with his own emotions, trying to keep from showing his sorrow at learning that Leah was indeed the dead body about which Regina had called. He regretted that he had not considered exploring the UP yards along I-10, but there are so many freight yards there, and they are strung out for ten or more miles. Most of the hobos down there are headed east, and they never come up into the center of San Bernardino, unless they are going to catch a bus or look for narcotics. He would have gladly gone down there if he had thought that Grifty or Leah might be there, but he had no clue. Finally, he said, "You should report Grifty to the cops, Lorenzo. They may not do much to him, but they need to know. If you don't, they may come after you. After all, the ambulance drivers will remember that it was you that made the first call and then showed them how to get to that girl's body."

"I was thnkin' the same thing, bro. You right, bro. I'm goin' to the cops."

Ross took a deep breath and heaved a sigh, trying to blow off the emotions he was feeling. "I can take you to the morgue in San Berdoo, bro. That is where the cops will be gathering. Just tell them what you just told me. I'll go along to talk to the cops and be nearby when they question you."

"Then let's go to the morgue, bro." He puffed another large cloud of smoke from his cigarette, and it flowed out across the top of Lorenzo's window.

Ross pulled off the freeway at a diner near Manning and left Lorenzo alone in a booth. From the men's room, he called Regina to tell her what he had learned from Lorenzo and that they were returning to San Bernardino together. She wept to learn of the inevitability of Leah being the body they had found in the freight yards. She agreed to meet Ross at the morgue. "When we get to the morgue and they make positive identification, Ms. Borrego, would you do me a favor?"

"I'll do anything I can to help...Ross."

"With the fingerprints, dental records and other things I have in Leah's folder, positive identification should take only a few minutes after I get there. After positive ID, I am going to ask you to call Reverend Tasker and have him break the news to Rachel Waters. That's more his line of work and he's much more experienced at that sort of thing than I."

Ross pulled into the San Bernardino county coroner complex, which could have passed for a large, well-groomed funeral home. Its driveway was lined with palm trees. He parked his car, and made an entry into his journal.

Tuesday, October 18. 11:15 a.m. Arrived at the Sheriff-Coroner in San Bernardino to meet Regina Borrego. Lorenzo in tow, ready to tell the Sheriff's investigators everything he knows about Grifty and the unattended death of Leah.

He removed the Leah Waters folder from his backpack, and then he and Lorenzo walked up the sidewalk to find Regina waiting for him just inside front entrance. She said, "The Watch Commander is waiting for you. He is anxious to inspect your identity documents of Leah, and share them with the coroner, along with your custodial order, if needed."

Ross gave his file of Leah to a secretary and she took it straight to the Sheriff Coroner's office.

Lorenzo looked abjectly confounded, and Ross motioned for him to follow over to an isolated corner of the lobby where they sat in two visitors' chairs. Lorenzo said, "What's going down, bro? You're acting like a *cop*. Why do you say *Leah*?"

"I'm not a cop, Lorenzo. I'm a private investigator from El Paso, and my real name is Ross—Ross Spencer. I have a contract with Leah's mother to find her daughter, whom you call Linda. Don't worry about anything. I'm going to do everything I can to help you. I do not think you are in any trouble at all.

You've been a lot of help to me, and now I can tell you the truth about me, and everything. I will also go with you to tell it to the sheriff's investigators. Just be honest with them and tell them everything you've told me about how Leah died."

Lorenzo's hands began shaking, and he said, "Could I go outside and have a smoke?"

"Sure, you can, Lorenzo." They got up and headed for the main exit. Ross did not think that Lorenzo would try to back out of testifying, or run away, but he said, "I'll go out there with you."

"Thanks, bro."

After a cigarette, Lorenzo regained his composure and affirmed that he was ready to go to the investigators' office and tell them everything he knew about Leah and Grifty.

At a little after 12 noon, the Watch Commander called Ross, Regina and Lorenzo into his office and introduced himself.

The Lieutenant's face grew dour. He said, "With the fingerprints, dental records and photo of Leah Waters, the forensic pathologist has made a positive identification."

Regina said, "Then it *is*...?"

The lieutenant nodded. "I'm sorry to tell you that the body definitely has been identified as that of Leah Waters."

Regina broke into tears.

"Sadly, we were almost a hundred per cent certain of that," said Ross. Then he introduced Lorenzo to the Watch Commander. "Lorenzo here helped me solve the mystery and he wants to tell you what he knows about Leah and how she died. He knew Leah's companion, Grifty. Lorenzo was the one to direct the ambulance to the deceased's body."

Ross and Regina Borrego got up to leave the Sheriff Coroner's office, and looking at Lorenzo, he said, "We will be right outside incase we're needed."

In a few minutes a stenographer carrying a writing pad walked into the Sheriff Coroner's office.

After about an hour, the Sheriff Coroner and the stenographer emerged from his office with Lorenzo. He told Lorenzo that a deputy would take him to lunch and bring him back to the coroner's office. Then, the Sheriff Coroner turned to Ross and said, "I just got a call from the forensic pathologist and his preliminary finding is that Leah Waters probably died due to a drug overdose. Everything is consistent with what Lorenzo told us and we really appreciate his cooperation. It looks like a mix of alcohol and barbiturates, but the pathologist is going to run some more tests before issuing a death certificate. We have a lot of work to do before a press release. If they try to question any of you, just refer them to me. The homicide detectives are on their way here to talk with you and Lorenzo, Ross, and take statements. It looks like we can wrap up all the loose ends in a couple of days. Homicide will arrange to have Lorenzo put under a witness protection program, but all that will be worked out later. That character, Grifty, has a lot of questions to answer, when we locate him. The chief investigator told me about some of his other suspected crimes, including welfare fraud. They also mentioned possible charges in this case for his failure to report an unattended death, for providing drugs to a minor and for a possible negligent manslaughter charge. By the way, as co-custodian, you have a legal right to view the body, if you want."

Ross shook his head slowly. "No. I see no purpose. Since I actually never saw the victim in life, I prefer to remember Leah as...just a beautiful picture. She was a young, innocent, vulnerable girl that made some very bad choices. I hope her case might save some other young girls from getting awestruck with these older, smooth-talking con artists that prey on them on the Internet, and elsewhere."

The Sheriff Coroner said, "These silver-tongued guys can induce even older women to take up with them—but they usually prefer the young girls who think they are something like celebrities."

In a little while, the Watch Commander escorted Lorenzo and Ross to the lobby to join Regina Borrego and to await homicide investigators. There, Regina told Ross, "Reverend Tasker just called a few minutes ago and affirmed that he has advised Rachel Waters of her daughter's death. He said that Mrs. Waters is on her way to L.A. by plane. Reverend Tasker will meet her at the airport and the two of them will come to the morgue as soon as she arrives—later tonight."

The watch commander said, "That's great, Ms. Borrego. We probably do not need any more proof of Leah Waters' identity, but it is customary for the next of kin to complete the positive identification by viewing the body. Investigators will want to talk to her and maybe take a statement from her.

Ross called Rachel Waters on the phone to offer his condolences. She was at the El Paso airport getting ready to board the plane for L.A. She thanked him and seemed to take the news stoically. He knew that after the shock wore off, she would be in deep mourning.

Lorenzo left for lunch with a deputy, and Ross and Regina Borrego left to have a late lunch together at a nearby diner. He said, "Regina...I'm really grateful for your assistance in helping solve this case and everything you've done to help bring this case to a close."

"Leah has become the daughter of all of us that know about her." She added, "I hope we'll meet again someday...Ross." Their use of familiar, first names, marked a new point in their relationship, but it did not worry him. She was beginning to feel like family. He wished that she had a man in her life, and hoped that she might meet a good one. He remained a little worried about her hosting couch surfers. Loneliness can make anyone, man or women, vulnerable to the machinations of dishonest suitors. It can lower a respectful woman's guard. If she had been his sister, he would have warned that there are a lot more con artists out there besides Grifty. However, some are smooth operators and pose as respectable Middle Class men. He had known of case where one recently escaped convict had spent a lot of money on clothes and cheap jewelry on a lonely widow, and had attended church with her regularly in order to have a roof over his head, but soon robbed and dumped her and moved on as soon as the heat wore off. She was a rare survivor— a very fortunate survivor from hooking up with a professional con artist.

CHAPTER SIXTEEN

After the meeting with homicide detectives, Ross sat in his rental car and made another entry in his journal:

3:55 p.m., Tuesday, October 18. Completed interviews with San Bernardino detectives and departed for El Paso by auto. The detectives advised that Lorenzo would be put up into a nearby safe house by the SBPD. Departed for El Paso.

Upon leaving San Bernardino, Ross knew that he had performed his contract faithfully with Rachel Waters, yet he felt defeated. Grifty was still running free out there somewhere, perhaps already enticing some other naïve, young girl into the pernicious drug scene with his Svengali charms. There was a ray of hope that the authorities would eventually bring him to justice, due to several outstanding warrants; but since the rogue could change his identity at will, Ross wondered whether the police would ever arrest him.

Ross drove east along I-10, putting distance between himself and the more populated areas of Sothern California. He turned his satellite radio onto a classical music station. Driving and enjoying the scenery, once he was out of the traffic jams, relaxed him, inducing him to reconcile nature with energized, reflective thinking.

He noticed quite a number of hitchhikers going both directions on the freeway. He remembered, from his border guard days what a railroad yardman once told him: October is a month of mass movement of hobo transients. Like wild geese, they migrate from the northern states to the warmer climes of the southwest when the weather gets cold. For a fleeting moment, he again envisioned himself, living life on the road, actually doing a research project, not just role-playing. He wished that he were really writing a book on the subject. Maybe someday he and Rocio could make a hobo trip together. Are you nuts, Ross? That would probably be her question to him, if he proposed such an idea to her. He wondered if he would ever have the perseverance to write a book length story on that—or on any subject. Had he missed his muse's calling? Was it laziness, or insecurity, that had kept him on the Government dole for so long. He was still engaged in a job dealing mostly with the dregs of society, but most importantly, he was his own boss. Staying solvent had become a sidetrack—along with his busy schedule. Perhaps poverty and excessive leisure time was the real incentive that spurred great writers, like Gogol and Twain. He needed to find a way to avoid squandering the good memories during freight yard patrol in El Paso. Colorful characters riding the trains, and their intriguing stories should not go untold. Neither should his own experiences where he had witnessed firsthand the occasional discovery of bodies of inexperienced riders who made fatal errors, either in mounting trains, or in selecting their riding companions. Real writers studying and reporting the subject of hobos would envy his extended, vantage point. However, police writing was best left to retirees, not to those still full of energy ready to take on the criminals.

Driving while listening to classical music always stimulated in Ross daydreaming and philosophical thought. He passed a group of four illegal aliens hitchhiking from a Beaumont on-ramp, smiling and laughing while they waited for a ride. They were clearly oblivious to any fear of being picked up by authorities in their newfound, presidential sanctuary.

However, those smiling victors in the lost war of the Great Invasion have their mental problems too and the inevitable encounter with truth. Some, especially in California, feel secure in the sanctuaries and fantasize themselves as irredentists that have a warped concept of some kind of "right" to unlimited immigration to America. Some extol the "virtues" of their failed third world countries and failed socialist doctrines and delusional legacies. As parents' and grandparents' unpleasant memories of their true heritage will rapidly fade, replaced by romantic nostalgia for the "old country," they suddenly think that things "down there" in Latin America or Mexico were not as bad as their parents and grandparents had thought; they avoid rehashing the reasons they left. The world of illegal immigration, like American government bureaucracies, is fraught with mental departures from reality by a coalition of its perpetrators and left-wing co-conspirators. Today's third world immigrants, most of whom get here illegally, resist assimilation and struggle in vain to find a respectable legacy in spite of its inevitable clash with factuality. They mentally reconstruct the past that brought about their need to emigrate, and they try to escape guilt by justifying it with counterfeit irredentism. Most of them never really "fit" in the country they came from; if they had, they would not have left it, and most do not want to "fit" in America, but want to remake it in the delusional image of the country they left.

Ross shook off such unpleasant thoughts of his country's leaders' stupidity in allowing this condition of arrogance and smugness of illegal aliens to obtain. He thought about picking up an American hitchhiker for conversation and for a source of information, vaguely visualized actually writing about the subject someday. Every hobo he had talked to as a border guard in the freight yards was a different soul, and each had his own interesting story. Sociologists call hobos homeless, but transients were keenly aware of the symbiotic relationship between themselves and the social workers. Some of the "homeless" boast of being skilled poseurs, dutifully playing the role that the do-gooders expected of them in this game. "It's a skill and duty of the trade," an old self-educated hobo philosopher called "Dwight," had once told him. Dwight sat cross-legged on the front porch of a hopper car and peered at Ross with mischievous, yet wise eyes beneath the brim of a beat-up fedora. He said, 'I guess you call it sort of teamwork. Half the team is living in a make-believe world—that would be the do-gooders—and us, the so-called homeless in the real world. I don't knock them for their naiveté, mind you—I mean, Hell, they can be useful sometimes, but only for short periods of time." He further explained, "The bygone days of begging for food at back doors that the old timers told me about when I first started riding the rails, is outdated, and those fellows are long gone, but I remember a few of them. To those that survived into their seventies, those days were a bad memory. When I was young, they were a vanishing breed, and only a few could remember the Great Depression. Nowadays most homeowners protect their back yards with fences and mean dogs. People that used to give handouts at their back doors have grown suspicious of strangers, especially bums, due to their lack of good grooming and personal hygiene. The older hobos' message seemed to be that society needs losers so that it can have winners. The do-gooders that perceive themselves as winners have a need to feel needed. We all know, but only a few of us admit, that socialism is rapidly closing the gap between loser and winner. Soon, unless a Joan of Arc leader emerges and awakens us from our lethargic slumber, the socialists will complete their redistribution of the remnants of our national wealth. Few of those profession-al "slummers" that enjoy looking down their noses at bums will have anything themselves worth flaunting or bragging about. However, until the crash comes, today's drifters have an important role: creating jobs for liberal arts majors to look after their needs so that the young graduates do not have to bus tables at Starbucks. Memories of Dwight's perspective always brought a smile to Ross' lips, and he wondered if the old philosopher were still alive.

Ross again weighed the idea of picking up a hitchhiker. He considered that there aren't very many out there like Dwight that could share interesting and exclusive views on the human condition, and he'd not want to get stuck for a long drive with a bitter, sullen ex con or prison escapee on the lam. It was risky business, picking up hitchhikers, but from a motorist's perspective, those that smile, look fairly clean and have very little baggage are usually the best prospects for interesting company. The thought clashed with his thoughts of soon seeing Rocio again and taking that planned vacation to Vegas. He was in a hurry, and today not totally in the mood to meet new people. Ross remembered that his grandfather used to pick up hitchhikers, but times have changed since he was a small boy. There are too many bad characters out there on the streets and highways to make the practice a habit. Ross would be a difficult target for a criminal, for he was a fighter, always armed, and too cautious to let any suspect get the drop on him; but why take the risk? He heaved a sigh, accepted the limitations of a vicarious life of a bum, increasing his odds to live to write about it someday.

Ross cruised through Banning on I-10, and on the outskirts noticed a hitchhiker sitting on the guard rail of an eastbound on-ramp. The hitchhiker was smiling and had a backpack and sleeping bag on the ground in front of him; but his dress was not particularly appealing. Ross was fighting off the temptation of picking him up when something about this hitchhiker grabbed his attention. The hitchhiker wore a faded, red baseball cap, and on the front was a sewn patch—one that looked like a marijuana leaf. Whoa!

Ross stopped about fifty yards beyond the hitchhiker and beckoned him by tapping the car horn. He watched in his rear view mirror as the hitchhiker grabbed his gear and started trotting toward his car. Ross quickly pulled his pen scanner from his shirt pocket, set it on voice record and put it in the card slot of the dashboard, just in front of the gearshift lever.

The hitchhiker opened the passenger side door, still smiling, exposing a missing, left-upper dogtooth.

"Just put your bags in the rear seat bro," Ross said. "Where ya headed?"

"El Paso. How far ya goin' in that direction?" asked the man in a high-pitched voice with a southern accent.

"All the way, bro."

"That's great, bro. It was beginning to get boring sittin' there on that rail. Not as many people pick up thumbers as they used to."

"I'm Jake," Ross said, extending his right hand.

"Mitch," said the longhaired man. His hand was coarse and weathered.

If this guy is not Grifty, he must be a clone, thought Ross. He said, "I'm an aspiring writer and I'm collecting stories from guys like you out on the road."

Mitch smiled and said, "Well, I could tell you a few hairy tales, Jake. You mind if I light up a joint?"

Ross thought for an instant about the legal repercussions, but if this guy turns out to be Grifty, he wanted him to be as talkative as possible, and wanted to keep him as a passenger. "Go ahead," said Ross. From the control panel on his door he opened the window on Mitch's side about an inch in order to let his fumes flow out. Marijuana, like tobacco and booze, loosens tongues. Ross just hoped he didn't get pulled over by a police officer. It would put him in a legal jam from which it would be difficult to extricate. Nevertheless, in his assumed role as a writer, Ross needed to be freethinker, and so far, his dissembling had been good enough to lead this guy to treat him as a fellow member of the demimonde. Mitch opened a small, red, metal container and offered Ross a joint. "No, thanks, bro. Maybe later. I don't use anything while I'm driving."

"Good idea, bro," said Mitch, removing a lighter from his shirt pocket. "I haven't driven a car in years, but I wouldn't smoke a joint while driving. Not just because of the cops, but, well, it makes you feel good, but feelin' good ain't always good...know what I sayin?"

"I get your drift."

Ross was feeling good because he was hitting it off with "Mitch," or whatever his real name was. He was almost certain that he'd stumbled onto Grifty, but he needed to slip in some subtle questions to verify it. After the two exchanged small talk for a few minutes about the demise of riding the rails, about ten miles out of Banning, Ross said, "Y'know Mitch, I think I've seen you before."

Mitch jerked his head to face Ross. His pupils were dilated and his gray eyes unblinking. After a brief hesitation, he asked, "Really? Where?"

"When I was doing some research down on San Julian Street in L.A. I think I saw you in the Jehovah-Jiveh soup kitchen."

Mitch laughed, lifted his joint and let the wind blow off some ashes through the opening at the top of the window. "You may well have seen me there, Jake. I've grabbed a few free meals there."

"Yeah, Mitch, it's coming back to me. It seems you were with someone...a cute little blond..."

"Yeah...?" Mitch's response had the inflection of half question, half answer.

"Yeah, I'm sure it was you she was with, but like all men, my eyes were mostly on *her*."

Mitch laughed. "Yeah, she was a cutie. That must have been Lena. She's the only *blonde* I've been hooked up with in the past couple of years."

"Her name was Lena, huh?"

"Yeah, the hobos gave her that name because of the way she boarded and got out of boxcars, sort of clumsy. Originally it was *Leaping Lena*."

Ross had trouble controlling his breathing and pulse rate. The name Lena or Lorena or Linda was not as relevant as Grifty's confirmation that "Leaping" was part of her name. "I agree she was a cutie—she looked like a *keeper* to me. How'd you disconnect with *that* little fox?"

Mitch took a draw from his joint, hesitated slightly, and said, "Aw, she got homesick and went home to her mom."

"Too bad, bro."

"Ah well," started Mitch, hesitating again, and then continued, "There are a lot of cuties out there—especially in El Paso—where I first hooked up with her, after we got together on the Internet."

206

"You got a point there, bro. There are plenty of cuties out there. I guess all good things must end. I never had much luck hangin' on to those I'd classify as 'keepers.'"

"*C'est le vie*," said Mitch with a shrug.

I'll bet all of your clichés really charm the young chicks, thought Ross. Ross now had recorded evidence he needed to identify this creep as Grifty. He began to devise a plan.

As Ross approached Indio, California, he said, "Hey Mitch, how would you like a good, hot meal on me?"

"That sounds cool, bro."

Ross pulled into a chain restaurant off I-10 in Indio and parked near the entrance. "Just leave your baggage in the car," he said to Mitch. "I'll lock the car so no one can steal anything. I always try to park close to the front door of restaurants where I eat. It makes it easier to keep an eye on the car."

The two travelers settled on stools at the counter, and Ross said, "Say, bro, I gotta go take a dump. When the server gets here, order me a hamburger, fries and a Coke. You order anything you want."

In the restroom, Ross pulled out his cell phone along with the calling card of the San Bernardino County Morgue Watch Commander. "Sir, I'm in Indio, and I've got Grifty, the guy you're looking' for in the Leah Waters case. I picked him up hitchhiking near Banning, and he thinks he's going to ride with me all the way to El Paso."

The Watch Commander said, "Did you say you're traveling with *Grifty*?"

"In person."

"Okay, Mr. Spencer. That's super. Just stall him there at the diner as long as you can. I can't ask you to use physical force to hold him, but right now I'll call a sheriff's deputy I know there and let him know we got an urgent case going down."

Ross gave the Watch Commander a description of their car, where he had parked it and where they would be sitting at the counter. Before he returned to the dining room, he made an entry in his journal.

Tuesday, October 18, 4:40 p.m. Got Grifty in Indio. Waiting for detectives to take custody.

He returned to his counter stool and the two each finished off hamburgers and started on their second cup of coffee. Ross started thinking of plan B. *If the deputies don't show up to take Grifty soon, I guess I'll fake diarrhea and make another trip to the john.* Just then, three Riverside County Sheriff cars pulled into the parking lot and stopped near the front entrance.

Four deputies went directly where Ross and Grifty sat. They grabbed Grifty simultaneously, without resistance, handcuffed him and led him outside the restaurant to their patrol car. Ross paid with a twenty-dollar bill and told the cashier to give the change to the server.

The deputies leaned Grifty against the trunk of a patrol car, searched him, and found a baggy of marijuana, a crack pipe and three tiny bindles of crystal meth. In Grifty's backpack, they found six different social security cards, all with matching drivers' licenses, and other counterfeit identity cards with Grifty's picture on them.

After the sheriff deputies read Grifty his rights and summarized the charges against him, he did not show a lot of worry. Obviously, this was not his first rodeo in the arena of the justice system. However, Ross and the law had a surprise waiting for him: the upcoming damning, testimony of Lorenzo regarding his wanton behavior in the death of Leah. Ross knew that all the evidence that the two officers found on Grifty, along with the apparently stolen, or counterfeit welfare documents, would probably be bundled by prosecutors as the fruit of this single arrest. With plea bargains, Grifty's plight might not be very serious, but their star witness, Lorenzo, might work to get him a couple of years of hard time.

An Indio deputy told Ross, "We'll keep him right here until the San Bernardino County deputies arrive to take custody of him. They're on the way here right now."

Ross waited for the San Bernardino deputies to arrive, and then followed them back to San Bernardino to assist in the investigation.

At the San Bernardino County Sheriff's Office, two homicide detectives, Dave Gertloch and Bill Wesstel invited Ross and the morgue Watch Commander, whose office was nearby, to watch the interrogation of Grifty through a sound proof one-way mirror-window. Through a speaker, they could listen to the interrogation.

Grifty told them that his real name was Ed Courtney Griffin, which may or may not have been one of many aliases, and he said that he was twenty-eight years old. He was truthful only about the facts with which he knew the investigators were already familiar. They found no records under the name "Griffin" that they could attach to him. Soon, Investigator Gertloch confronted him with Lorenzo's sworn testimony, now a part of the official investigation, and now labeled as Exhibit A. Grifty now had to know that the San Bernardino deputies were not bluffing. They knew too much about him, Lorenzo, and other damning facts, to be bluffing. Grifty remained defiant and did not show a lot of worry. The rogue soon decided to alter his story. He said, "Okay, I was with that girl, but when I saw she was apparently sick, I left her down by the rail yards to call EMC, but I didn't kill anybody. Now I don't want to say any more until I have a court-appointed attorney."

Investigator Gertloch rejoined, "You'll get your lawyer, but you should feel real proud of yourself—leaving Leah there unconscious—or dead— and taking it on the lam, like the coward you are. Your companion, Lorenzo, was the one that gave her mouth-to-mouth to try to save her and saw to it that the ambulance did arrive. There are laws against that type of negligent behavior, especially when a minor's life is involved."

Grifty never showed any remorse or admitted any blame in Leah's death. Homicide investigators locked him up on charges of possession of drugs and paraphernalia; and, due to the difference in Grifty's age, twenty-eight, Leah's age, seventeen, they charged him with contributing to the delinquency of a minor.

They were able to get bond denied temporarily due to the ongoing investigation. "We are going to use DNA to try to hook him up to a statutory rape charge," said Investigator Gertloch to Ross during a break in the interrogation. "However, the prosecutor thinks that charge is a little shaky. This guy needs to be put away for as long as possible, and we'll try our best, but I'm thinking he's just a low-level scumbag. I'm sure we can eventually work up multiple welfare fraud charges against him, but it will take time to get all the evidence. His lawyer will probably ask for a reduction in bond, so keeping him locked up until we make the other cases may be problematic. We have sufficient charges to keep him in jail for a couple of years, and that might give us the needed window of opportunity to develop the welfare fraud cases. Unfortunately, welfare fraud has become a way of life and a bunch of overpaid jellyfish State investigators do little to improve it."

"Tell me about it," said Investigator Wesstel. "I used to be a deputy in Lubbock, Texas, and I knew a welfare investigator who must have traded brains with a cowbird and threw his balls in to boot. I guess they've learned that in order to survive in a bureaucracy, you have to conform to the status quo, and soon they lose whatever common sense they may have ever had."

Deputy Gertloch looked at Ross with a grin and said, "That was sort of poetic, wasn't it. Did you get that cool alliteration?"

Ross was inured to bureaucratic incompetence, but he understood the need for humor to these officers. They see dead bodies almost daily, some never identified. For over a hundred years, San Bernardino had been literally a railway crossroads, and on any given day, hundreds of transients pass through the city and its multiple railroad switching yards. Not only the FTRA, but also other criminals have left bodies strewn around the railroad yards. Like immigration law enforcement, these officers' jobs could become depressing, if they should lose their sense of humor. However, presently, Ross could not share in it. He said to Deputy Wesstel. "You're right about the welfare's light regard for fraud. As a Border Guard, I used to report it when I was a rookie, before I learned better. My reports probably never got any further than immediate supervisors, and I'm sure that most, if not all of them, wound up in File 13."

Gertloch agreed and said, "Government agencies are not known for their civic responsibility of cooperating with other agencies, and these days local and state authorities don't co-operate much with the Border Patrol. Illegal immigration is so out of control that if you took it seriously, you'd wind up ba-by-sitting illegal aliens most of the shift—if you detained them for immigration authorities. They don't get in a hurry."

"Too much crime is now acceptable by society," said Deputy Wesstel."

Soon, the investigators released Ross and told him that he could resume his trip back to Texas. The homicide investigators told him that they doubted the case against Grifty would get big enough to subpoena back from El Paso. It would probably end with a plea bargain, after Grifty and his lawyer learn that Lorenzo is a witness against him.

After Ross left the San Bernardino Sheriff's Office, he called Rocio on his cell phone and brought her up to date.

"It's great that you got Grifty so he will have to answer for what he did to Leah."

"Well, I'm sure that someday he'll screw up big enough to maybe spend the rest of his life in the pen, but this time we did the best we could."

"When can I expect to see you, Hon?"

"Well, you know I really haven't ridden as many freight trains as I'd like. I was thinking about turning in my rental car and going down to Colton and catch an eastbound Union Pacific tonight. If I make good connections I should be in El Paso by...let me calculate..."

She interrupted, "Have you lost your *marbles*?"

Ross chuckled. "I was kidding, Sweetheart. I have had all the freight train riding I want for a long time to come. I'm leaving right now for El Paso—in my rental car."

The End

ABOUT THE AUTHOR

Walter LeCroy was born September 9, 1934 on a farm in Terry County, Texas and attended high school in Hockley County. He served seven years in military service.

LeCroy retired from the DHS in 1994 (then, the Justice Department's INS) where, among many other places, he served ten years in the Border Patrol in El Paso, Texas. There, he earned a B.A. degree in creative writing from the University of Texas at El Paso while working nights and attending classes in the daytime. He served at duty stations in all four southwestern states as a commissioned officer, and served as a criminal investigator, and other positions, in Los Angeles. He traveled as far north as Chicago on temporary assignments as an officer with the INS.

LeCroy has done graduate study in creative writing at The University of Texas at El Paso and at Texas Tech University. Most of his woks deal with conflicts and drama on the Texas-Mexico international border where he draws heavily from personal experiences—as he does in this story. He has published five novels, including a historical one based on the life of *Paula Maxwell*, the girl that Billy the Kid wanted to marry.